HEDGE WITCH RISING

THE UNCHOSEN LIFE SAGA

FRANZ MCLAREN

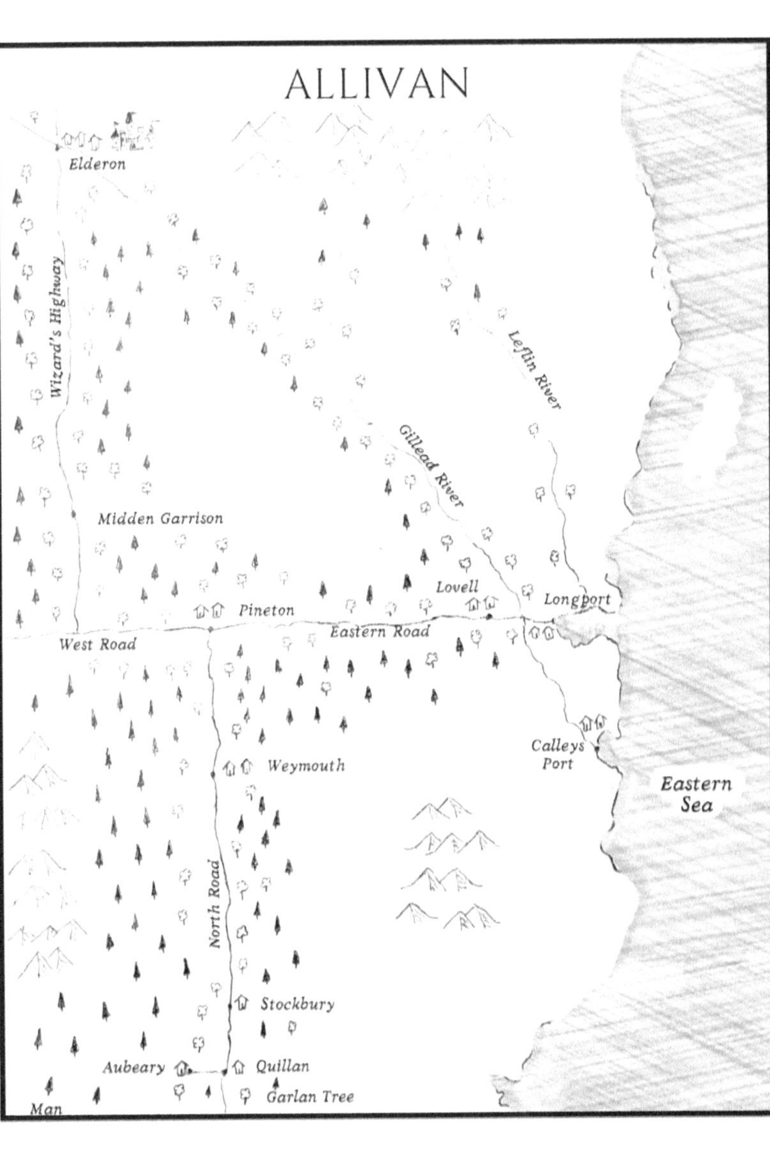

ALLIVAN
Elderon
Wizard's Highway
Leflin River
Gillead River
Midden Garrison
Lovell
Pineton
Longport
West Road
Eastern Road
Calleys Port
Weymouth
Eastern Sea
North Road
Stockbury
Aubeary
Quillan
Garlan Tree
Man

PROLOGUE

Robart inspected the small, exhausted group of soldiers as they passed. These tattered stragglers were the last free humans, and they were dying.

He admired these men. They marched through the long, chilly night without complaint. But as he watched the remains of his army shuffling in the mounting late-morning heat, he slumped in his saddle. Frustrated tears of shame and sorrow clouded his vision. They, and thousands more like them, had trusted him, depended on him, and he had failed. Countless fathers, sons, and husbands once followed him and believed in him. Now, only thirty remained. They staggered forward, heads bowed in defeat and shoulders hunched as if expecting the enemies chasing them to appear at any moment. Few walked without support from the bone-weary scarecrows trudging next to them.

As the men passed, Robart counted weapons: three bows, a dozen knives, and one sword, which was his. Most weapons and all armor were scattered along the path behind them, discarded in the futile hope of saving their dwindling strength for escape. Only his horse remained, and its over-stressed flanks quivered with fatigue as if shaking off invisible flies. When the last of the horses fell exhausted this morning, each battered soldier realized that evasion was no longer possible.

Oppressive silence, broken only by the weary shamble of his troops, grated on Robart's nerves. No animals scurried away through the thick carpet of dried leaves blanketing the forest floor. No birds or insects flitted through the relentless sun rays that beamed down through gaps in the canopy overhead. The fiery shafts of sunlight baked the surrounding bushes brown, toughening the shrubs' limbs and entangling the legs of the unfortunate men as they struggled to carve a path through them. Shaded areas beneath the forest's canopy helped little as the broiling heat sapped their remaining strength.

His steed could go no farther. With a gentle tug of the reins, Robart steered the weary animal to the rear of the small column and sat, listening. A shiver crawled up his spine as he detected only ominous quiet. Their enemies must be close. Soon, his troops would have nowhere left to run.

A man stumbled and fell.

As though this was a signal, the group shuffled to a stop, sinking boneless to the ground, most fainting from exhaustion before their heads settled on the thick, leafy bed of the forest floor. The others sat with their forearms resting on bent knees, heads hung in defeat. All sensed the end of the chase was near. No strength remained to rise for one more effort. They waited only for capture and certain death, but not before enduring endless, painful lives as slaves in the orcan mines.

Robart had no heart to urge them further. They had no reserves left, and with so few weapons and no armor, any attempt at resistance against the pursuing horde would be laughable and futile. Their cause was lost. He prayed their ends would be quick and painless, but in his heart, he knew it could not happen.

A sudden, thunderous chaos of shouts and snarls from the pursuing swarm rose like the hungry braying of a ravenous dog pack, shattering the ragged army's small peace. Only minutes of freedom remained. Fatigue and despair prevented any hope of escape. The screech of branches rubbing against armor chest plates and the crushing of metal boots on the dry leaf bed signaled that their enemies were near and closing in on all sides.

Think. You have to think. There must be some way to escape. Have we struggled for so long, been through so much, only to face humiliating defeat? Useless thoughts darted through Robart's brain. His mind refused to settle on a single idea long enough to examine it. The noise was too distracting.

A human-sized, green creature with spindle-thin legs and arms stepped into the clearing. For a moment, Robart thought its pointy ears appeared elflike. However, the milky-green pupils glaring at him from within a pair of angry red eyes and its long, drooping nose destroyed all doubt that this was anything but a goblin. In seconds, a group of similar skinny, well-armed beasts, each with pot bellies and long limbs, surrounded the exhausted men. Several hundred more pressed against the backs of the first arrivals, grunting and drooling as they thickened the circle, fighting for a glimpse of their prize.

Mumbled complaints rose from the green mass as a wedge of enormous walnut-colored brutes forced a path to the front. These dark giants stood a head taller than humans but with much broader shoulders. Like the goblins, this group wore shiny new armor. Long brown hair protruded through the gaps between joints in their protective suits, fading to black in the shadowed areas of their dark skin. The orcs were a race dedicated to the torture and destruction of everything human.

A crushing anvil of defeat settled on his shoulders as Robert dismounted and sank to his knees, compressed by the unbearable knowledge of complete failure. Dropping his head, acknowledging his disgrace, his eyes were drawn to an industrious black ant scurrying across the face of a withered leaf. This insignificant creature, born to a life of servitude, had more freedom to live a life that suited it and die a far less painful death than anyone in his group.

Robart refused to raise his head to watch the orcs strut around the circle and assume positions at the front of the crowd. He did not want to face the encircling mass as they stood frozen like statues, unspeaking, letting tortuous minutes creep by.

They're waiting for something. But what?

His insides tightened at the thought of seeing their eyes gleaming with conquest and hatred, with every mouth curved up in anticipation of his men's screams and pleas. He waited, kneeling, head bent toward the ground like a condemned man expecting the sharp kiss of an executioner's ax. No, a convicted person knew their imminent death meant an inevitable release from pain. Robart and the men who followed and trusted him knew their deaths would only end when their screams ceased to please the evil horde surrounding them.

His fingers slipped into his tunic to stroke the bark of the crooked Garlan Branch, the symbol that had led them to this defeat, where it dug against his ribs. What good was it? Since the war began, he'd tried everything he could think of to release its power, waving the Branch in every conceivable pattern while shouting various commands, then hopes, and finally wishes. But every attempt had failed.

Life seemed so uncomplicated on that Midwinter night when he'd found the Branch. Like everyone in Allivan, he'd listened in rapt attention as storytellers shared the legend of Skylar, the first wielder of a Garlan Branch. According to legend, when Skylar waved his Garlan Branch five centuries ago, orcs and goblins either died or fled in fear.

Six months after Robart found the Garlan Branch, orcs and goblins flooded his homeland. As a young man of twenty-two, he knew his forces would be invincible with this symbol of freedom in his possession. With the Garlan Branch on their side, human victory was as inevitable as the sunrise. No one doubted that the Garlan Tree had selected the best candidate. As a lord's son, he was born a natural leader. Robart rallied an army, using the Garlan Branch as a symbol that their cause was just and the enemies' defeat unquestionable. Filled with the confidence of preordained victory, he'd unified the country's armed forces and men from all towns and villages and led them into battle.

At first, human resistance surprised and unnerved the orcs and goblins. Early triumphs went to the human army without using the Branch. The effortless victories did not last. Within weeks, in battle after battle, an inexhaustible supply of the ugly beasts appeared as though by magic. The creatures rushed into action, wearing armor that deflected the sharpest steel arrowheads and wielding weapons that cleaved through human swords as if they were twigs.

Far too late, Robart discovered he did not have the skills to use the Garlan Branch. Something vital was missing. Gone for five hundred years, Skylar, the uneducated son of a farmer, left no writings. His wand disappeared at his death, and in time, fanciful and useless legends grew to replace any truth about how to activate the Garlan Branch.

The tides of war changed while Robart struggled to discover the Garlan Branch's secrets. Sweeping it like an artist's paintbrush failed, as did concentrating on a command for it to reap the hordes before him like stalks of grain. Aiming it at individuals and commanding their destruction had no effect. As his despair grew, he waved the Branch in wild desperation while invoking the name of the Garlan Tree. Everyone knew the Tree only released a Branch to one it selected as worthy to defend Allivan. However, nothing he tried worked. The Garlan Branch remained as inert as a baker's spoon.

With their victories mounting, the orc and goblin battalions separated into two devastating forces. Several continued to engage and defeat Robart's armies. Other hordes raided unprotected villages, capturing entire populations and marching them off to slavery in the southern lands. Although Robart's troops killed thousands of orcs and goblins through winter and spring, new legions multiplied like Hydra's heads. By midsummer, fewer than five hundred human soldiers remained, forcing Robart to change tactics. Instead of engaging in battle, he led orcs and goblins into traps and ambushes, hoping to wear down their will to fight. The invaders suffered tremendous losses, but it did not matter. Fresh enemy troops would soon appear to take their place. By the beginning of harvest season, only these thirty human soldiers remained.

Surrender was out of the question, and an appeal for mercy was a waste of time against an enemy with no concept of the word's meaning. Neither orcs nor goblins knew compassion. Therefore, Robart led what remained of his troops into the thick northern forests, hoping to evade further conflict and capture while struggling to master the secret of the Garlan Branch.

The ant disappeared to the underside of the leaf. Using the last of his willpower and strength, Robart looked at the slumped shoulders of men who knew hopeless defeat at the bottom of their souls. No one returned his gaze. He had promised them victory. But in his pride at being chosen to carry the Branch, he delivered only broken dreams.

Robart forced himself to his feet, feeling old beyond his years as he eased the Garlan Branch from his waistband. He stared at the inert stick, concentrating, begging it to give him the knowledge to make it work. Could desperation be the secret to releasing its power?

For the thousandth time, he regretted not being a wizard. The Branch was intended for someone more knowledgeable and more capable in the mystic arts, someone able to use it. When he had the opportunity, his ego prevented him from asking a wizard for help. Now, that option no longer existed.

All the wizards and everyone else in Allivan were dead or captured.

He needed to redeem himself, but how? He had used every idea, every wild thought, seeking the key to activating the Branch's power. His brain refused to respond. It moved with the slow pace of a clogged drain, useless in these last moments when he needed it most.

Raising the Branch, he pointed it at a goblin, wishing the ugly creature an immediate death. Nothing happened. Slicing broad strokes through the air before him, he whipped the Branch like a scythe, mentally commanding it to tear a wide swath through the beasts' ranks, all with no effect. Smiles rose on the faces of his enemies as frustrated tears trickled down his shame-reddened cheeks.

Desperate beyond rational thought, he pointed the stick at an orc and, with every fiber of his being, willed the evil thing to fall. The orc's lips rose at the corners, revealing razor-sharp teeth between the upward-thrust fangs, bracketing its wicked smile.

Skylar, why didn't you leave something to tell me how to use the Garlan Branch?

His arm dropped. His chin sank to his chest. *No, this is not the time for self-pity.* With immense effort, Robart lifted his head and scanned the surrounding crowd. *Maybe I can pull my sword before they notice and take at least one enemy with me to the fields beyond.*

Orcs and goblins clenched and unclenched their claws around their weapons, waiting for him to move. They wanted him to resist. Each relished the thought of chopping his arm off before his weapon cleared its sheath. Several snickers echoed from the crowd, warning him that a massive humiliating wave of laughter would rise before his severed hand plopped to the ground.

Spittle dripped down the creatures' chins. Their anticipation of long, satisfying torture sessions pulled at his soul. They were ravenous to see the humans suffer prolonged deaths, screaming and crying in agony, begging for their forgiveness. They would make his death so memorable that none would ever consider defying them again.

Why are they waiting? The silence tore at his stretched nerves while the beasts stood mute. Gleeful, victorious hate gleamed in their eyes. Soon, the horde would reduce him to a mass of tortured flesh. His teeth ground at the thought as his insides quaked with dread and tension.

"Come on! Get it over with!" His shout echoed and faded through the forest. Above, panicked birds fluttered away in terrified flight. Rasping chuckles rose from the surrounding circle as they stood, unmoved by his outburst, waiting for something or someone.

Silence fell over the crowd as if cut by an axe as familiar sounds rose through the surrounding trees. Squeaking saddle leather and clicks from a horse's bridle rose in the silence as a rider forced a path through the encircling crowd. Round-eyed fear replaced the hungry eagerness on every goblin's and orc's face.

An oversized steed broke the circle, pacing toward Robart and forcing him to step back or have his feet crushed by the animal's massive hooves. The mount shone a startling white. A black-haired human with equally black eyes, wearing a long ebon robe, sat in the saddle. A chill crept up Robart's spine as orcs and goblins drew back and kneeled, heads bowed, shivering in fear.

Robart's thoughts reeled. Orcs and goblins hated humans, yet this one controlled them. *How can this be?*

"Ah, Robart, at last, we meet." The size of the steed made the rider appear imposing. Without this horse, he would be shorter than average. His small stature made the orcs' and goblins' fear even more confusing.

"You have led us on a merry chase these past few weeks." The man leaned forward, resting his forearms on the pommel of his saddle like a friend sharing a secret. A smile rose on his face as he scanned Robart's exhausted troops.

"However, since this ragged group is the best you can muster,"—he snorted with small head shakes, looking at the human skeletons—"I am certain you know your resistance is over."

Robart's heart sank as his troops withered under the man's scornful look. As his hands knotted into fists of frustration, the useless Garlan Branch pressed a deep furrow in his right palm.

"But you're human," Robart said. "How could you do this to your own race?"

"I did not give you permission to speak!" The man's eyes blazed at Robart as he straightened in his saddle. He halted, composed himself with visible effort, and leaned forward, again resting his fore-arms on his saddle's pommel. The lifeless smile returned to his face.

"But let's put that aside for the moment." His tone suggested that Robart would soon pay a high cost for his insolence. "It is true; I was born a human. But I have made myself so much more. You know, I was not born Halsey, nor was I born in this land." Lost in his visions, the man seemed to talk to himself. "However, those facts are for another tale and of no matter here."

The man's eyes lost focus as he slipped into the past.

"I was born the son of commoners in an unremarkable village, a place so dull even destiny did not linger there. As a child, I realized I was gifted with a natural talent for magic unlike any possessed before me. In their jealousy, my gift caused others to fear and plot against me. Despite the envy of those around me, I rose above my low birth to find acceptance in an academy where others, more knowledgeable in magical arts, agreed to teach me."

His vision refocused on Robart, eyes blazing.

"Do you know what it's like to develop in an environment where every person wants to control your talent? Where every individual views you as a stepping-stone for their gain? Where each instructor, each student, strives to hold you back for fear you will grow too mighty for them to control?" He glared at Robart. "No, of course you don't."

His eyes, which cleared for this interrogation, dulled as he faded back into his memories. "No one else can imagine its loneliness. I lived in a world where no one understood the power within me. However, I survived. I learned. And, in time, my tormentors paid a dear price for ignoring me." Without resurfacing into the world around him, the man breathed a deep sigh. "But that also is for another story.

"From birth, humans scorned me. They refused to acknowledge my superiority and grant me the rights my powers demanded. Many sought to undermine me, to defeat me. They even exiled me twice. So, humans must suffer.

"Since my exile, I dedicated several hundred years to studying, learning, and using the knowledge gained to plan my ascension. Now, my time is here. I won. All remaining humans in this land will serve me, and they will suffer and die until I feel avenged. I assure you that will take a long time indeed. In fact, I suspect no humans will be left alive long before that day comes."

Robart shivered beneath the angry madness in Halsey's eyes, revealing an insanity that allowed no appeal to justice or reason.

This creature's lived so long with his evil dreams that they've become his reality. His twisted mind believes torturing and killing every human will somehow make his life perfect. And I can do nothing to stop him.

"And now"—as though the action would make him appear more intimidating, Halsey drew his sword and raised it above his head like a staff of retribution—"my defeat of humanity will be complete." Walking his mount toward his victim,

Halsey bent forward, preparing to deliver the blow that would end Robart's and humanity's resistance.

The back of Robart's neck tightened rock-hard as he crouched in a defensive ball. Blindly, he raised his right arm, the hand still clutching the Garlan Branch, to protect his head against the incoming blow of Halsey's sword.

For a second, his vision blurred as his heartbeat swelled, growing within his chest. His face flushed red as warmth rose within every part of his body like a bright sun appearing from behind a black cloud. Power blossomed and surged through his being, growing as it infused his brain with energy. The Branch seemed no different, but now it called on him to act. Clearing his mind, he let the Branch guide his thoughts.

Halsey's sword raced down. The lethal blade stopped as if smashing against an invisible force. Shock washed over his face, replacing the evil sneer. Rising in his stirrups, he pointed his sword at Robart's chest.

"Kill him! Kill him, now!" His high-pitched screech shattered the forest's silence.

Orcs and goblins surged forward, tightening the circle. Robart needed to act now. Forcing the iron-strong tension from his neck, he relaxed his mind.

Confidence and strength roared through his being as the Garlan Branch fed knowledge into his mind.

For the first time in days, Robart stood straight. Pointing the Branch at Halsey, his mind commanding the crooked wand to aid him. Wonder flowed through every cell in his body as a blanket of dazzling light spread from the Branch and settled over the evil wizard and his troops. Halsey froze, immobilized, silenced by the Branch's power. As though deflating, the wizard shrank and aged. His horse stood unconcerned as it diminished along with its master. In seconds, a trembling, aging man sat atop a worn farm pony.

Robart pulled his eyes from the feeble, broken man as a collective gasp rose from goblins and orcs. Fighting to maintain concentration on Halsey, he scanned the encircling army. Fewer than two dozen orcs and goblins surrounded his group. Those remaining presented a pitiful sight. Gone were the fantastic weapons and armor that ensured their effortless victories. Now, they clutched only sticks, and their bodies were draped in the meanest rags.

Where are the others? Did Halsey create and arm them using magic? He must have.

Robart turned his attention back to the aged rider to find a child-sized, emaciated, shrunken-cheeked elderly man breaths away from his final weak gasp. He lowered the Branch before it completed its work. Death was an insufficient punishment for this creature.

The figure atop the scrawny pony was ancient beyond measure. Now, too weak to sit, the man's thin stomach lay along the animal's back. His knuckles strained white, clutching the mane to keep from sliding off. For one so frail, the short distance to the ground onto the pile of brown leaves would not spare his brittle life.

The Garlan Branch remained meshed with Robart's mind as he slid the stick behind his belt. Whimpers rose beneath the tear-stained cheeks of the withered husk of a man clinging to the pony's back. Moving to the aged mount's side, Robart grasped Halsey's snow-white hair, lifted the defeated sorcerer's head, and stared hard into dark, lifeless eyes.

"You've drained my power." Even those closest to the two men were challenged to understand Halsey's words as his voice crackled and grated like an unoiled hinge. "How?"

Halsey's eyes stared at Robart, filled with hope-less pleading, as his neck and shoulder muscles strained to free his head from Robart's firm grasp. He failed. The effort was too much.

"My army." Tears sparkled twin paths down

Halsey's cheeks. "My army." Glistening saliva leaked from the corners of his mouth. The lips went slack as Halsey's words faded to silence, and the light of intelligence dimmed from his eyes. Robart could only tell the man was still alive when he drew a slow, rattling breath.

Robart turned to the surrounding group of rag-covered goblins and orcs. "Who's in charge here?"

The small group shuffled together into a protective clump. After a quick, whispered conference, a goblin, shoved from behind, stumbled forward. With a jerky motion, it dropped its shabby stick, once an invincible sword, as though ridding itself of a flaming ember.

"I am, yer lordship." The scrawny beast trembled in fear. "Tho truth isss, we no want be here." The creature pointed at the drooping figure on his skinny, age-weary pony. "Him makesss usss, sssir. Mercy, please?"

Falling to its knees before Robart, the creature's trembling head bowed.

Anger and fear-driven adrenalin drained from Robart, replaced by near-debilitating fatigue and an urge to make things right. He needed to sit, relax, and let his mind drift. But this was not the time.

"We won't kill you unless you give us reason to. There's been enough unnecessary death to last this world an eternity." His voice reflected his weariness and disgust at the waste caused by one human's madness.

Robart pointed at the listless man. "Take him and take your troops. Leave this land and never return. If I hear even a whisper that you've entered this country again, I will hunt you down and end your threat forever. Do you understand?"

The kneeling goblin shivered as Robart glared down at it.

"Yesss, yer lordssship. Thank you, yer lordship."

The creature knee-walked forward, head lowered, intent on kissing Robart's scuffed, dust-covered boots. Robart jumped back.

"Go!" His shout startled the goblin to its feet.

With short, choppy motions, the goblin leader hurried to the pony and gathered its lead while chattering unintelligible syllables to its troops. The goblins and orcs dragged a half-dead wizard and his near-dead pony into the underbrush without looking back. Within minutes, the forest settled into the soothing rhythm of birdsongs and animals rustling through the forest's leafy carpet.

Robart turned to his exhausted troops.

"Rest, men. You've earned it. Tomorrow, we begin rebuilding."

ONE

Sixteen-year-old Leena Goodwin, the tailor's daughter, fought to concentrate on her mum's words. She wanted to listen. The tale was fascinating, but tonight's sunset was less than three hours away. With every passing moment, anxiety mounted within her. She dared not reveal her plan to anyone, even Riana, her eighteen-year-old sister and best friend. *Riana might not tell Mum and Da, and I love her, but confiding in her now is not worth the risk.*

Her mum's light brown eyes stared at her, awaiting a response.

Uh-oh. What did I miss? Did she ask a question, or does she expect me to ask one? Leena searched her mum's face for a clue. Her scrunched forehead prompted Leena to say something.

"So what happened to Halsey?" Leena asked.

"No one knows." Ellowin smoothed out the wrinkles of her blue flower-patterned dress and moved to the brick and clay wood-fired oven. Grabbing the charred paddle, she removed a browned loaf and set it on the sideboard."Robart sent him away two hundred years ago, and he disappeared. Some say he lived the rest of his life hiding in the Eastern Mountains. Others believe he still lives, planning to return someday to complete the destruction he started so long ago. I wouldn't worry about him too much. With Robart as our Great Wizard, Halsey would be a fool to try anything if he's still alive." She stirred the chicken stew in the black iron pot hanging by its wire handle in the kitchen fireplace. "Anyway, it's time for you to set the table. Your father will be home soon."

Leena hummed a lively tune as she scurried across the kitchen to get the plates from the cupboard. Like all the children in Quillan, she had heard the tale of Robart the Great Wizard and how he defeated Halsey with the Garlan Branch. No one in all of Allivan would ever wield as much power as Robart the Great Wizard. Leena could only dream of such things. Wizards still existed in faraway lands, but Leena had never seen one in person. Her mum had met a wizard traveling through town years ago. He needed a potion for his itchy feet.

Leena's mum was the village hedge witch, a local practitioner of nature-based care using herbs, plants, or magic spells that often controlled the four elements—earth, air, fire, and water—to heal and protect the villagers and their crops and livestock.

Riana was beginning her sixth year of training to be a hedge witch. When she completed her training in two years, as the older sister, she would serve as their mum's assistant until their mum retired. Then Riana would assume the duties of Quillan's hedge witch. The senior female in their mum's bloodline had served as Quillan's healer for as far back as anyone in the village remembered.

Since each town or village required only one hedge witch, Leena, the second daughter in their long line of hedge witches, would have to leave Quillan when she completed her training and search for another village that needed one. The thought of leaving home filled her with anxiety and excitement, but she still had four years to master her spells.

Despite the intriguing story, Riana sat at the kitchen table and drifted into a light nap, soothed by her mother's tone and the wood-burning oven's comfortable heat. Leena smiled as she passed her sister on the way to the shelves by the kitchen window. The temptation to give her sister a slight nudge in the ribs was more than she could repress.

Riana's head snapped up, searching for the source of her rude awakening. "Okay, Leena, wait until you fall asleep listening to one of Mum's tales and see how you like a jab in the ribs."

Leena, carrying a load of ceramic plates over to the table, couldn't help but giggle at Riana's dainty fists raised in a playful rendition of a carnival fighter with her cute face scrunched up in mock anger. Though younger, Leena, with the broad, solid shoulders and grace of a natural athlete, stood half a foot taller than her mum's and Riana's five and a half feet. Both girls knew Riana would have no chance in a physical battle. But even if someone was imprudent enough to attack her, Riana did not need to use physical violence to subdue an opponent. Her training so far included spells to soothe or neutralize even the most hostile patient or anyone else if she felt endangered.

"Eek," Leena responded to Riana as she set her burden on the table and then returned to the cupboard to gather four mugs. She studied her sister as she distributed the table settings, admiring how Riana always looked so refreshed and beautiful. She envied her sister's light brown, almost golden eyes, slender figure, and long, braided walnut brown hair, unlike her dark brown eyes and thick, unruly black hair she'd inherited from her da.

A wave of nerves suddenly overwhelmed her. She had big plans tonight and couldn't tell anyone about it. *I've never kept secrets from my family before.* Leena turned away as though looking for more dishes to set on the table, letting the excited flush drain from her cheeks.

The front door burst open. Sliding the last mug into place on the table, Leena rushed toward her da as he stepped inside, followed by a snow-laden wind blast that whitened his boots and ruffled his trousers as he struggled the door shut. She gave him a big welcome home hug.

"Whoa, little one. What's all this?" A pleased laugh rose from Janon, Quillan's village tailor, as he leaned forward to absorb Leena's charge. She swirled into a winter-chilled embrace against his chest and squeezed him like their separation had been for days, not hours. Her da, several inches shorter than Leena, pushed her back to arm's length and looked up, his critical face studying her expression.

Leena forced a smile. *Oops, I shouldn't have given him that lingering hug.* She had to be more careful. Her usual quick welcome-home hug would have been enough. Family meant everything to her. She hated deceiving them, but tonight was important. They couldn't find out where she was going. *Come on, Leena, act natural.*

"Nothing, just glad to see you." Butterflies fluttered a dance in her stomach under his suspicious, probing stare. She dared not look away. That would only make him more suspicious, and she could not lie to him if he asked probing questions. "And I thought I'd give you a big younger-daughter hug before Raina gets here."

Leena studied his face to see whether he believed her story. She suppressed a relieved sigh when he pecked his lips against her forehead, then removed his snow-covered boots and set them on a woven mat by the front door to dry.

WITH THE LAST cleaning swipe of her dishrag across the table, Leena followed Riana to the family room. Dinner had been excellent, as usual, and crowded with a lively conversation between delicious bites. Now, her da sat before the fireplace, absorbing the heat as he lounged in his oversized chair, fingers interlaced across his trim stomach. With his hunger soothed, he relaxed, his suit jacket removed, and his shirt collar's lacing loosened.

"So, whose turn is it to choose the game tonight?" Her da asked this question every evening, even though they all knew whose turn it would be. They rotated each night from Da to Mum, then Riana, and finally Leena.

"It's mine," Riana spoke before Leena could answer, "and I choose Ten Pins."

Leena looked out at the darkness beyond the window. "That might not be the best choice since it's pitch dark with three feet of snow on the ground." She flashed an innocent grin toward her sister. "And you chose last night. So tonight, the choice is actually mine, and I choose Save the Maiden."

Leena made an internal vow to concentrate on the game. Each minute at dinner had seemed like hours as she struggled to act and look normal. With luck, Save the Maiden would consume her attention for the next few hours.

Leena raced to the bedroom she shared with Riana and snagged Bessie, the doll her mum had sewn for her as a birth gift when she was just a bump in her mother's stomach. Although worn from use, Leena ensured Bessie was always clean and dressed. Returning to the family room, she set the doll on the floor away from the fire and handed each family member a rope ring.

"Now," her da said, "since it's your night to choose, you get to create the story's first sentence."

The game's rules were simple: Each player tried to throw a rope ring to settle around the doll. If successful, they added a sentence to a story that developed throughout the game. Each successful player would try to concoct a sentence that made adding another logical sentence difficult. When seventeen sentences were added, the person who added the most won.

Stomach knotted, Leena concentrated on the game and pretended tonight was just an ordinary evening at home. She was eager for the game to be over so she could begin her night's mission.

Leena smiled in anticipation of delivering a challenging sentence the others had to scramble to follow: "Once, an evil ogre captured a beautiful princess and stole her away to his hidden cave in the forest. " She looked at her father. "Okay, Da, your turn."

Eying his target, Janon lined up his shot and, with a curl of his wrist to add spin, sent his rope hoop sailing across the room to settle over Bessie with ease. Everyone clapped, even though he rarely ever missed.

"However, no one knew the ogre was really a cursed prince. So, that's two sentences, leaving only fifteen more to complete the tale," her father said. Again, everyone applauded at the masterful way he diverted the story in a new and exciting direction.

Ellowin's toss hit Bessie on the head and rolled into a corner. Chuckles vibrated the room as Riana's toss fell two feet short of the target. Leena lined up her first throw. The hoop sailed in a graceful arc across the room and settled atop the ring thrown by her da as though drawn there by magic.

"The ogre prince did not want the princess, but he needed to drink her blood to help him return to human form." Nervousness fled as Leena allowed the game to consume her thoughts.

In the next three rounds, Ellowin and Riana each added a sentence to the story. As usual, Leena and her da competed to add the most outlandish twists to the story, hoping to prevent each other from providing a new or challenging sentence. Ultimately, her da won the game with eight sentences to Leena's seven. In the end, Janon left the ogre to live his life as a freak in a carnival show, and the princess married a handsome tailor. Tired but happy, the family retired to their beds.

For the next two hours, Leena lay in bed, staring at the ceiling, watching moonlight shadows creep across the wall. Time inched by as minutes stretched toward hours. Leena feared her racing heartbeats were loud enough to wake her sleeping sister, just six feet away. Usual creaks from the house settling in the chilled winter wind made her palms sweat as she clutched them into tight fists beneath the thick, down-filled quilt.

Are Mum and Da awake? Did they notice my nervousness at dinner? Are they sitting in the family room waiting to see what I'm up to?

She dared not rise too soon. Tonight might be her only chance. She had to ensure her family slept before she dressed for the chilled night ahead. Moonlight crept across the bedroom floor. After waiting and watching for an endless lifetime, the silvery glow touched the third floorboard, and her patience reached its limit. She had to leave now.

Easing her cover off, keeping her movements so silent they would not disturb a mouse, Leena lowered her bare feet to the cool wooden floor. A nervous rumble rose from her stomach, shattering the bedroom's quiet. Before a squeal could escape, she clamped her lips between her teeth and halted as stiff as a statue. Only her sister's soft breaths disturbed the silent room.

With infinite care, Leena donned warm clothing, pausing every few seconds to listen for any noise that might destroy her plan. Willing her feet to move, she crept through the house to the front door.

Her hand grasped the latch. This was where her plan would fail, if at all. A silent prayer rose within her that the cold would not cause the hinges to squeak or the wind outside to rush in and howl through the opening, as it did when her da arrived home. Leena lifted the latch, pulled the door open, slipped through, and eased it shut behind her. As though stuck, her hand refused to leave the door handle.

Let go. Leena sent the mental command to her stubborn fingers. *No matter how this turns out, I have to go.* Her fingers straightened, and the hand dropped. Turning her back, she stepped away from her home.

TWO

On Midwinter Night, the longest night of the year, earth-magic forces aligned to prepare for spring's unfolding. Only a well-trained, experienced witch or wizard—protected by their most effective wards to fend off foul spirits—would dare venture into the forest on this night. And they would only risk the dangers because this was when winter herbs were most potent.

Unschooled in the hideous consequences the creatures of the night could demand from a lone, defenseless girl, Leena huffed clouds of warm breath as she struggled against accumulated snow, darkness, and the bitter chill. Looking up, she searched the frozen stars dotting a pitch-black sky above the forest's winter-barren branches. The view showed no change. But she knew time raced as the bare legs beneath her long black woolen skirt fought endless inches forward through knee-high snow, slowing her progress to a crawl. She tried to ignore her freezing, mitten-encased hands tucked beneath her armpits and the bitter air burning her face behind her shawl's insufficient protection.

She thought the trek would be the easiest part when she had developed this plan. Now, she chastised herself for not leaving sooner. *Why didn't I think about this stupid deep snow and freezing cold slowing me down?*

Time was her biggest enemy. The stars told her midnight had passed. Her heart sank. The farther she traveled, the more the winter fought against her. Her quest would fail if she did not reach her goal before sunrise.

Only her movements broke the thick silence. Her labored breathing huffed long fog clouds while her red, chaffed legs carved a draining, time-devouring path through the frozen snow. Her chattering teeth provided a backbeat to her struggling symphony.

The shining full moon disappeared behind a patch of thick clouds. With only the pale star-glow to guide her, Leena struggled to see nearby trees. Shivering, she pulled the heavy woolen shawl tighter around her ears, hoping to extract a little more warmth as the gnawing cold nibbled away at her internal heat.

Her thoughts drifted to the hedge witch wand tucked behind her skirt's waistband. How long could she resist casting a heat spell? It would create a warm, comforting envelope around her, and she could use a simple illumination spell to light her way. Her hedge witch wand was more than sufficient for these tasks. But a near-silent voice told her that using magic before she reached her goal would jeopardize her mission.

As though to tease her, the cold and fatigue created internal visions of a fire crackling and leaping in a hearth, its heat flowing over her as she snuggled in a comfortable chair wrapped deep within a warm blanket. *No!* Shaking her head, she dispelled the image before tears of doubt and longing could trail frozen streams down her cheeks.

Why am I doing this? Uh-oh, that's the wrong question. Spirit, protect me. I didn't mean it. A lump rose in her throat. *Has that thought ruined my quest? Maybe I should turn around now. I might get home before anyone wakes.*

Crack!

Leena jumped as ice snapped a large branch above and it thudded to the ground. The vibration of its impact shuddered in her chest. With her vision hindered by the lack of moonlight, an unseen shower of frozen powder settled on her face. She swiped her frigid cheeks with an armpit-warmed mitten, smearing icy snow into sensitive, reddened skin.

The surrounding forest grew darker. Her trek's end was close.

Resettling the stiff shawl over her head and around her face and shoulders, Leena slapped her hands together to dislodge the snow and ice clinging to her mittens. She needed a moment to regain her bearings.

She couldn't back down now. Not when she was on a mission to find a Garlan Branch.

Her thoughts scrambled through her brain. *I wonder how large it will be. Should I have brought a bag to carry it? What if I succeed? Can I keep my hedge witch wand if I'm selected?*

Closing her eyes, Leena opened her mind. She needed to remain calm. Her mind drifted to her mum's tale of the Garlan Tree.

The Garlan Tree was older than legend. No one had seen the Garlan Tree other than Skylar, the first holder of the Garlan Branch, and Robart, the current Great Wizard. Not even the oldest person in Allivan knew where it stood. The tree was more ancient than time and possessed magic beyond imagination.

According to legend, the Garlan Tree enabled humans to settle in this forest. If the tales were correct, it took two things for the Garlan Tree to bestow a Branch: a time of great trouble and a worthy hero.

Centuries ago, goblins and orcs ruled the forest, using its resources to provide for their needs, giving nothing but destruction in return. The Garlan Tree sensed humans—a hunted and dying breed—and summoned them to the forest. Then, using knowledge gained over thousands of years, it spread the fear of man throughout the goblin and orc races. Over the next few decades, the goblins migrated south to the wastelands, and the orcs wandered southwest to the mountain caves. They returned only twice in the next thousand years, reuniting and attempting to reclaim the forest. Both times, the Garlan Tree selected a hero to defeat them.

Leena had dreamed of being a hero from her earliest memories but knew she had little chance. Everyone expected her to settle into a life of caring for her chosen village with little prospect of ever performing heroic deeds.

But she still dreamed. Sometimes, when looking for herbs alone in the forest, she pretended her hedge witch wand was a sword. Swiping the wand as though in battle, she dueled bloody pirates and giant, terrifying monsters.

During one of these ferocious battles last summer, she'd discovered the Garlan Tree. After taking a mighty blow from the staff of an imaginary giant, she fell backward and struck an invisible force. It stopped her fall and repelled her through the air, where she'd landed in an awkward tumble of skirts and shrieks.

Stunned, she wondered what she'd hit but saw nothing. Leena had gathered herself and approached the area. Her extended fingers encountered a force so gentle it could shift the path of any creature, guiding it away. She'd pushed her hand against it, but it resisted. The barrier was a magical shield. But she saw nothing beyond except an open space in the forest.

Something was not right in the protected clearing. As with the surrounding forest, dappled shadows covered the ground. Something invisible inhabited the space.

Then Leena had raised her wand and cast a discerning spell. Something resisted her spell. She sensed a force washing through her mind, determining whether it wished to be revealed. The air before her shimmered. As by magic, the Garlan Tree appeared. There could be no question. Once exposed, its majesty and strength were undeniable. A sense of fathomless age rippled around it.

In that moment, Leena had stood there, stunned. *The Garlan Tree exists! The tales are more than legends, and I've found it! But what does it mean? Am I destined to be a hero, or have I stumbled upon something I should never have seen? What will be the consequences of this discovery? Will I be allowed to leave the forest with this knowledge?* A thousand thoughts and questions had flooded Leena's mind. *Why did the Garlan Tree appear to me? How does one get a Branch from an unapproachable tree?*

She had searched the ground for a twig that could have fallen from the Garlan Tree. Under the summer sun, leaves and small twigs covered the ground, but none that could serve as a wand. Carefully, keeping one hand on the protective barrier, she circled the invisible wall, finding only a few tiny stems. The border was so far from the tree that no branch could fall beyond it.

Feeling frustrated and confused, Leena had thumped to a seat on the forest floor. Closing her eyes, she slowed her breathing to clear her mind. Her hands formed cups in her lap, ready to receive whatever knowledge might come. If legends were true, two others had secured a Branch from the Garlan Tree. She was determined to be the third.

As she sat that summer's day, her inner vision faded into a nighttime winter forest. Although warm sunshine surrounded her, she saw and felt the chill of an encompassing iced-coated woodland. Within its protective shell, the Garlan Tree stood untouched by the winter cold, impervious to the icy forces biting at the surrounding woods. With a sudden snap that shattered the frozen calm, a Branch flew from the upper reaches of the Garlan Tree. As though hurled by an unseen hand, it flew outside its protective barrier and submerged in the deep snow of the surrounding Midwinter Night. As if in a dream, Leena watched her hand—red and chapped from the cold—reaching toward a new crooked furrow in the snow beside her. Something had fallen and buried itself there.

For six months, her dream vision of where the Garlan Branch was located had consumed her. For six months, she had waited for this night. She couldn't fail.

The memory of last summer's warmth faded as the wind bit her cheeks. She scanned the area. With the barest hint of dawn outlining the horizon, her hand reached toward a crooked black line carved into the white-powder blanket beside her. She hesitated.

That can't be it. Something that small and thin

could not contain such power. If I dip my hand into that rift and the Garlan Branch is there, will my life never be the same? What will this mean for my family? I'm not ready for this responsibility.

There would be a high price to pay for this gift. Once accepted, her life would cease to be hers. The forces that required the Garlan Tree to give up its Branch would govern her future. *Do I want this? Am I worthy of accepting it? But the Garlan Tree would not have revealed itself if I wasn't meant to have it. It's older than time and far wiser than me. Who am I to argue with such an intelligent and powerful entity?*

As though controlled by someone else, her mitten curled and uncurled, flexing over the crack in the snow where the Garlan Branch might rest. Hesitating, it hovered above the crack and withdrew as she inspected the winter forest.

I can't do it. It's far better to walk away now and spend the rest of my life trying to forget the Garlan Tree exists.

Leena removed her mittens, closed her eyes, huffed warm breath into her cupped palms, and rubbed them together, producing friction-generated heat. Warmed, she prepared to put her mittens back on, leave this place, and try to forget everything that had happened tonight. Maybe she could still get home before her parents awoke.

Then, as if it had a will of its own, her bare right hand flew down through the deep line in the snow and grabbed the Branch faster than she thought possible. Retracting it, she stared at the fourteen-inch-long, crooked, normal-looking, bark-covered twig.

I did it. Oh Spirit! I did it!

Her body and mind jolted as though struck by lightning. The winter's chill flew from her like rust flakes from an iron bar dropped on stone. Unsuspected power flowed through her, energizing everything within.

This is not a hedge witch wand. This power should belong to a mighty wizard or maybe only the Great Wizard himself.

An angry bull of doubt crashed through her mind. How dare she assume she had the right to touch a Branch from the Garlan Tree?

I'm not worthy. I'm a sixteen-year-old girl who daydreams of fame and glory. A hedge witch whose training has barely begun. I have definitely overstepped my bounds. I don't doubt there'll be a high price for this audacity.

A lump rose in Leena's throat as tears of shame and fear fought to surface. *What will Mum and Riana say? I can't keep this secret from them. What have I done?*

Maybe she could give it back. Leena opened her palm and rotated the Branch toward the ground. It stuck fast, as though glued to her hand. *Is this a curse? Can I never again release this wand?*

Jumping up, she whipped her arm over her head, trying to cast the Branch as far as she could, but it stayed attached. A blue spark shot from the Branch's tip as her hand reached the end of its throwing motion. With a crack that shattered the forest's peaceful silence, the tiny sparkle ignited a leafless tree a hundred feet distant. Dancing orange flames, crackling like an angry fire demon, flared against the pale pink of the increasing dawn. Leena grabbed the hedge witch wand from behind her skirt waist with her left hand and cast an extinguishing spell before the fire could spread.

How did that happen? I didn't cast a spell. I don't know any Garlan Branch spells. In welcome silence, she watched a finger of gray smoke rise from the blackened tree. Hand shaking, she stared at the Branch, highlighted against the early morning-pinked snow. Her mum was fond of saying, "With great power comes great responsibility." For the first time, she truly understood what that meant. Maybe she was growing up.

THREE

The Branch's rough bark trembled in her hand as a warning vibration flowed within it. Her eyes flashed around the area. Something was coming, something that threatened her and the Branch. Dread grew within her. The approaching danger drew nearer, growing with each second. Becoming too powerful to ignore. She had to hide, but where?

No shrubs peeked up from beneath the white blanket around her, and nearby trees stood winter-darkened and leafless. Scanning the area, she realized she did not know which direction the danger was coming from. But every sense told her something lethal was speeding toward her.

She had to hide now. But where? There was no shelter nearby.

The Garlan Tree was once again cloaked and invisible within its protective barrier. She, however, stood in an open forest. She had to do something. Her brain felt as slow as winter tree sap.

Move! her mind screamed.

A high flicker of motion to her right warned she had no time left. Without stopping to consider, she flung herself headfirst—hands up to protect her face—into a high snow mound. She thanked the Spirit for finding her a windblown drift, not a snow-covered bush.

Kneeling, hunched into a ball, Leena remained statue-still as the frigid pile collapsed over her, resettling into a new mound indistinguishable from others in the surrounding forest. Breathing air trapped beneath her upper body and her knees, she shivered as small snow piles settled beneath her shawl and trickled down her spine.

Hiding within the frozen refuge, Leena knew her shivering would be noticeable to whatever approached. But she dared not use the Branch again without knowing how to control its power.

Slow inches at a time, her left hand snaked down to the hedge witch wand pressing against her stomach. As her fingers touched it, her mind sent a warming spell. Her shivering ceased. She needed a strategy now. It would not take long for her increasing body heat to melt her snow shield.

She needed to see what was coming. Careful not to disturb the protective barrier, Leena used her new Branch to poke several holes in the sides and top of her mound and peer through the openings. Beyond one of the small tunnels, the charred tree, with its tendril of gossamer smoke, painted a restful scene against the deepening rose of the coming daylight.

Something flickered across the snow. A midnight-black silhouette rippled across the white mounds at the burned tree's base. In the winter's silence, a large, vee-shaped shadow drifted across the moonlit ground cover like an ebon phantom. *Oh no. What is that?* Before she could see enough of the creature's outline, the phantom passed over her hiding place and beyond her limited sight. Leena breathed a relieved sigh. *How long should I wait before it's safe to come out?*

In less than a minute, the shadow reappeared, larger, gliding toward the tree.

Icy dread flooded her being as a night-dark raven, as massive as a dray horse, flew in ghostly silence. Gliding lower, it circled the smoking tree. With a wingspan broader than a barn door, it soared in graceful circles above the fuming embers like a vulture preparing to dine on carrion. Its head constantly swiveled as its soulless eyes scanned the frozen landscape.

The dark specter was searching for something.

It's looking for me.

A voice inside told Leena that she was the object of this horrid shadow's hunt. Someone had dispatched this dark seeker to locate and destroy her. A graveyard chill shivered through her. She was trapped. Running now would be useless. She had no hope of surviving the wicked creature's beak and talons. She dared not breathe for fear the beast would discover her whereabouts.

The black phantom circled wider, searching the ground. The scorching light of its glowing, yellow eyes passed over the mound where Leena kneeled hidden. Her eye looked into the creature's depthless glare for the briefest instant. Her pulse quickened. She had never sensed so much concentrated hate. *Did it see me?* She felt small and helpless, captured and immobilized by its glare. Her stomach tightened like a drum as her bowels threatened to release.

The eye passed on, freeing her gaze as the massive bird glided silently over her mound, continuing its scan. A deep sigh broke the silence within her snow mound. *It didn't see me. That was close.*

A tear emerged from a bottomless well of fear

and trailed down her cheek as the bird circled overhead. She felt like an infant abandoned by its mother, all alone and defenseless. Tension gritted her teeth, aching her jaw. She longed to burst from her feeble shelter and run screaming home to her family's protective arms, never to leave their safety again.

The world remained silent. Nothing moved but the gentle smoke column rising from the scorched tree and the ominous bird circling above. Seconds crawled past like hours.

How long do I have to remain hidden? How will I know if it's safe to leave?

A furious wind surged with the fury of a cyclone from behind her hiding place. The blizzard threw blinding snow past her mound, hiding the smoking tree behind a swirling white curtain.

The monster landed behind me. It's here. I've been found.

Hot, fear-driven tears flowed along her cheeks. Her throat closed as if an apple had lodged within it. Her heart pounded, a living thing fighting to escape, desperate to burst from her chest. She wanted to sniff back the salty flow dribbling from her nostrils, but she didn't dare move.

Spirit, please make this a dream.

But it was no dream. The adventure was real this

time, and Leena did not feel like a hero. She felt small, frightened, and helpless.

Her mind took on a life of its own, darting about, seeking wisdom, answers, or some solution to this situation. *Maybe I can break out of this mound before the thing destroys it. Then I can dive into another pile to hide. It won't know I'm here if it can't see me. Right? All this swirling snow should conceal me. Perhaps it just landed here to look around.*

The beast's footsteps crunched on snow as it circled her haven, looking for an entrance into her half-destroyed hiding place. The plodding of the creature's oversized feet paused. Dread drove all reason from her brain. She crouched, waiting.

Like a dragon's roar, a deep howl rose, its thundering resonance smothering all other sounds. Snow blew around her, pelting her, forcing her to shield her face from its icy shards. Eyes clenched shut against the storm, Leena frantically grabbed at the swirling snow, trying to catch it, rebuild her walls, and restore her glacial hideaway.

As quickly as it began, the storm eased when the creature looming before her slowed the flapping of its enormous wings. Leena fought to open her powder-encrusted eyes. Through frost-blurred vision, she found her snow mound protection no longer existed. She crouched, helpless, exposed to whatever evil the creature might unleash upon her.

Leena gasped. The demon bird towered before her, refolding its massive wings against its horrible body. Her stomach rolled from the reek of rotting flesh drifting through the air with its movement.

The beast seemed twice her height, with a curved beak made to tear flesh and long, sharp nails capable of digging deep into body tissue to hold its prey as it feasted. Fear clenched her soul as she imagined the burning agony of skin and muscle being torn from her back by a razor-sharp beak and digging claws as she screamed her throat raw with no hope of rescue. The creature's evil, unblinking golden eyes stared at her with a pitiless look of triumph, destroying all hope of escape. She was going to die the slow and painful death of a captured prey.

Still, a little voice in the back of her mind spoke. *When hope is gone, there's nothing left to lose. If I must die, I'm going out in style.*

Without hesitation, Leena rose, standing tall, a dwarf challenging the leviathan before her. Perhaps, in her last instant, she could raise some doubt within the creature. Maybe her actions could at least plant a seed of confusion in the thing before it took her life.

The massive raven tilted its head like a dog, wondering how to react to a new command. Its golden eyes sparkled as it stared down at her, enjoying the fear it created before it devoured her.

She jabbed the beast in the chest using the Branch as a sword. "Ha!" she cried. "Take that!" she yelled in her best hero's voice. Confusion flickered across the merciless eyes. Then, the creature's body expanded as if bloating by an irresistible pressure within. Its chest stretched gaps between the midnight black feathers, and its eyes swelled in their sockets, growing larger with each second.

Wide-eyed, Leena eased backward.

Sensing something solid looming next to her, she risked a glance. *Oh good. It's a gigantic tree. Just what I need.* Drawing a deep, relieved breath, Leena leaped behind the tree. Before she could exhale, a loud pop exploded the creature, scattering its remains in a flurry of feathers and red meat chunks.

Stepping from behind the tree, Leena stared at the bloody mess decorating the snow. She stood immobilized by what she had done, unable to form a coherent thought. White-knuckled, she gripped the Garlan Branch.

This Branch is most definitely not a hedge witch wand.

She stared at the Branch that had caused so

much destruction. It looked like a typical twig. Nothing about it suggested the stick could obliterate a monster with so little effort.

Leena's stomach turned. It could hold back no more. With frantic haste, she tore the shawl from her face, fell to her hands and knees, and spewed the ground with the vile acid of fear. From far off, she heard sobbing behind the gut-wrenching spew. After several minutes, she recognized the heart-felt cries as hers. Rolling away from the nauseating stench of last night's dinner remains, she surrendered to the gasping relief of tears.

Her cries shattered the forest tranquility, but she could no more control them than she could change the seasons. Release flowed from the center of her being, exiting her lips while inviting the earth to comfort her. Words gushed from her, penetrating the forest peace like regular heartbeats mixed with the hoarse bellows. "Mummy, Mummy, Mummy," she sobbed over and over, unable to stop the one-word chant warding off her residual fear.

Over time, her cries diminished to hushed moans, then faded to soft sniffling whimpers. Fatigue replaced fear and relief. The night had been endless. As she looked toward the rising sun peaking over the horizon, her eyes misted as her eyelids drifted shut. Leena snapped to attention. She needed to get home and slip into bed before anyone woke up.

Her weak legs wobbled as she stood. Fighting her fatigue, she took a step forward, then another, but her body felt heavy, and she could go no further. She collapsed to her knees. *Spirit, help me get home.* She rose with all the strength she could muster, only to fall back down. Her energy was drained. She let out a whimper. *Mum and Da are going to kill me if they wake up and I'm not there.*

Leena looked toward the clearing where the Garlan Tree stood. Gripping the Branch, she closed her eyes and let her mind sense the protective enclosure hiding and protecting the tree. Like a welcoming hearth after a winter's trek through harsh wind and knee-deep snow, the giant tree called to her. Unthinking, she allowed the silent promise of sanctuary to draw her frozen feet forward, carving a trail through the thick winter blanket and into the eternal sunshine and warmth within the tree's protective shell.

The Garlan Tree let me in. How? She now knew the Tree had a protection spell that hid it from all but a holder of the Garlan Branch, but she didn't know if she had the ability to invoke it. Her eyes felt heavy, and she had trouble keeping them open. *I'll just rest for a bit before I go home.*

The vast power that permitted her to enter enveloped and protected her in a comforting warmth while restoring her strength. Feeling secure, she touched the hedge witch wand nestled behind her skirt's waistband to ensure it had survived the battle. Its rough texture, warm from contact with her skin, soothed her mind. For the moment, this conflict was over. She had survived. A wave of mental and emotional exhaustion flowed through her mind, pulling her body down. Her eyes closed before her head reached the ground. Unseen, unsuspected by anyone save the Garlan Tree, Leena slept on an invisible dry patch within the snow-covered forest.

FOUR

A hooting owl's call echoed through the dark trees, dragging Leena back to a forest basking in the pink light of a setting sun. Beyond the Garlan Tree's protective barrier, dark tree shadows lengthened against the forest's snow-covered ground as another night approached. Closing her eyes, she fought to recall the half-remembered dream lurking at the tattered edges of her awareness. In her dream, she saw smoke and flames. Women were running, carrying their screaming children. She shivered the nightmare away. She had more than enough to worry about now.

Lying with her face pillowed on a soft bed of winter-darkened leaves, Leena opened her eyes. A two-foot-long black feather, caught by its quill end in a small mound of snow beyond the barrier, waved at her like the mitten-encased hand of a departing friend.

Oh, Spirit. I slept the day away. She bolted upright. *I am in so much trouble! How can I ever explain this?* Memories of the conflict flooded her brain. The Garlan Branch was still attached to her hand, and the raven-black feather proved it wasn't a dream. She needed to get her thoughts straight, review the events, consider what they meant, and figure out what to do. *But not now. I have no time.*

Leena searched the growing darkness. How could she sleep through an entire day? A new dusting of snow sparkled in the winter outside the Tree's protective shell. Except for the waving feather, snow covered all evidence of the raven's destruction.

Now, two nights and a day will pass before I reach Quillan. How can I possibly explain my absence? Even if I could run through this blasted snow, I can't get back before morning. Oh, Mum, I am so sorry.

With no warning, red pain flared in her legs, clouding her vision. Her muted groans drifted through the trees as her hands rubbed and kneaded tight calves, trying to reduce the painful knots induced by her arduous trek. Stabbing cramps lit her brain with agony as her thumbs dug deep to prod the spasms away.

Oh, Spirit. Where's my brain?

She touched the hedge witch wand behind her belt with her left hand and sent a mental healing spell into the screaming muscles. Leena let herself enjoy the relief as her legs released their tension.

Inspecting the Garlan Branch in her right hand, she wondered whether it would allow her to store it beside her hedge witch wand. Palm sweating, she slid the stick behind her waistband, uncurled her fingers, lifted her hand away, and heaved a relieved sigh as it stayed snuggled against her abdomen. Since she couldn't discard the Branch, this would at least allow her to carry it comfortably while it remained hidden from view.

Leena combed her fingers through her tangled hair, removing the twigs and bark. She then brushed leaves and twigs from her tunic and skirt before resettling the shawl around her head, face, and shoulders. *I need to go home now.*

As Leena exited the Garlan Tree's forever-summer shelter, a white-feathered owl, startled by her movements, lifted in silent flight from a nearby tree and disappeared against the snowy background. Her boots sank into the deep snow. Touching her hedge witch wand, she sent the mental command to cast a warming spell over herself. At least she could be more comfortable on the way back to Quillan.

Light from the bright, silver-coin moon flitted through the trees above, keeping pace as it marked her progress through the winter forest. Her footsteps crunched a regular beat through the dry, powdered snow, settling a soothing peace within her, and she let her thoughts drift.

She had told no one about finding the Garlan Tree last summer. First, she feared no one would believe her, and second, it was personal. The Garlan Tree had selected her. Even if she had been at the right spot and had fallen just as she had, the Garlan Tree could have shifted her around its protective bubble, none the wiser.

But the Garlan Tree chose me. What did that mean? Was there going to be a time of great trouble? She was lucky with the raven, but she was no hero. She was a half-trained hedge witch. The little magic she knew only provided healing and good fortune for others. Maybe the Garlan Tree wanted her to give the Branch to someone else, but to whom? Her mother?

Mum! Oh, Spirit! What will she be thinking by now?

Feet stomping up and down, hips swinging wide with each step, and elbows pumping in agitation,

Leena struggled to force her body faster, trying to plow through the deep drifts as if they did not exist. Within a hundred yards, her breath came in deep, heaving gasps with little increase in speed. She slowed to a more comfortable pace.

An hour or two won't make any difference. I'm already in more trouble than I can imagine.

Would her mother think she'd been with a boy? *No, surely not.* A vision of Thomai in his father's shop, bare to the waist, a sheen of sweat glistening on his chest as he worked the bellows, filled her mind. Every girl in the village admired him. He'd shown no interest in Leena. But he was kind and handsome, and his hands were so strong. The thought of an emotional attachment to Thomai made her stomach tingle.

Stop it! This is just a silly little girl's daydream. Focus.

She could see her mum's worried face. Would she think wolves had taken her? No, hedge witches didn't fear wolves. Maybe there would be a concern if foraging for food was difficult. Still, despite the season, game creatures were more than sufficient now to satisfy the wolves' hunger. Besides, she could cure the unfortunate animal's hunger with a wave of her wand. Her mum knew wolves posed no danger to her.

Perhaps she could say she went seeking a winter-blooming moth flower. Rumors of their existence and remarkable healing powers had been circulating as far back as anyone remembered. Her mum would think she was a little child to chase such a rumor.

What am I thinking? I can't lie to Mum. I need to tell as much of the truth as possible and hope she understands.

Her feet dragged, heavy with dread, as she continued her journey. This trip would end the special closeness she shared with her mum. She would understand and accept whatever Leena told her. Still, her mum knew Leena so well and would know her daughter was withholding information. The inability to tell her mum everything would create a rift in their relationship that time could not heal.

Leena was not a Skylar or a Robart. They were mighty warriors who barely succeeded. She was only a teenage girl. Despite her dreams of glory, her chance of surviving the calamity she now faced was nonexistent. She could not let Mum worry about her safety for the rest of her life. The thought slowed her feet even more.

Her da's response would be a different story. Despite her dread at arriving home so late, Leena giggled and did a one-footed spin with her arms held wide and head thrown back, anticipating her da's reaction when she told him of last night's adventures, never letting on that the tale was based on fact.

Since Leena had learned to talk, her da encouraged her to tell tales of wonder about her daily activities. In trade, he shared stories of exciting, fantastic adventures that kept her awake and fantasizing into the wee hours. Living the peaceful life of a village tailor, he could only dream of exciting exploits, knowing they could never be more than wishes. She could hardly wait to tell him about the raven. He would never believe her story, anyway. Her mum would cluck her tongue and walk away, shaking her head and smiling at the special bond Leena and her da shared.

The last sunlight disappeared beyond the horizon. As Leena continued through the moonlit forest, her thoughts turned to her older sister. Riana was always there for her and was more than a sister. She was a second mother and her best friend. She had taught Leena the spring dance, watched over her selection of herbs and wildflowers, and helped her through awkward spells.

Besides a few silly younger sister dreams, Leena had kept no secrets from her sister. Everyone said

Leena and Riana were closer than twins. Like their mum, Riana would accept what Leena told her, but everything would change. For the first time in their relationship, Leena would have to hide an important part of herself from her sister. She stopped.

I have to go back and try to return the Branch. Her head hung as her throat grew thick and tears threatened. *No, I've had enough tears for one night, and it would be useless, anyway. For whatever reason, fate's chosen me. Wherever it leads, I'll have to fulfill my destiny. I'm not even sure I want to be a hero anymore. Not if it means losing the closeness I share with my family.*

This trip had been nothing like her fantasies, and she suspected her vision of a future with the Garlan Branch would not match her girlhood dreams of an adventurous life. She never even considered what possessing a Branch would do to her family and friends. In her daydreams, she would secure the Garlan Branch, return home, and dispatch whatever threatened her world. After that, she would become a partner with the Great Wizard. Her job would be to venture forth and protect Allivan citizens from all future threats. Heroes in the bards' tales always won and then lived happy lives, sharing their adventurous tales, fame, and wealth with their loved ones.

I've been so naïve. That oversized bird terrified me into uselessness. How could I ever consider facing an attacking army of orcs or goblins? I'll probably be too busy crying for my mum.

Like her mother and sister, Leena was born gifted with the power to heal. The women in her family had always been hedge witches and always would be. Their job was to use natural magic to treat animals, people, and crops. Her vivid imagination had blinded her to that fact.

Leena stumbled over a hidden branch. The night was dark, and the trek was long and challenging. Fighting the deep snow for hours was taking its toll. Her fingers slid to the Garlan Branch against her stomach, but she dared not use it to try casting an illumination spell. Any mistake might end with her burning the forest to a mass of cinders. She lifted her hand away. The Garlan Tree might have limitless powerful spells. Still, she dared not experiment with its capabilities until she knew what had summoned the raven.

Touching her hedge witch wand, Leena sent the mental command to cast an illumination spell. The magic light threw long, dark shadows that rolled and flowed in dancing patterns on the snow.

She grabbed a fallen branch that formed an arched bench and brushed a small avalanche from its surface. The night had passed while she walked and thought. To the east, the sun's bright yellow arc peeked above the horizon. Pulling her skirt tighter around her legs, she sat and let the growing sunlight seep into her.

A muffled silence cloaked the land. The scurry of night creatures returning home had ceased, and the tentative movements of daytime animals had not yet begun. Dawn's hush blanketed the world.

Leena let the forest's peace comfort her. With her eyes closed and the rising sunlight warming her face, the world shined fresh within her. She let her worries and fears flow into the ground beneath her, cleansing her mind as they returned to the Earth Mother. With deep, healing breaths, her lungs drew in the crisp, early-morning fragrance of winter trees. Touching her hedge witch wand, Leena collapsed its illumination spell and enjoyed the dawn. She inhaled the fresh winter air and became one with the forest. After a few minutes, she opened her eyes. Arms of black tree shadows reached for her across golden dawn-lit snow as though the awakening forest was offering itself for her protection.

It was time to move on.

A chill snaked up Leena's spine as she stood atop the last hill overlooking Quillan. Her palms moistened with sweat as uneasiness crept up the back of her neck, tingling within her skull. For a moment, she tried to convince herself that her fear was because she needed to explain her whereabouts to her family, but her drum-tight stomach muscles told her otherwise. The still air warned her that the golden, late-morning sun hid ominous secrets. Her mind screamed that something was not right. A small voice within said that her life was in as much danger now as it had been when she faced the oversized raven.

The village was too calm, too still. The sounds of

citizens moving about and starting their day should rise to her ears. Even in the chilled midwinter, some townsfolk should be shopping. But there were no echoes of men chopping wood for stove and hearth fires, no shouted greetings and gossip as store-keepers and shoppers added to the village's tran-quility.

She could not stop the growing alarm within her as she stood listening, hoping for some sound, some sign of a wakening village rising to her welcoming ears. Although a dim haze shrouded the town beyond the trees, no smoke trails rose from kitchen fires, reaching to touch the cloudless blue sky with soft, dark fingers. A faint, smoky aroma filled the air, concealing a dark, heavy odor of decay deep within. The gentle air reeked of exhausted fires. Quillan was now a town shrouded in the memory of flames that destroyed, not nurtured.

Her eyes and ears told her what happened here had occurred some time ago. Leena charged forward, forcing her way through the snow toward her home beyond the town-encircling hedge. Halfway down, her feet slid in the deep, slippery ground cover, and she fell, tumbling, gathering a snow blanket from the soft, deep powder. As her shoulders touched the buried hill base, she sprang to her feet, a puffy, snow-covered bear, to continue her mindless charge. Tears clouded her vision, blurring the landscape.

As she neared the village, the foul odor of old smoke overpowered all other scents. The aroma held an undercurrent of something putrid that grated on her nerves, commanding her to increase her speed.

She approached the snow-buried South Road into town. Her flying feet stopped, skidding twin trails through the loose white powder. Ripples marred the road into town like something large had carved studded paths beneath the concealing snow. Like a puppy digging for a buried bone, Leena squatted to clear a patch of road with her bare hands, heedless that her mittens had been stowed in her skirt pockets as a safety measure in case she needed to touch her wand. Her fingernails scraped an impenetrable, frozen surface. Throwing snow wide, she cleared a two-foot circle. She found that the six inches of fresh snow hid a layer of solid ice compacted by countless hard-soled boots, as if a massive army had marched into her village.

Tingling dread crawled up her spine as she rose. Leena turned toward the town, not wanting to look but knowing she must. The thin lingering smoke could not hide what little remained of her village. All the roofs were gone. Charred edges around the tops of the houses' stone walls showed that thatch no longer protected families within from the elements. Several walls had fallen, and only the black teeth of scorched chimneys protruded into the hazy air.

Waves of horror, fear, and overwhelming sadness washed over her. It was too much. She closed her eyes against the horrible sight. *Please, Spirit, let this be a dream.* She opened eyes, now blurred with tears. Her village was gone. Destroyed. Her body shook with anger, and her stomach reeled. She kneeled to vomit in the snow. After last night's fear-filled adventure, only a thin stream of bile dripped out. Who had done this and why?

Why wasn't she here when her family needed her most? She could have...what? Scared the vandals away with her hedge witch wand? Maybe she could have warned them, and they would all have escaped together. The point was, she could have done something if she hadn't been roaming around in the woods playing girl hero.

Maybe her family was still here. Hope blossomed and grew in her mind before another thought took hold. *What if the vandals who did this are still here, pawing through their destruction now that the fires have burned down to smoldering embers?* But that didn't matter. She had to get home and find out. And after she found them, she would help anyone else she could.

There was no time to waste, but she couldn't be reckless. She needed to stop and think before rushing in. Leena shivered from the unnerving silence. Charging into town without knowing what to expect was foolish. With the slow steps of a condemned person shuffling toward the gallows, she crept toward the quiet village, breathing through her mouth to reduce the stench of charred dreams.

Reaching the stable and blacksmith shop, Leena backed against the wall, listening. The world was quiet, like a town that had never known living beings. Only the outer walls remained to show this place once had a purpose.

Crouching, she peeked through the corner of a window. The interior was black with soot. Tools, bent and twisted by unimaginable heat, lay scattered like a child's forgotten playthings. Only the mighty anvil, lying on the dirt floor beside a pile of ash, seemed undamaged by the fire.

Edging to the front of the building, Leena peered around the ruined wall at the town's main street. No chickens pecked the road. No dogs or children romped around. A charred wagon wheel lay in front of the ruined baker's shop. That blackened circle was all that remained of the baker's wagon. It gave no hint whether anything remained of the baker.

Grasping her hedge witch wand, Leena stepped into the street, tense and ready, expecting someone or something horrifying to charge at her. Nothing moved in the eerie silence. Only smoke-misted daylight filtered through the jagged teeth of broken glass in every window. No building remained intact.

Seeing the destruction up close, Leena raced through the village toward the hedge wall surrounding it and her family's home beyond. Her heart dropped when she saw scorched stone walls from a distance. Like the rest of the village, her family's roof was gone.

She slowed as she neared the wooden slat fence, where only jagged, fire-blackened slivers poked up at odd angles through the fresh snow. Smoke shadows clawed up the stone walls above the site of the destroyed door and shutters as though they had struggled to escape the blaze.

Her lower lip trembled as tears rimmed her eyes, and her throat constricted, preventing her from calling out. Only thin, wheezing air huffed from her mouth. She tried to swallow, to moisten her vocal cords, but no words would pass. For a moment, she stood numb and mute with panic.

Mum, Da, Riana. Where are you?

Terrified, Leena shuffled toward the ashes of her front door. She froze, a jarring unease racing through her as a slight breeze lifted a specter of powdery snow and danced it in a miniature tornado around her yard. With her heart racing, she started forward again. Her foot touched the front stoop.

I can't go in there. Leena blinked, struggling to dispel the fear-generated tears misting her vision. Closing her eyes, she sucked in air, fighting to calm her racing heart. *I have to see.* She opened her eyes, then stepped across the threshold into the destroyed family room to find the burned and broken remains of the table and chairs in the kitchen where her family had spent countless pleasant meals. Only the brick and clay oven had survived the fire. A quick look in the bedrooms confirmed no one hid there. Thankfully, she saw no lumps that might have once been people.

I don't know where they've gone, but I hope they have their wands.

Rushing to the charred herb cupboard, Leena jerked the doors open and jumped back before black falling debris could touch her. Inside, random ash piles disguised what the objects had once been.

Nothing in the ash piles could tell her if they had secured their wands before disappearing. However, since a wand couldn't be burned or broken after being enchanted, there was a good chance Mum and Riana took theirs before the raiders could find them. At least, she hoped they did. Without wands to focus their spells, their magic was limited to herbs and potions.

Of course, they took their wands. But where are they now? Maybe someone was still alive in the village who could tell her what happened and where her family had gone.

As she searched house by house, her hopes dimmed with each ruined structure she entered. In several, she found the twisted, charred remains of familiar friends. These victims had been old, feeble, and defenseless. They were people that she, Riana, and her mum tended to many times.

How could anyone do this? They were too frail to protect themselves from whatever ravaged the village. Where are the others? When she left Quillan, over four hundred people lived, worked, and shared each other's lives here. Now, only nineteen charred bodies remained.

By mid-afternoon, Leena had found no living person, only blackened skeletons. A confused stupor settled over her, growing with the discovery of each fresh horror. The unimaginable had occurred here, and her mind was finding it impossible to accept. Her brain felt wrapped in cotton as it struggled to insulate her from the mental effects of the surrounding devastation.

As if dreaming, Leena searched the east, north, and west roads. Growing more despondent at each discovery, she refused to think or consider the implications of her findings as she used her bare hands to clear new patches in the snow coverings. The east and west roads showed only regular traffic. Tracks beneath the snow told her that whatever attacked the village had come from the south and departed to the north.

Daylight was fading. It seemed so long ago when Leena had last shared a dinner with her family. Only constant warming and rejuvenation spells kept her moving, but at a cost. Coupled with the lighting spell she'd cast in the forest and the magic she used to clear snow from each building during her search, her energy levels were almost drained. She needed food and sleep to recharge her core.

"Mum, Da, Riana, where are you?" her whisper rose into the stillness.

With no warning, tears sprang from her eyes. No longer able to restrain her fear and despair, she howled in an agony of loss and pain, wailing as though her heart sought to leave her body with each wrenching sob. Her soul poured into her tears, and she crumpled to the snow. Lying and weeping, beating her chilled fists against the powder-covered street, she let her sorrow flow into the ground.

She would never know how long she shared her tears with the unyielding earth.

A silver moon, balancing like a mage's coin trick on the nighttime horizon, provided soft illumination to the silent village. Less than three hours after falling asleep, Leena's warming spell failed when her energy level diminished too low to maintain it. Her chattering teeth woke her from a dreamless sleep, warning her she was freezing.

Something pulled at her cheeks as she creaked to a sitting position. Her numb fingers traced a path from the edges of her eyes to her upper lip. With small ticks, her thumbnails pried away the icicle tear tracks frozen on her face.

I need to build a fire.

Sleep-deprived, Leena struggled to her feet like an ancient, exhausted crone using chilled muscles that wanted to refuse her commands. Dizziness washed over her in a wave, and she found herself back on one knee. Again, forcing reluctant arms and legs, she struggled to her feet.

She needed shelter and warmth. Shuffling through town, she searched for a house with a roof or even a clean room with a fireplace where she could rest with a warm fire to help restore her magic reserves. She found none. Quillan's business district offered the best chance to find supplies to sustain her. Although the town square was exposed, she had a better chance for a rapid escape using the cross-roads than she would struggling through a single narrow entrance or a small window in one of the town's houses.

Warmth was her highest priority. Fire-black-ened boards lay scattered throughout the town. Shuffling with slow, weary movements, Leena gath-ered small charred boards of life-restoring fuel. For an endless hour, she forced herself to drag planks, one at a time, and heap them in the middle of the crossroads at the village center.

After pulling a few boards into a tiny pile away from the volatile stack, she tugged the hedge witch wand from her waistband. Swaying, her mind numb, she waved her wand over the miniature pyra-mid, but no flames leaped from the stack. Concentrating, she pointed the wand at the boards and, with the last of her magic reserves, formed the mental command for it to light.

A tiny smoke wisp rose. Deep within the wooden heap, an ember flared. It would not be enough. Falling to her knees, ignoring the burning cold of snow against her bare skin, Leena blew gentle breaths on the tiny glow. With patience, the tender breeze from her lips fanned the weak radiance into a bright, blood-red flame. It flared and raced along the charred plank, spreading its heat to the rest of the structure.

She had a fire. Leena basked in the heat as the flames crackled, sending sparks toward the star-dotted night sky. The heat replenished some of her reserves, helping to protect her from an immediate frozen death, but she needed more. She needed to eat and regain sufficient strength to use her wand and restore her health.

I'm so hungry. How long has it been? Two days ago, we had dinner together. Her mind stopped, unable to bear the memory of that evening. Cheeks flaming with self-reproach, her mind floated back to the girl who had been so eager, hoping to receive a Garlan Branch and return home a more mature and powerful woman. *It seems so long ago. I was so naïve. I should have been here instead of playing the heroine. A real hero would have been here to save them.*

But this was no time for self-pity. Now it was time to find out what happened and what she could do to fix it. But first, she needed to eat.

Leena surveyed the burned facades of the surrounding shops, illuminated by the fire's flickering glow. After seeing the destruction of the villagers' houses, the damage here seemed less severe, as though the invaders had been more interested in rounding up citizens than pillaging the shops.

Why? They had to be searching for someone or something in particular from the total devastation of the homes. She gasped. Did someone know that she had the Garlan Branch? *Were they searching for me when they raided the town? Are my family and the other villagers doomed to a life of slavery because of me?*

The village had no answers for her silent queries as she studied Quillan's business district. The Garlan Branch, tucked securely in her waistband, seemed to call to her. Her hand slowly reached for it, but then her stomach growled, breaking the silence, and she quickly pulled her hand away. Leena's eyes stopped at the northeast corner of the town square. Sculley's Market. Maybe something in there survived the fires.

Using her hedge witch wand's light, Leena followed its reflection on the snow toward the remains of the market. Inside, crumbled piles of burned wood and ashes showed where a counter, shelves, and tables once stood. The merchandise they once held lay scattered in misshapen, unidentifiable chunks. Along the walls stood several black cylinders, still encircled by charred iron hoops. Barrels that once held apples, pickles, and grains. Lifting the lid from one ruined cask revealed only round, black lumps. *What were these things? Apples? Potatoes? Why did they have to do this? These things might have saved me. It's not fair.*

Leena slammed the lid back down. Several charred slats tumbled from the side of the barrel, scattering a midnight-dark wave of charcoal and ashes. Dozens of fresh, ripe-red apples spilled from the center of the barrel. Like stampeding children freed at school recess, they tumbled across the blackened carpet before settling on the scorched wooden floor. Leena snatched one up. The precious life-giving fruit was undamaged. These lucky few apples, secured within the middle of the barrel, had been insulated from the inferno's destruction.

Fresh, cold juice squirted into her mouth with the first bite as her grumbling stomach chastised her for waiting so long. Sweet liquid streamed down her chin while Leena devoured one apple after another, six in all.

It's late, and I'm too tired to think now. So, tonight, I'll sleep and recover. Tomorrow morning, I'll figure out what to do.

Leena loaded another half-dozen apples in her shawl. As she stepped onto the front porch, a low, appreciative rumble flowed from her stomach across the silent village like a ghost's moan. Recognizing her gut's response to the welcome feast, she could not stop the braying laughter that followed. Like a dam bursting, shouts streamed from her wide-open mouth. She sank to her knees on the floorboards, hugging herself and howling into the night. Tears flowed from her eyes, but these were tears of release. With each bray, tension flowed from her like an unwinding spring.

With one last hiccup, her laughter subsided. Scrubbing a sleeve across her eyes to dry them, Leena took a deep breath and moved to the fire. She lowered her cargo to the ground next to her log seat like she was laying tender babies in their cradles. Replacing the shawl around her head and shoulders, she sat and stared into the black outline of warped and jagged shadows beyond the firelight.

The gravity of the situation weighed on her. *Who did this?* Trade in this part of Allivan was sufficient to allow everyone here to live comfortable lives. But Quillan was not prosperous enough to attract bandits like the larger towns in the north. It couldn't be the Great Wizard's troops. Robart saved this country. Had some army invaded Allivan? Did the Great Wizard know what had happened here?

Leena's palms grew moist as the answer drifted into her mind. Dreading what she knew it must be, she touched the Garlan Branch at her waist. *Whoever it was, they had to be searching for the Garlan Branch. Nothing else here is worth this much effort. Mum told us that no one but Robart and Skylar had ever seen the Garland Tree. But what about the Branch? If I can see it, can't everyone else see it? Tales often tell of wizards willing to sell their souls for ultimate power. Merchants could ask for a prince's ransom when offering to sell a Branch to one of them. I need to keep its existence a secret.*

But if the Branch was the reason for this destruction, someone already knew it had been discovered. How could they know? It had been two days since she found it. Was it possible that someone could have gotten here, destroyed Quillan, and taken the people away while she'd been gone? She didn't think so.

Fatigue washed over her as her thoughts

tumbled. She didn't have enough information to make any rational guesses.

Sliding to the ground with her back nestled against the log seat, Leena snuggled beneath the blanket of her shawl, enjoying the radiant heat against her face provided by the leaping flames.

The growing pile of red coals was mesmerizing, drawing her most profound, most heartfelt thoughts to the surface. The words leaped into her mind, shattering all other considerations: *Tomorrow, I will do what I can to set the spirits of the dead here to rest. Then, I swear, I will do whatever it takes to rescue my family and bring them home.*

SEVEN

Arose-colored sun peeked above the horizon when a tingling at the back of her neck pulled Leena from a deep sleep. She was being watched. Her rapid heartbeat told her this awareness was not the residue of a fading dream. Remnants of yesterday's physical and emotional exhaustion swallowed all memory of last night's dreams. Someone or something hid nearby, observing her. Experience had taught her to trust her senses. Although she had never felt a human watching her before, the hedge witch's ability to detect and locate injured animals now alerted her she was no longer alone in the village.

Without moving, Leena scanned the area, frustrated to discover the rising smoke from her smoldering fire hid everything beyond it from view.

Trying to appear casual, she sat up, stretching to ease the cold-induced kinks from her body.

She'd searched the village yesterday, but no one was there except her. Keeping her expression neutral, she smoothed her blouse as though worried about its sleep-generated appearance. Brushing ashes from the cloth confirmed both wands were still nestled beneath her waistband.

Combing sleep-matted hair from her face, Leena surveyed the surrounding unobstructed areas. Only the deserted village greeted her. No one ducked from sight. No muffled footsteps hurried away. Whoever or whatever watched her was not ready to make themselves known. For the moment, she would pretend she did not know anyone was there and go about her business until they revealed themselves.

Adding several boards to the fire, Leena sat on the log seat and munched on an apple for breakfast. Much of her energy had returned. She would be back to full strength with sufficient food and another day of rest.

But what should I do until then?

An ache grew within her chest as she studied the fallen walls and missing roofs. The charred remains of nineteen friends lay within those destroyed buildings. All had been old and harmless.

Why were they killed? The silence provided no

answer. They deserved to receive proper burial rites. A Holy was supposed to teach people about the Spirit, perform birth and marriage rites, and help those who had passed to transition to the fields beyond. But there was no Holy here.

Visions of the contorted, blackened bodies passed through Leena's mind.

She wasn't a Holy, but a hedge witch could perform certain rites when necessary. Her mum had taught the rituals to Leena and Riana. *Okay, so I'm not a hedge witch, and I'm only half-trained, but I can't let their souls wander lost.*

Selecting another apple from her small stockpile, she stared into the crackling fire, basking her face in its comfortable heat. A nervousness swelled in her chest as she pondered what she would do after she helped the poor unfortunates transition to the fields beyond. She needed to find her family, but how? She was sixteen years old and far from finishing her hedge-witch training. There was so much that she needed to learn. Panic flared within her, chasing logic from her brain. *What can I do against the horde that devastated Quillan?*

Images of friends and family starved and abused grew more intense as each fear-generated vision fought to erase rational thought from her mind.

Tears clouded her sight and her breathing increased as fear rose within her.

No! A voice screamed against the growing, dancing black spots stealing her vision as they swirled her toward unconsciousness. *I'm the missing villagers' only hope. No one else knows they've been taken. I must find them and do what I can to save them. But first, I need a plan.*

The darkness receded while she concentrated on controlling her breath and heartbeat. Leena stared into the mind-calming fire as she devised a plan. She would take the North Road. Based on the snow-buried footprints through the village, whoever did this went that way. It was all she could do for now. Maybe she would find someone in that direction with information that could help her.

After breakfast, Leena trudged toward the Woodsmans' house, fighting the urge to turn and run from this village. Everything in her wanted to head north now and forget all that had happened here while she searched for the Garlan Branch.

The Woodsman couple lay as she had left them yesterday, just inside the door to their bedroom. In death, their half-charred remains held each other for support, just as they had throughout their seventy years of marriage. Leena swallowed a lump in her throat.

The bodies crackled and flaked black skin to the floor as she slid her hands beneath them. She pulled her hands back. She needed to find a way to move their bodies without damage.

Another warning tingle slithered along her neck as she stepped from the house. Her watcher had returned. As though stretching kinks from her limbs, Leena yawned, her biceps flexing above her shoulders as she turned her head left and right to ease neck and shoulder strain. She focused her senses, scanning for any sign of the watcher. Someone was there.

Okay, so far, they've done nothing threatening. Whoever's there could have captured or killed me as I slept if that's what they intended. I'm done worrying about it. I have more important things to do.

She headed toward the destroyed blacksmith shop to retrieve a cart. Old Hotchkiss, the blacksmith, used a handcart to transport tools when he traveled to outlying farms. His creation was like a plank table with two handles at its back end. An iron front wheel and two rear legs formed a stabilizing tripod beneath, enabling the vehicle to be used as an offsite work surface.

The cart rested in the blacksmith's vast backyard as if enjoying the morning sun while waiting for its master's return. Old Hotchkiss and Thomai, his son, often strolled through the village, taking turns pushing this barrow loaded with anvil, ingots, small brazier, bellows, and tools, chatting with villagers as they passed. Leena lifted the two handles to raise the legs from the ground and pushed forward. The front wheel would take most of the weight.

She soon found maneuvering the cart was a learned art. The creation was far heftier than it looked. Sweating as she mumbled under her breath, Leena fought to control the unwieldy beast. As though having a mind of its own, the creature left abstract designs in the snow, followed by Leena's slipping and sliding boot prints, leaving a trail like a drunken snake had danced intricate patterns through the yard with an unwilling partner. A suppressed giggle disturbed the silence when the pushcart tipped, almost falling on its side as she attempted a too-sharp turn.

The hairs on the back of her neck stood on end. Someone else was near, close enough to see her efforts. She suppressed her reaction while struggling the cart upright. She'd become too used to the feeling of being watched and needed to be more careful. *What do they want? Why are they staying hidden? Could it be a vandal waiting for other members to return before attacking? Maybe they're a survivor of the attack.*

Leena considered shouting for the watcher to show themself, but what would that gain her? She was new to hedge witch training and could only cast an immobilization spell on a single being with her hedge witch wand. What if her newfound ability to sense people could discern only one watcher at a time? She needed more experience testing its limits. She now possessed the most powerful wand in her world but had no idea how to use it. Maybe her watcher hoped to trick her into revealing the Garlan Branch's location. Questions swirled in her brain with no answers.

Okay, ignore the creepy watcher for now and see what happens.

After an hour's practice, the blacksmith's barrow yielded to many of her commands. She was not yet an expert, but she could almost steer the cart in a straight line. Her hedge witch wand would make the job easier, but instinct warned her not to reveal her magic to the watcher until she knew why the person hid and what they wanted. Magic might be her only defense if the watcher was hostile, and she had no desire to face a person ready to protect themselves against magic.

Forcing the cart on a crooked trail through the deep snow, she struggled a path into the Woods-mans' house. Her heart warmed at the sight of the embraced couple. Despite their condition, they looked loving. She needed to figure out how to get them on the cart. They were too unwieldy to lift together, and she didn't want to separate them.

Scanning the area beyond the Woodsmans' doorway, she saw no one, but that meant little. Her senses warned her that the watcher was near. Positioning herself between the barrow and the door, she drew her wand. Using a levitation spell, she raised the joined couple and floated them, still joined, onto the cart's rough wooden surface. Stashing the wand beneath her blouse, she grabbed the cart's handles and pulled the heavy barrow back through the front door.

"H'lo."

Leena jumped as though lightning seared the ground next to her. The handles ripped from her hands, and the barrow's rear legs bounced the contraption forward to a stop. She spun to find a boy standing next to the door.

"I'm sorry, m'lady. I din mean to startle you." The boy looked alarmed and terrified by what he had done.

Heart racing, Leena looked at the lad. He seemed about twelve, though small for his age, with blond hair and dark brown eyes. A thick brown jacket hid the waist of a pair of blue linen trousers with legs stuffed into the tops of worn leather boots.

"Who are you? What do you want?" The harsh words were out before she could stop them. A bit of her heart melted as his lower lip trembled, preventing him from answering. *Is this the watcher? Yes, he startled me, but it's not his fault that I have nightmare visions running through my head.*

"I'm sorry," Leena said. It was the only thing she could think of that might slow the tears streaking down his dirty face. "I've had a hard few days. I didn't mean to take it out on you."

Squatting, placing her hands on his shoulders, she looked into his eyes. Within them, she saw a depth that seemed far too old for his years. She wondered what he had been through and what he had seen.

"Are you hungry? I have some apples."

"I'm starving, m'lady. It's been days since I've had anything to eat."

His accent was strange, almost archaic.

"Well, come on then. I'll finish this later. Let's get you fed." She wheeled the cart toward the town's center crossroads. The boy lagged several yards behind her, unwilling to engage in conversation.

A dozen questions filled her brain: *How did he get*

here? Where is his family? Why is he here? How did he escape the disaster that destroyed Quillan? But this was not the time to intimidate him with a barrage of questions. She suspected there would be plenty of time later.

Parking the cart near her apple trove, she tossed one to the lad and waved a hand toward the log seat. The boy grabbed another apple and arced his first well-gnawed core into the fire.

This boy's going to need a lot more than a few apples. After throwing a few more boards onto the fire, Leena left the boy sitting by it, enjoying the warmth as he munched through her dwindling food supply. Leena returned to the store to see if she could find more food. She rushed across the surface-blackened floorboards toward the counter. Crouching down, she swept away the cinders, revealing an iron ring resting in its floor depression. Sadness washed over her when she remembered Sculley's lively chatter as he disappeared through the floor entrance to his underground storage shelter.

I might as well get used to it. Those days are gone.

Although the iron ring was blackened but undamaged, the fire-swollen hinges squealed like a butchered pig as she lifted the door to peer below.

The first three rungs of a sturdy ladder were visible, unmarked by fire. Beyond, darkness cloaked the cellar like the beckoning entrance of a bottomless cave.

Maybe I should return to the fire and get a torch? No, taking an open flame into a basement with a dry, scorched ceiling would be stupid. She could use her hedge witch wand. The boy must have seen a hedge witch before. Every village had a hedge witch or one nearby.

She shook her head. She didn't know if he was alone. *What if he's been sent here to win my confidence and gain my trust? Showing him I'm a magic user might be just what he wants.* She needed a candle, but the fires had likely consumed them all.

Standing, glancing through the doorway, Leena saw the boy still sitting, munching apples, staring into the flames as though mesmerized. Something about this child made her nervous. Something about the depth in his eyes, the way he watched her every move, and his physical coordination seemed much more advanced than his age. None of these added up to a twelve-year-old boy.

Whoever or whatever he is, I'll have to keep a watchful eye on him and use magic only when he can't see me.

Descending to the dirt floor below, she shut the trapdoor before casting an illumination spell. Its light revealed that the fire had damaged nothing in the cellar. They would not starve.

Sacks, cloth-wrapped bundles, corked earthen jars, and covered wooden containers crowded the shelves. Large bags and barrels lined the walls. The cellar was fragrant with the enticing scents of dried fruits, spices, cheese, and grains.

Leena unwrapped a cloth protecting a large cheese round. She broke off a sizeable chunk and rewrapped the bundle. A large wooden box revealed several dozen bread rolls. After laying her shawl on the floor, Leena loaded it with cheese and a dozen rolls and looped the makeshift pack over her shoulder. Darkness settled over the cellar with the intensity of a moonless, midnight graveyard when she collapsed her illumination spell.

She stepped onto the ladder's first rung and reached up to open the trapdoor. It would not budge.

This doesn't make sense. The door has no latch, only the ring to lift it open.

Descending and setting her bundle down, Leena again mounted the ladder and pushed both hands against the trapdoor. The ladder creaked with the strength of her effort, but the door remained as rigid as a stone wall.

This can't be. Leena fought to calm her rising panic. *I saw no damaged roof beams that could have fallen to cover the door. How can it be sealed?*

A slight creak from the floor above broke the silence. Someone or something heavy had crept in, making no noise, and now stood on the door.

The boy can't weigh over sixty pounds. The door should have moved when I pushed. What's his name? Drat, I forgot to ask, and he didn't tell me.

"Boy! Are you up there?" Her shout met only silence. "Boy! I'm down here. Can you lift the ring and let me out?"

That was stupid. What if it's not the boy? Fighting to control her racing heart, Leena's hands slid from the sweat-lubricated ladder rung, and her feet thudded to the dirt floor.

Think, Leena. Maybe an opening spell would work, but it would use a lot of her energy. She sat on the floor with a huff. This cellar had plenty of food, and she could wait until whoever was above got bored and went away.

As her eyes adapted to the darkness, dim light in the room above outlined the overhead floorboard cracks with pale lines. Soundless, a dark phantom flickered across the cracks, gliding toward the front door. Had that been the boy's shadow creeping across the floor? Or could it have been a large raven flying over the charred and roofless building?

"M'lady?" The boy's voice came from the front door. "You still in here?"

Leena sprang up the ladder to find the trapdoor opened with ease.

"I'm here," she said as she emerged. "There's a cellar, and I went down to get more food. Were you in here just a moment ago?"

"No, m'lady. I finished the apples and noticed you'd been gone a while, so I came looking for you."

Goosebumps dotted her arms. Rubbing them for warmth did not help. *Perhaps fire-warped wood wedged the door shut, and in the silent darkness, I imagined the rest. Or maybe the boy was here and afraid to admit it, fearing I would...what? Make him leave? Hurt him?*

Arvin stared at her, unblinking, like a snake. She could not imagine what was going through his mind behind those expressionless eyes.

"Come on, let's go eat some proper food." She nodded toward the door.

As they warmed by the fire, Leena broke off a chunk from the cheese wedge and passed it along with two rolls to the boy. They sat munching, staring into the flames, lost in thought.

"What are we to do now, m'lady?"

Leena glanced at the barrow holding the Woodsman couple. "Well, first, we'll have to build a pyre large enough to hold nineteen people. Once that's done, we can lay them to rest properly. That'll take most of the day. After that, we can decide what we'll do tomorrow. Okay?"

"Are you a Holy, m'lady?" His eyes had gone round with wonder.

"No, my mother was the village hedge witch here. I'm no hedge witch, but I suppose it would be all right for me to send them on their journey. Anyway, I'm all there is. Unless you're a Holy?"

"Oh no, m'lady." He looked so appalled at the thought that Leena could not help giggling.

"I'm teasing you, but please, call me Leena."

"Leena?" The color drained from the boy's face.

"Yes, Leena. Have you heard my name before?" She searched his wide-eyed expression, trying to imagine what caused his surprise.

"No, m'lady...er, Leena. It's just not a name I'm familiar with."

I know he's hiding something, but what? How can a twelve-year-old boy be a threat? She needed to put him at ease and then try to get some answers.

"What is your name, and where are you from?"

Leena kept her voice calm, as if they were discussing the weather.

"Arvin. I'm from Wedgelin to the north."

Leena had never heard of Wedgelin. "How did you end up here? Where are your folks?"

"It was the Great Wizard's troops, same as here."

"What?" It was unthinkable. Arvin must be mistaken. The Great Wizard ruled and kept peace in Allivan for over two hundred years. He was the symbol of all that was good and just. "I don't understand," she said.

"Me neither, but a bit more'n three weeks ago, the Great Wizard's troops attacked our village at dawn. They burned the town just like here. Then they killed all who was too old to work, captured everyone else, and sent them north."

"But why?" It was a rhetorical question, and Leena expected no answer.

"Some of the troops said they was looking for a Garlan Branch. They said they would release everyone if someone was to turn over the Branch to them. Otherwise, they would all work as slaves forever."

Leena jumped to her feet and paced back and forth. With each step, the Branch's rough bark rubbed against the skin beneath her tunic. Her thoughts spun in confusion. Surely, the Great

Wizard could not know about her Branch. She had told no one about her trip.

Through the chaos tumbling within her brain, Leena noticed the boy's intent stare following her every move, gauging her expressions. She could not read the ideas developing behind his blank face. She had to think of something to say.

"Has someone stolen the Great Wizard's Garlan Branch?"

"Don't know. Guards didn't say nothing 'bout that. My guess is the Great Wizard's Branch is protected by such magics that it's impossible to steal. That'd mean there's another, don't you think?"

Arvin's tone and narrowed eyes were so probing that Leena dared not look at his face and reveal the anxiety growing within her with every word he spoke. Was the Branch against her belly making her paranoid? She had to change the subject before she said something she might regret later.

"So...your parents were taken?"

Leena resisted the urge to expel a relieved sigh when the boy turned away. Staring into the fire, his trembling lower lip and the tears in his eyes were answer enough.

"How did you get here?" she asked quietly.

"I was gathering wood for the morning fire when they came. I tried to get back to save my ma and pa, but I tripped on something under the snow and hit my head against a tree. By the time I woke, all the villagers was roped. The head guard said if they turned over the Branch and the girl who had it, everyone would be set free to go on about their lives."

A chill shook Leena. She felt his penetrating gaze.

"Did they mention the name of the girl they were looking for?"

"I'd rather not say."

"Arvin, you've been through a lot, and I think we can work our way out of this mess together, but it means we have to trust each other. What was the name?"

He stared at her for several moments, his lower lip tight with control. With no warning, he jumped up, screaming. "Leena! Leena! Leena! It's you they was looking for. You've got the Branch that can save my ma and pa. It was 'cause of you the whole village was destroyed!" he shouted, pointing a dirty-fingered accusation at her face.

Without warning, he spun and ran away up the North Road. The sounds of his cries diminished in the still morning air.

~

LEENA SPENT the rest of the day building a pyre and loading the charred bodies. Her anxious mind worked on the implications of Arvin's tale. His agony seemed genuine, so she had no reason to doubt his story. Her heart ached for him. His parents were missing, just like her family. If he returned, she would try to explain that she doubted giving up the Branch would save his parents.

She should have known the Great Wizard would sense a disturbance in the Garlan Tree. Only he could have foreseen a time of great trouble was coming. But since the Great Wizard was still alive, why would a new Branch be necessary? And, with all his power, why wouldn't he just come and take it from her?

Maybe he feared her Garlan Branch would be more powerful than his. After all, his Branch was over two hundred years old. Perhaps it had lost some of its power in that time. Maybe his plan was to capture and enslave people to use as a ransom for her Branch. That would mean the Great Wizard had to keep her parents and sister alive.

She sat on her log seat before Sculley's Market, her arms and legs aching from the manual labor. Her head throbbed as though it might explode with questions raised by Arvin's tale.

Why did the Garlan Tree give me a Branch? I'm no

hero. What can I possibly do against a time of great trouble? How many villages are between the Great Wizard's castle in Elderon and here? Scores, maybe hundreds.

But if the Great Wizard's army descended on Wedgelin three weeks ago, how did he know then that someone would have a Branch now? And how could he possibly know her name? Did a Branch grant the ability to predict the future? Could the Great Wizard's destruction of villages and the enslavement of Allivanian citizens be the time of great trouble her Garlan Branch was supposed to combat? If so, Leena could not give up the Garlan Branch, even to save her family. Once she surrendered it, there would be no incentive for the Great Wizard to stop his pillage. When the time came, she would have to use the Garlan Branch to fight whatever trouble appeared to save her mum, da, and Riana.

Her head throbbed from the speculations. She had no proof that what Arvin had told her was true. Therefore, she had no choice but to follow the invading army north and gather more information before developing a plan. But now she needed to tend to her village.

Dusk bathed the ruined town in an orange glow, extending sharp-toothed shadows from the destroyed buildings. The nineteen bodies on the pyre waited for Leena to complete the ritual to release them from this world.

Leena checked her senses to ensure no one was spying on her and, with her last words, ignited the dry wood with her hedge witch wand. Yellow flames crackled, reaching toward the darkening sky. As the fire grew, the remains on the pyre settled, sending the departed spirits up in firework displays of dancing red sparks and gray smoke.

Leena cried as she bid each friend farewell and wished them a long and pleasant rest in the fields beyond. She sat watching the consuming fire through the night, her numb mind reviewing untroubled times and happy moments with each of the deceased.

When the bright morning sun cast a golden glow over the ash pile, Leena waved her hand over the spent pyre to ensure no lingering embers remained. They held no heat. Summoning a wind with her hedge witch wand, she scattered the ashes back to the earth. Calmed, knowing her friends' spirits were at rest, she returned to Sculley's Market.

Descending into the cellar, leaving the trapdoor open, Leena selected a variety of foodstuffs to load into her shawl. The heavy bundle was awkward to carry, but its size and weight would diminish as she traveled north.

At the edge of town, Leena turned for one last look at the roofless walls and blackened stone. In her memory, she saw the once-bustling village as it had been and vowed that someday she would return to restore it.

EIGHT

Sadness slumped Leena's shoulders as she shuffled toward Stocksbury. Only distant, sharp-edged building silhouettes, high-lighted against a cloudless star-specked sky, suggested that civilization spanned the road ahead. The city had always been the trading hub of nearby villages. Fond memories of planting seasons and harvest festivals distracted her thoughts from Quillan, bringing recollections of past joys to her heart. Stocksbury had more than a thousand residents. During the annual festivals, that number swelled to over five thousand revelers and celebrants from outlying villages. Wagons and tents would blanket the surrounding post-harvest fields like late fall crops, sending waves of music, singing, and dancing toward the bright nightlights of the city.

Visions of hayloft sleeping quarters, shared with scores of laughing children bedded down in heaping piles of fresh hay, filled her mind. She remembered the safe comfort of the stable loft, their temporary home and imaginary kingdom, where a few dozen children played, gossiped, and told stories until the wee hours during the festival's three nights.

Happy memories faded as she neared the town's entrance. She gasped at the jarring sight of the desolate city of Stocksbury. Like living shadows, a few skeleton-thin dogs roamed the streets, sneaking between the scorched buildings and sniffing for food amidst the ruins.

How many people have the invaders taken? How many died here? Leena felt small and helpless against this backdrop of carnage. Tears rolled down her cheeks as she vowed to the Spirit that she would master the Garlan Branch, save her family, and someday restore Allivan to its former glory.

Leena found less damage as she penetrated the town, as if the intruders' need for destruction decreased once their atrocities created a proper level of fear. Pulling her scarf tighter around her neck to ward off a chilly breeze, she closed her eyes and sensed the waiting city. The stillness in her mind told her no living people remained.

The town's largest inn emerged through the

darkness as she approached. Undamaged, its two stories towered over the surrounding shops and houses, an enormous night-darkened specter looming like a mother hen guarding her chicks. She crept down the grave-silent street toward the building's entrance. The twin doors stood wide as though the management no longer concerned itself with heating the interior.

Pausing on the wooden porch, Leena listened for any sign of living creatures hiding inside, but nothing moved. She cast a lighting spell with her hedge witch wand. Holding the glowing rod above her head like a torch, she entered and closed the doors behind her. The vast common room was crowded with round oak tables, each surrounded by a half dozen stout wooden chairs perched like cattle around a watering tub, anticipating patrons who would never come. A dozen wooden stools stood in a precise row against an extended counter. A fireplace large enough to roast an ox graced the far wall.

An enormous cauldron was suspended from an iron arm in the fireplace. Leena could not stop her feet from rushing to inspect its contents. A smile rose on her face when she spied a deep red ice block of vegetable soup. As though fearing the soup might vanish at any second, Leena threw her bundle on a table, then whipped her hedge witch wand toward the half-burned logs beneath the cauldron. The fire ignited, its orange glow leaping up as the flames caressed the black kettle, heating the room. After warming her hands, palm extended toward the cheery fire's glow, Leena explored the area behind the long counter, her wand's light bouncing shadows across the wall behind her. Her stomach emitted a pleased growl as she discovered four frozen loaves of whole-grain bread tucked into a nook below the bar's sideboard.

While the soup heated, Leena explored the inn. Her family never had enough money to eat in this hotel. Despite this, her father would spend long evenings here during the harvest festival, sharing a pint with seldom-seen friends while catching up on current events. To Leena, the inn had been a place of mystery and wonder where men laughed and sang and travelers in fine clothing retired to hidden rooms upstairs to enjoy the inn's luxuries.

Several rooms contained made beds and fireplaces prepared for the customers' arrival. Leena mentally confirmed she would stay in one of these wondrous chambers tonight.

After inspecting six identical rooms, Leena came to another door and peered inside. A tall metal cylinder stood along the rear wall, and firewood was stacked on a steel plate beneath its four metal legs. A pipe ran to the long wooden tub before the water heater, and a long icicle dripped from its tap above the tub. It was a bath. She had heard about these but had never actually seen one. At home, they bathed in a round wooden tub, using well water warmed to boiling in pots suspended in the fireplace.

With a quick flick of her hedge witch wand, she sent a mental command to light the well-laid fire beneath the reservoir. While the ice melted and the bathwater heated, Leena prowled the rooms, looking through abandoned luggage to find clean, sturdy traveling clothes. After spending more than an hour choosing just the right outfit for her first meal in a hotel restaurant, Leena returned to the bath. Laying her foraged clothes on the wood-plank changing bench, she opened the bath taps to fill the tub before removing her worn and dirty attire.

Pulling the Garlan Branch from her skirt's waistband, Leena tried to set it on a chair next to the bath. As she lifted her hand, the Branch remained stuck to her palm. Brisk shaking and attempts to throw the Branch from her hand failed.

Come on, Leena, how would a trained wizard free the Garlan Branch long enough to bathe? Use your brain.

Clearing her mind, concentrating on releasing the Branch, she willed it to float to the chair. Her small chuckle echoed in the silence as the twig obeyed, although she felt its strong reluctance to leave her. The Branch remained on the chair at her command, but she felt its constant presence in her mind, pulling at her to take it back. At last, she slid deep into the bath's warm luxury.

Leena descended to the common room, feeling like a princess in her all-new winter outfit. The air was fragrant with the aroma of stew bubbling merrily in the cauldron. Lifting a dish from a stack behind the bar, she ladled a heaping bowl full of steaming goodness, then grabbed a chilled bread loaf and sat at the table nearest the fire. Restraining the urge to gulp down her meal and burn her mouth, she dipped the bread loaf's end into the bowl to thaw and soften while cooling the soup enough to eat. Her eyes closed when the first savory spoonful touched her lips. She could not remember when she had last eaten a meal that tasted so good.

With her hunger satisfied, Leena pushed her chair back and stared into the fire's mesmerizing depth. Fatigue dragged at her eyelids, and her head bobbed up and down. She snapped her head up. She'd almost fallen asleep.

It's late, and I'm too tired to think. Come on, Leena, it's time you got a good night's sleep in one of those heavenly-looking beds upstairs.

With effort, Leena rose and trudged up the stairway. She chose the first bedroom she came to, lit the fire, and snuggled beneath the thick comforter's chilled embrace. Letting the world pass her by, she drifted into a dreamless sleep as firelight shadows danced over the room's walls and ceiling.

NINE

Warm sunlight pulled Leena into a world of birds' soothing, window-muted calls. She opened her eyes to a fairyland of dazzling rainbows as sunshine passed through the cut-glass windowpanes.

She lay relaxed and content beneath the comforter for a few minutes, reluctant to leave its luxury. It would be so pleasant to stay here, warm and cozy, letting the days drift by. But she couldn't. There was so much she had to do. First, she had to find her family and rescue them. But how? Arvin said the Great Wizard's troops had taken them, and they were heading north.

She stared at the Garlan Branch stuck to her stomach beneath her waistband. *Why didn't you come with instructions? Then you could help me. But since you can't, I must find someone who can. But who? The Great Wizard knows how to control the Branch, but I can't ask him, or can I?* She only had Arvin's word that her family had been taken by the Great Wizards' troops. She didn't even know if his story was true.

Logic said the closer she came to the Great Wizard's castle, the more people would know about him. If she found the right people, they could advise her on approaching him without endangering herself or anyone else. Her mum said he was a sensible man. Maybe this was just a misunderstanding she could clear up if she could engage him in a rational conversation. It wasn't much of a plan, but it was the best she could do for now. Leena eased out of bed.

The morning sun was above the horizon when she finished a hot soup and bread breakfast. Full and rested, she adjusted her scarf and stepped outside, shouldering a borrowed inn sheet, heavy-laden with the foodstuffs gathered from Quillan and this hotel.

She suspected the town contained many bodies that should be properly laid to rest. But several towns and villages lay ahead of her. She could lose days, maybe weeks, trying to tend to them all. The sooner she got to the Great Wizard, the sooner this mess might end. With her makeshift pack and a half-formed plan, Leena walked away from Stocksbury on the North Road, feeling the burden of her responsibility weighing heavy as she struggled to keep her hopes alive.

Leena had never been this far north. The land was new to her. So far, it looked the same as yesterday's landscape; a forest of pine trees and winter-bared oaks, with only the white-powdered depression of a hidden road showing that humans had traveled here several days ago. She had never seen a map, nor would she know how to read one. Arvin said the Great Wizard had ordered the captives from Wedgelin, his hometown, to be sent north. These were the only directions she had. They would have to be enough.

Though uncertain whether she trusted Arvin's story, she prayed to the Spirit that the boy was unharmed. Was he on his way back to Wedgelin? Was he nearby watching her? She did not think so. After the last few days, she trusted her senses to warn her if living creatures were nearby.

Pulling the scarf closer around her head, she closed her eyes, enjoying its warmth. Although a warming spell from the hedge witch wand protected her from winter's bitter cold, the garment's soft touch reminded her of the time spent and her mother's loving patience while weaving it.

Oh, Mum, I wish you were here with me. She shook the thought from her head. Reminiscing would not help her now.

Her thoughts turned to Arvin. How could he survive in this cold? Perhaps she should have chased after him. It'd be better to have him near, to watch him and determine whether he could be trusted. But she couldn't hold him a prisoner. Leena shook her head. He was gone, and she could do nothing for him now.

The monotonous crunch of snow beneath her boots pulled her mind back to the Garlan Branch. Nothing distinguished it from any branch found in the forest. Could it be used the same way an ordinary wand could? She was surprised that the Branch listened to her when she commanded it to leave her hand while she bathed. She wondered what else it would do for her. For instance, could it keep her warm?

She removed her hedge witch wand's warming spell. The shocking cold bit through her clothes as its icy chill sent the white moisture wraiths of her breath dancing before her. With chattering teeth, her shaky hand moved toward the Garlan Branch tucked into her waistband. If this didn't work, she'd be lucky to last five minutes in this weather.

According to legend, it had taken Robart months

to learn how to control the Garlan Branch. But Robart wasn't a wizard then. Also, she had heard no stories of Skylar having trouble using the Branch, and he was just a farmer. Maybe it was no more complicated than using her hedge witch wand. Just concentrate on the spell and...

Her racing thoughts stopped as the creaks and groans of an approaching wagon, accompanied by several male voices, rose beyond the rise ahead of her. *Uh oh. Someone's coming.* She resettled the hedge witch wand warming spell over herself.

Heart thundering, Leena searched the roadside for a hiding place. Racing to the distant trees would leave footprints in the snow. She had to be careful. The raiders had left no one behind, and Arvin only escaped because he hid in the woods.

She touched the Branch at her waist and hesitated. No, this was not the time to experiment. Leena raced toward the roadside woods, her boots skidding in the deep white powder. Sliding behind the snow-dusted bark of the nearest tree with her back against its trunk, she closed her eyes and tried to catch her breath. *Okay, they shouldn't see me here.* She leaned around the tree to see who approached.

Drat! Footprints lead from the road to her hiding place. They might not see her, but they couldn't miss her tracks in the snow. Touching her hedge witch wand, she cast a wind spell. A small blizzard rose, rolling toward the road. She smiled when the storm's fury died down, watching the white funnel sink at the road's edge. The powder settled like mist, leaving slight indentations of tracks that appeared several days old.

The voices and commotion grew louder. From beyond a far hill in the road, a pair of massive, white oxen plodded into view, trudging forward, uninterested in the men's noise or the surrounding scenery. Behind them, an ox-cart driver appeared above the rise, his face hidden beneath a dirty, thick woolen shawl. The cart bed behind him clinked and rattled from a small mountain of jumbled goods. Beyond the cart, a floppy forest-green peasant cap, followed by the head that wore it, appeared above the rise in the ice-covered track to the north. Another head crowned the hill, this one sporting a battered helmet. In minutes, she counted thirteen men, one driving the wagon and twelve following. Her muscles tensed as she watched the motley-dressed crew approach. She stood alert and ready to run at the first sign that anyone noticed her.

These men looked dangerous and filthy, wearing various articles of ill-matched clothing. Each sported random pieces of armor and carried weapons of all shapes and sizes. All eyes scanned the area for danger. Her head dove behind the tree as several looked in her direction, but none raised an alarm.

The low rumble of their conversation increased as they neared. Within minutes, they were close enough that Leena could understand their words.

"How's our little piggy doin', Ned? I ain't heard nothing from him in a while," the man in the peasant hat called back to someone in the group. His low voice carried, echoing through the peaceful forest.

A heavyset ruffian, walking behind the wagon in an ill-fitting helmet and mismatched armor, poked his spear at something hidden from Leena's view. Laughter filled the air as a piercing, agonized scream echoed among the trees.

"Did ya hear his squeal of pleasure? He seems happy we found him, Bert," the big man called forward. Another round of laughter rose, rolling through the countryside.

The group drew closer. Leena gasped as the object of their ridicule appeared. *Arvin!*

The boy's jacket was missing. A ragged length of rope bound his hands to the rear of the over-laden wagon. In the sunlight, two icy tracks of frozen tears sparkled on his cheeks. A small blood trail oozed from a fresh wound, staining the left side of his trouser seat. Leena heard his chattering teeth clacking like castanets above the tramping boots and rattling cart.

Fear for Arvin's safety and anger toward this band of ruffians swelled within Leena. *I have to do something. But what?* Anything she did would alert these men of her location. And without knowing how to use the Garlan Branch, it might cause more harm than good.

"Don't damage the goods too much, Ned. We need him to keep the boggles away from our camp tonight." Again, the laughter.

Think, Leena. She could cast an immobilization spell with her hedge witch wand, but only on one person. What could she do to subdue the others?

Her thoughts froze as Bert stepped to the roadside to enjoy the boy's misery, his back less than fifteen feet from Leena's hiding place. Bert held up a hand, and the group halted.

"He looks a bit cold, don't he, lads?" Bert called out. "Perhaps we should warm him up some, just to give him a preview of what's in store later. What d'ya say?"

Again, laughter rose from the group as several voices mumbled agreement. Bert's cold glee reflected on every face. *These men enjoy inflicting pain. What kind of animals are they?*

"Anton, Lank, if you'd be so kind as to untie our little piggy and hold his arms wide."

Two men stepped from the group and worked on the knot securing Arvin's wrists. Bert loosened and slid a wide leather belt free of his trouser waist. The man's cold eyes contradicted his smile as he waved the black, threatening weapon back and forth in front of the boy while he talked.

"It's time you started learnin' to be a good little piggy. The first lesson is you squeal when I tell you to squeal. That'll scare the boggles away. But you must be a quiet little piggy when I don't tell you to squeal, or you'll let the boggles know where our camp is. Do you understand me?"

Arvin's knees trembled. Round-eyed, the boy stood shivering and transfixed by the belt's swing.

Pain coursed through Leena's jaws as her teeth clenched in anger. Her hands squeezed the tree in front of her to stop herself from charging out to challenge these jackals.

"Okay, it's nighttime, and the boggles are coming. Do you understand?" Bert shouted into Arvin's face, his mouth so close that Leena saw spittle freezing on the boy's cheeks. Arvin's face paled as his head bobbed in frantic jerks. Round-eyed, the boy stood shivering and transfixed by the belt's swing. His mouth opened and closed in silence as his knees trembled.

"You know, I really wish I could believe you, but sometimes little piggies lie. Ain't that right, men?" Laughter and agreement rumbled through the group. "So we just got to make sure. Stretch him if you would, please, gentlemen."

The two men grabbed the boy's wrists and jerked his arms straight out to the side. Pain contorted Arvin's face as his feet rose from the snow-covered ground.

They were going to beat Arvin for no other reason than his pain gave them pleasure. Leena restrained the urge to scream. She needed to stop them.

Bert nodded approval. "Now, it's time to be a quiet little piggy."

Before Leena could react, the belt raised and flashed down, driven by a powerful, full-armed swing. The weapon slashed across the boy's thin cotton shirt with a crack that resounded through the barren trees. Arvin's head flew back as he screamed toward the sky. The cords in his neck stood out like bowstrings as his deafening howl shattered the forest calm. Angry, frustrated tears blurred Leena's vision as Arvin's body twisted in an anguished dance, his shoulders tugging against the men's grip, struggling to free his arms. His frantic movements pulled against the restraining hands, and his feet touched the ground, running in place as his boots slid over snow-covered road ice.

"I guess you're a slow learner. I told you it's time to be a quiet little piggy." The belt rose again.

Leena clenched her fists. She couldn't stand by and watch these creatures torture the boy. *Here's hoping I don't destroy everything in the neighborhood...*

She touched the Garlan Banch and concentrated on the hedge witch wand immobilization spell her mother taught her. As though she had called it, a different, more powerful immobilization spell entered her mind and activated.

What the...where did that come from?

Arvin's terrible wail ended as if chopped with an ax. Men and boy stood unmoving, lifeless as statues. The belt in Bert's upraised hand dangled back and forth like a mesmerist's charm in the slight breeze. Arvin stood frozen in a twisted pose, one shoulder bulging forward, the other wrenched back, his hips bent in the opposite direction, his body contorted in agony. A wide-mouthed mask of fear and pain deformed his face as a large, red welt swelled across his right shoulder to the left side of his waist.

Wide-eyed, Leena stared at the frozen group. Her hedge witch wand's immobilization spell only affected one person at a time and lasted an hour. She rubbed her fingers where she had touched the Garlan Branch. Somehow, she had cast a much more powerful spell using the Garlan Branch. *But how did I know the spell? And how long will it last?* She needed to be more careful. The Garlan Branch wielded mighty power. She could do significant damage until she learned how to control and use it. But there was no time to worry about that now.

Peeking around the tree, Leena mended and soothed the boy's injuries by casting a healing spell with her hedge witch wand. The livid welt across his back faded as she stepped out from behind the tree trunk. With no idea how long the Garlan Branch immobilization spell would last, now was the time to act. She touched the Garlan Branch. Even though she knew it might be reckless, Leena focused on Arvin, preparing to attempt lifting the immobilization spell from him.

The rough bark of the Branch trembled against her stomach from the disquieting warning vibration flowing within it. She froze as a wave of dread washed over her, the same feeling she experienced when the raven appeared at the Garlan Tree. *Oh Spirit, what have I done?* Throwing her head back, she searched the sky, dreading what she might see. Something ominous approached. Everything within her felt it. Fear flooded over her as if pouring from the sky above.

A distant dot appeared, its size doubling with every passing second as it sped toward her. In less than a minute, the black raven circled above. Before she could move, the creature tilted its massive head and dove toward the ground with dropped-anvil speed, as though sensing where she stood. Mindless panic rushed through her as she ducked behind the tree trunk.

I have to run. Leena's eyes scanned the frozen tableau on the road. She needed to dismiss the immobilization spell so Arvin could escape. But this was no time to see if she could remove the spell from only one person. Even if it was possible, what about the ruffians? Could she leave them to die? What if the raven was only after her? There was no time to deal with the frozen figures. She had to lure the creature away from here. She could figure out what to do about the others later. If there was a later.

Hunching forward, arms pumping above her long strides, Leena raced to the road and ran north over the rise and down its far side. From there, the raven could not see the immobilized men, but she still needed a hiding place.

Like an avenging demon, the giant bird

screamed toward her over the hill, twenty feet above the ground.

This was the second time a raven appeared when she used the Garlan Branch. It had to be searching for the Branch. A bird appeared at the Garlan Tree after she accidentally set a tree on fire, so this one might have flown here when she used the Branch to cast an immobilization spell. It must sense when the Branch is used to cast a spell.

Indecision tore at her. She needed a safe hiding place now. She didn't know if another Branch protection spell would hide her from the bird. With her luck, casting another spell would call another raven, and she doubted she'd even survive this one.

Panicked, Leena raced toward the trees to hide. Three steps into her flight, the raven landed behind her. A blizzard rose before the creature's mighty wing strokes, hiding her within a buffeting snowstorm. The trees before her disappeared in a white whirlpool.

Blinded by the snowstorm, she froze, then pivoted, careful to make no sound. The dark creature stared in her direction as if it knew where she stood, but could not see her until the snow wall dispersed. Head darting left and right, the raven searched for her location.

Would a hedge witch protection spell work

against a magical creature? This was no time to experiment. She didn't want to use the Garlan Branch, but she had no choice. Leena eased her hand toward the Branch, intending to throw a protection spell on herself. Her fingers brushed the rough bark. Like a bright light, the mental command for a much more robust protection spell flared in her mind. She jerked her hand away before she could activate the spell.

She couldn't use the Branch. The risk of calling another bird was too great. But maybe the new protection spell would work with her hedge witch wand. Touching her wand, Leena cast the Branch-enhanced protection spell on herself.

Dread tightened her stomach as the monster's enormous wings unfurled and flapped. *Couldn't it wait another two seconds? Does it expect another flap will clear the snow? It'd be nice if this thing is unmagical and dumb. Then I might have a chance.*

The world before Leena disappeared behind another smothering blizzard. As the growing ivory wall touched the edge of her protective shell, it flowed around the barrier, forming a four-foot-high, sloped snow wall between her and the bird, outlining the invisible sphere surrounding her. With a slow, measured tread, as though knowing its victory was inevitable, the black giant strode toward the white barrier, its eyes scanning as though searching for her. With every step the creature advanced, Leena's resolve weakened under the weight of its merciless, searching eyes each time they slid over hers.

What's it doing to me? Why can't I think straight? No, don't look into its eyes. Fight it! It's an enormous bird, but still just a bird. Just do what you did last time. If you time it right, you might get lucky again.

Like an approaching nightmare, the hulking raven paced closer, seeming to grow taller with every step as it neared. Its jaundiced eyes continued to search. Why did it keep looking around? Couldn't it see her? The demon's chest touched the invisible wall. Its eyes continued searching as the protective barrier shifted the creature to Leena's right. The raven continued past her as though unaware it no longer walked straight toward her.

Relief flooded her chest as the creature passed her protective shelter, walking as though still approaching its goal.

Wait, it not only can't see the barrier, it can't see me? That's never happened with my wand's protection spell before. Something's happened between the wand and the Branch.

The raven stopped, turned, and cocked its head, listening. Leena opened her mouth wide, breathing shallow, silent breaths. The giant bird paced back to the road, its eyes turned toward the rise where a feast of human statues awaited, frozen by the Branch's immobilization spell.

Oh no. She was safe from the raven, unseen within her invisible cocoon, but Arvin and the bandits were not. She had to do something.

As though possessing a mind of their own, her feet kicked through the snow wall, and she rushed toward the bird's back. Faster than she thought possible, the monster spun toward her. *It knew I'd come after it. This was a trap.* Its wing feathers, flattened against the beast's chest by her invisible shield, formed a barrier against her attack.

Leena drew the Branch like a trusty blade in her right hand. Her left touched the hedge witch wand as she sent the mental command to lower her enhanced protection spell. Maybe this bird would also explode if the tip of the Garlan Branch contacted its chest.

Seconds sped by too fast to notice. Leena extended her Garlan Branch sword, hoping its touch would prove as lethal as it had at the Garlan Tree. Looming above her, the raven spun its wing, slamming it into her arm and twirling her like a child's top. Spinning full circle, she fought to regain her balance. Her eyes met the monster's evil glare, chilling her heart. The raven spread its wings wide as its razor-sharp beak descended toward her skull.

No! Leena threw herself backward. Her hand slammed on the hard, icy road, halting the out-of-control spin as her face flattened against the frigid surface. Dizzy, her vision refused to focus. *I can't see. My head's spinning too fast. But I can't give up.* Her mind told her to roll onto her back and face the creature. *I will not let this thing kill me.*

Screaming her anger, she flopped onto her back, facing the leviathan's midnight black silhouette outlined against the bright blue sky. She threw her left arm up to shield her face from the attack. Fire raced along her arm as the beak carved a deep furrow from her wrist to her elbow.

I'm done. I have no strength left. She gritted her teeth against the growing red agony as strength flowed from her. Blackness closed around her vision as she struggled to find one more ounce of resistance. *No, you can't go this way. Not while there's any chance at all.*

Leena extended the Branch sword with her last remaining strength, propelled only by hope. Its tip touched the creature's chest. A burst of wild energy flowed around the Branch. The extended weapon emitted a fierce, crackling brilliance as it contacted the exposed breast feathers.

The bird was done. Touching her hedge witch wand, Leena cast her enhanced protective spell. As the Branch's irresistible pressure grew within the beast, she crossed her right arm over her eyes, hiding the sight of the creature's expansion. A small voice inside wished she could shut her ears against the sound she knew would come. A foul-smelling wind rushed over her as a loud pop scattered bits of bird meat and feathers across the face of her invisible protective wall.

All was quiet. Leena's lower lip trembled as she sat up, head hanging, eyes closed. It was too soon to look at the carnage left by that dumb bird. Relieved tears seeped from behind her closed eyelids, leaving sparkling streams frozen along her cheeks.

TEN

How late is it? Leena wiped a sleeve across her face, removing the evidence of her tears.

Clouds were moving in, hiding the sun behind their gray blanket. The sky had been bright blue when she'd cast the spell that called the raven. Now, the overcast was so thick she couldn't tell what time it was.

Leena inspected the surrounding carnage. Using her hedge witch wand, she raised a small snow blizzard to bury all evidence of the raven's messy passing.

As she placed her hands on the ground to help her stand, a burning fire shot through her left forearm. Wincing, she pulled back her sleeve. From elbow to wrist, congealing black-and-red blood outlined an inch-deep canyon along her arm.

That is going to leave a terrible scar. She wondered if the Garlan Branch could enhance her wand's healing ability. Touching her hedge witch wand, Leena cast a healing spell. Again, the spell she intended to send was overridden by a new, more powerful spell. As though following the raven's beak across her arm, the damage faded from wrist to elbow into a dim pink line, followed by a wave of normal skin. *Oh, good. That should keep me from becoming an old, scarred veteran when this time of great trouble ends.*

She stood up, feeling a bit dizzy. She needed to do something about Arvin and this bandit horde. Besides, it was time to figure out how to localize the Garlan Branch's effects. As awful as it was, she hoped only casting a spell would call a raven, not modifying or releasing one. She shuddered at the thought of fighting a raven whenever she used the Branch. *There's only one way to find out.*

Her fingers grazed the Branch at her waist as she concentrated on releasing the immobilization spell, focusing on Arvin alone. Arvin's boot-clad feet slid as he danced around, struggling to free his arms. Leena searched the sky. After several minutes, far longer than it took the last raven, no bird appeared. *Okay, it worked.*

She approached Arvin. Still clutched in the frozen ruffians' grip, unable to turn far enough to look behind himself, Arvin searched the area, confused. He didn't know she was here. She needed to be careful to keep him from injuring himself. It would be all too easy for him to twist and dislocate an elbow or shoulder while these thugs had their tight grip locked on his wrists. Still hidden by her protection spell, Leena crept behind the twisting, squirming lad. Five feet from him, she removed the invisibility-bestowing spell.

"Let me help free you." She pried the bandit's dirty fingers from his wrists.

"Where were you?" the boy screamed in her face. "Why did you let them get me? Do you know what they were going to do to me?" He was understandably upset.

"I just got here. I didn't know where you ran to or that anyone captured you."

"Yeah, sure. I bet you just stood there and watched while that animal beat me."

The accusation stung since it held a grain of truth. Leena hesitated because nothing in her experience warned her that anyone could be so cruel, but the boy would never understand that. She turned away as a shame-driven rose tinted her cheeks.

Now that he was free, Arvin began digging through the scrambled pile of goods at the rear of the wagon bed. He pulled out the jacket he wore in Quillan. His sniffles decreased as he pulled the coat on. Occasionally, a deep, hiccupping breath erupted. As though to punish her for not acting quicker, he rarely looked in Leena's direction. When he did, the accusation in his eyes increased her discomfort.

"You might look in the wagon to see if there's anything useful we can take with us," Arvin snarled. "You should also select a weapon that you know how to use. With the Great Wizard's troops out destroying the towns, I doubt this is the only bandit gang on the road."

His voice and the glare in his eyes told her she was stupid for not doing this already. She would have searched the wagon before they left here, but pointing that out now would do no good. His pride was hurt. In his mind, he was a boy, and she was only a girl. She had seen him beaten and screaming. It would take time for him to get over his shame and anger.

Inspecting the goods in the wagon, Leena suspected the band was on its way to loot the deserted town of Stocksbury. Her stomach jumped with fear at the thought that she might have been caught asleep and unsuspecting if the bandits arrived in Stocksbury a day earlier. A vision of her and Arvin tied and trailing the wagon flashed in her mind. She would have to be far more careful from now on.

The cart rang with clanging metal as Leena dug through its goods. Sifting through silver platters and candelabras, gold rings, jewels, food, and quality clothing, she found several sturdy leather bags that would serve far better for carrying their goods than the tied-together ends of the hotel sheets. The sturdy backpacks would hold all their remaining foodstuffs, with enough room left for spare clothing.

The wagon also contained several dozen death-dealing objects: swords, bows, arrow-filled quivers, crossbows and darts, knives, spears, clubs, and axes. Though she had never held a weapon before, having one at her disposal seemed prudent. She selected a short sword, not too heavy and small enough to maneuver with little effort. The six-inch leather-wrapped hilt fit her hand like it had been made for her. Drawing the blade from its scabbard, she found its two-foot length engraved with unfamiliar characters. Reseating the blade, she fastened the sword belt around her waist.

"Arvin, do you know how to use a sword?"

Receiving no answer, she stood and turned around.

"Arvin, no!"

The boy was standing behind the bandit, holding a knife at Bert's neck. His head snapped around at her call. His expression was blank as he turned and slashed a deep gash across the unmoving ruffian's throat. He smiled with grim satisfaction, watching the man's blood gush. Arvin's hand struck Bert's back with a meaty smack when the scarlet flow slowed to a trickle. The bandit's body toppled to the ground as though released from the gallows.

Bile rose in her throat as her eyes traveled over the gang's prone bodies, each adding their last lifeblood to the growing scarlet pools staining the ice below their necks. Adding insult to injury, Arvin stooped to clean his weapon using Bert's untucked shirttail. Her stomach threatened to lose the remains of her breakfast as the cloud-subdued light revealed the boy's blood-washed hands and several red trails painting his shirt.

"What have you done?" Leena's voice cracked, her throat constricted by the irreversible sight of the scattered bodies.

Arvin glanced at the strewn mass with slow head shakes. A sneer raised his upper lip as he threw her a condescending look. "If we'd let them live, they would only follow and kill us. You can't leave scum like this behind you. Now we won't have to worry about this band of filth."

"No, Arvin. There had to be another way."

"What would you do with them, m'lady? Leave them here to freeze to death under your spell? Turn them over to the next sheriff we see? When and where would that be, and how would we get them there?" He turned from her in disgust and started removing coin pouches from the dead men.

What have I done? Why did I cast the immobilization spell? I'd just finished telling myself I needed to resist using the Branch until I knew more about it. Too many thoughts raced through her brain. Leaving the bandits immobilized was a big mistake. These men suffered needless deaths. In addition, even a boy knew a hedge witch didn't have the power to freeze this many at once. After the casual way Arvin dispatched the gang, she suspected he would be looking for a way to disable her long enough to find the secret of how she immobilized so many. Leena shivered at the thought of those murderous hands roaming over her body. Maybe she just needed to escape from him.

As she sat on the heap of goods in the wagon, considering the feasibility of escape, Arvin combined the coins from the dead men's sacks into two pouches. He finished and returned to the cart, holding one out to her.

"Here, we can use these to get food and lodging if we come to a town with people."

Unthinking, she accepted the pouch. Leena searched her mind for an argument to refute the boy's reason for killing the bandits. She found none, and it bothered her. She sensed an old soul in the young lad's body. This Arvin was so different from the boy she'd met in Quillan. The trauma of his capture had changed him, and she feared most of these changes were not for the better.

Arvin wandered through the bodies, inspecting them. He stooped beside one to remove a belt and scabbard containing a short sword with a sparkling jeweled hilt. He stared at her with a challenging expression as he strapped it around his waist.

"To answer your question, m'lady..."

The boy drew the sword and performed an intricate and deadly dance. His blade flashed and glittered beneath the returning sun, his movements graceful, sure, and competent. *Where did a Wedgelin boy so young learn such skill with a weapon? Is he warning me of what will come if we stay together?*

Using her hedge witch wand, she cast a warning spell around herself that would tingle an alert in her mind if anyone intruded within ten feet of her. Watching the boy's swirling performance, Leena vowed to maintain the spell while they were together. Her nervousness grew each time she looked at him. His anger and hate were too unpredictable.

"Now, m'lady, if you're done with your rest, perhaps we should move along."

With effort, Leena forced her mind away from the disturbing thoughts.

"This cart's too heavy laden. It'll only slow us down," she said. "Even if it didn't, it would surely be too huge a temptation for another gang. I think it best to release the oxen, gather a few things we might need, and leave the cart here for whoever stumbles on it." Leena unstrapped the animals and shooed them away as she talked. "If the authorities find it, I doubt they'll suspect that a woman and a young boy caused all this damage."

Leena unrolled her sheet and stowed the food-stuffs and a few unbroken candles salvaged from the wagon into the two leather packs. She attached the bulging coin purse to her sword belt and shouldered one of the filled packs. Wrapping her shawl around her shoulders, she leaped from the wagon and held the other pack toward the boy when she landed.

A bowstring and the strap of a quiver filled with

arrows now crossed Arvin's chest. Having seen his display with the sword, she suspected he was also familiar with archery. She said nothing.

A sneer crossed Arvin's face as he noticed the sword at her waist. Still silent, he shouldered his pack and started north.

"Are you sure you won't need any armor?" The snide remark was out before she could stop it. *Oh, Spirit. Why did I have to say that? I have to be more careful about what I say.*

The boy stopped and turned to look at her. Grudgingly, as though hating to admit she might be right, he returned to the dead men. From one body, he removed a pair of sturdy leather gloves studded with short silver spikes at the knuckles. He pulled them on, flexed his fingers, and took a few enthusiastic swings in the air. Smiling, he seemed satisfied.

Arvin started walking away from the scene of his slaughter, then stopped. With a disturbing grin, he returned to Bert and removed the peasant cap from the nearly severed head. He pulled the hat over his unkempt hair like a king donning his victory crown.

"Now, I'm ready." He headed north between the fresh wagon tracks marking the snow-covered road.

Leena watched him for a few seconds, bothered by his callous disregard for the slain men. *I can only hope that, once his anger and embarrassment cool off, he'll be... what? Less hard? More human? More boy-like?* She was unsure what she wanted, but her heart told her that Arvin might remain harsh and cold for the rest of his life unless she changed his outlook.

As he plowed through virgin snow, Leena wondered if this might be the time to run. She could get into the trees, use the wind to cover her footprints, then hide until he left. But then what? This was the only road she knew of that went north. She still didn't know how long the Branch-enhanced protection spell would last. She'd have to face another raven if she used the Garlan Branch's protection spell to make her invisible. Two times facing one of those monsters was three times too many.

Leena shook the thoughts away. She needed a better plan before attempting an escape. Pulling her shawl tighter around her head, she hurried after the boy.

ELEVEN

H ours passed with only their footsteps, crunching through endless knee-deep snow, intruding on the winter's quiet. Leena abandoned the effort to open conversation after an unanswered attempt to break the speechless journey by asking the boy if he ever intended to stop and eat. She let her thoughts wander, reviewing their encounter with the ruffians, while Arvin stomped forward, lost in whatever fantasies fueled his idea of justice. In silent agreement, their hard-fought steps put as much distance as possible between them and the dead bandits. Head hanging with fatigue, Leena plodded for three endless days in the silent boy's footprints, sleeping on her shawl at night, protected by her hedge witch wand's warming spell.

"Hold up, m'lady. I thought I saw something on the other side of these bushes." Arvin's voice, rough from rare use, broke the peace of a crimson sunset.

Leena peered through the high, thick hedge bordering the east side of the road, amazed that his sharp eyes spotted a snow-covered cottage nestled behind the hedges in a small pine tree grove several hundred yards beyond.

Steel rasped against its scabbard as Arvin drew his sword. Leena's hand slid toward her wand. The boy approached the hedge and, with short, whistling slashes, carved an Arvin-sized archway through the base of the ten-foot-high barrier.

"You wait here while I see if it's safe." Sheathing the weapon, he edged his boots between the hedge's short, bared stumps toward the three-foot-thick snow blanket beyond.

Leena waited on the road, watching Arvin plow a path through the snow on his self-appointed mission to ensure the house held no nasty surprises. She needed the break. The cost of maintaining her hedge witch wand's warming spell was sapping her energy reserves to a dangerous level. The Branch-enhanced protection spell would remove her fatigue but render her invisible, and even if it didn't call a raven, she dared not risk alerting the unstable boy to this capability.

Every time she used the Garlan Branch, one of those stupid ravens appeared. Activating a spell with the Branch must attract them. But altering that spell by unfreezing only Arvin didn't call a raven. When she'd cast the Branch altered hedge witch wand protection spell, no raven came, even though the Branch put the new protection spell in her mind. It was a good thing, too. In the future, she'd have to remember to see if the Branch would give her an enhanced spell to use with her hedge witch wand before using the Branch.

Time inched by as dark shadows crept across the road. Leena struggled to maintain her patience. With every passing minute, her energy reserves drained. How long could she wait until activating the Branch-enhanced protection spell and escaping the half-mad child was no longer an option? The darkening hedge row gave no answer to the silent question.

A crimson sun perched on the distant skyline as though resting before creeping behind the horizon. Where was he? What was taking so long? Was this place a trap the Great Wizard's troops set to capture them? Maybe she should see if he needed rescuing again. Her indecision grew as her hand crept toward the Garlan Branch. *No!* Her hand snapped away from her waistband. The silence and the waiting made her nervous, but she couldn't risk using the Branch.

Another half-hour crawled by. Taking deep, calming breaths, Leena fought against worrying that something had happened to him.

Leena awoke to a strong breeze rattling the hedge leaves like dry, skeletal bones. A bright, full moon traced an arc above the horizon, its light painting long ink-black shadows from nearby trees across the glistening snow. Still, Arvin was nowhere in sight.

Where is he? Leena twisted her head side-to-side, loosening her sleep-stiffened neck muscles. She'd waited long enough. Gathering her pack and shawl, Lenna turned toward the hedge. *It's time I went to see what the little creature's up to.*

She froze as the boy reappeared at the side of the house, walking toward the boy-sized hole cut through the hedge as if he did not have a care in the world. As he neared, his face, glowing in the moonlight, wore the same merciless expression it held when he slaughtered the bandit gang. Several shiny, dark speckles marked his jacket. Were those new blood spots? The chill shivering along her spine had nothing to do with the weather.

Leena's heart raced as she tried to reconcile his casual gait with his fierce expression. *Did he kill someone else? It's as if the thought of killing relaxes him. What kind of boy is he?*

"Sorry I took so long, m'lady." Lifting his legs high to clear the low carved branches of his passage-way, Arvin stepped onto the road. "I wanted to make sure the place was safe for us. Seems there's no one there. I checked the fireplace, and the ashes were cold, so I suspect they've been gone at least a day. Maybe longer. Anyway, I lit a fire, so we'll sleep warm tonight."

"What took you so long?" she snapped.

"There's lots of tracks in the yard." He continued as if she had not spoken. "Could be some of the Great Wizard's infantry since there's no hoofprints. Course, it could be bandits. Hard to tell.

"If it's the Great Wizard's troops, whoever lived there has probably been taken to the nearest garrison for questioning, and it could be weeks, even months before they return. If it's bandits, they'll probably never be back. I suspect it's the Great Wizard's troops, though, since nothing seems to have been taken from the house, and there's still three horses in the hedge barn." He looked back through the hedge, lost in thought. "Those troops might not be thieves, but they don't care what happens to a detained person's worldly goods."

As she nodded in cautious agreement, the

sparkle of dark red stains on his jacket again caught Leena's eyes. Seeing her stare, Arvin looked down.

"I guess you're wondering about these." He touched a new shiny-wet, scarlet trail, then lifted his finger to inspect its moist tip in the bright moonlight. "I found a chicken in the barn, so I beheaded it and hung it up to drain for tomorrow's breakfast."

Leena decided not to question him any further about his extended absence. Perhaps he took extra time to search the surrounding area and ensure the house wasn't a trap.

As they rounded the side of the house toward the front porch, Leena discovered a yard where the snow cover between the house and the barn had been churned into a confused pattern of several hundred footprints, some sprinkled with a few red blood specks. For an instant, her mind reeled as unnerving images of the bandit gang's slaughter intruded.

No, his life was threatened by the bandits. His reaction might have been extreme, but that could be understandable under the circumstances. Here, there would be no provocation. You're jumping to conclusions.

Closing her eyes, Leena breathed deep, cleansing breaths, struggling to calm herself. These red spots could be from a chicken he killed. But he'd be careful to get as little blood on his shirt as possible, wouldn't he?

As a distraction, she studied the chaotic footprints in the yard. Many of the footprints could be from the Great Wizard's soldiers, and some could be Arvin's if he searched the area well before he came to get her. That would explain why it took so long. Most bootprints formed a wide column of four neat rows atop the yard's other jumbled boot tracks. The orderly prints crossed in front of the porch, skirted the barn's north side, heading east, and disappeared beneath a cluster of towering pine trees.

She looked around the yard, searching for anything more than the footprints to confirm soldiers were here, and took the residents away. Leena's eyes stopped at the porch when they met Arvin's angry glare. Moonlight glittered tiny sparkles in his eyes nestled within a shadowed mask beneath his eyebrows. Their gleaming beams radiated a flame of absolute hatred, burning like fire within her brain. Before she could convince herself the connection had happened, his head lifted. Moonlight softened his face into a gentle friendliness, dispelling the evil illusion.

If that look was sincere, maybe these footprints reminded him of what happened to his parents. Or perhaps I just looked his way at the wrong time.

"Sorry, I should have been more careful." Arvin's voice croaked, harsh and loud, through the frigid night air as his fingers smeared the new blood spots. He turned and opened the door. "I think we should grab a bite from their larder, then get some rest."

Uneasiness rumbled through her stomach as he entered the house. What was he apologizing for? What did he do? Leena fought to erase the memory of how he dealt with the bandit gang while weighing her chances of escaping as his back disappeared within.

Maybe she should use the Branch-enhanced protection spell and run away now, hiding her footprints in the soldiers' tracks while he's waiting for her to enter. She could be far away before he realized she was gone. But where would she go, and how would she survive? *I'm stuck. I have to depend on him for now.*

Leena mounted the porch and followed Arvin into the house.

DRAWN by the mouth-watering aroma of roasting fowl, Leena's rumbling tummy eased her from a dreamless sleep. Her satisfying yawn collapsed as she looked around the room.

*We've intruded into a stranger's house. I know we had little choice, but still...*She scanned the small bedroom, vowing to leave the room as she found it. She thanked the Spirit that this place had two bedrooms. She doubted she would get any rest if she had to share a room with Arvin.

Throwing the covers aside, Leena rose and removed the pack she had placed before the door last night to alert her if anyone had tried entering. In the central room, a fire crackled a merry welcome beneath the plump bird, dripping savory juices as it roasted on a spit in the fireplace. Her tummy rumbled another greeting toward the golden-brown goodness as the delicious scent filled her nose. Her morning joy diminished as the front door squeaked open, admitting a rush of frigid air when Arvin entered carrying his cap filled with rolled oats.

"I found these in the barn. I think the family that lived here won't miss them." He held out Bert's overflowing peasant cap for her inspection. Nodding toward the fireplace, he continued, "And having a hot meal will do us some good."

How does he know a family lived here? The room she slept in had clothes for a man and a woman. *Settle down, Leena. Maybe the room he slept in was for children.*

She fought to control the tears building as her

mind struggled to ignore memories of the fresh blood on Arvin's shirt last night. *Please, Spirit, let the family return soon and continue their lives here.* Her eyes wandered to the two bedrooms. *Surely, Arvin wouldn't do anything to innocent children.* Swallowing past the lump in her throat, she blinked to clear her vision while shaking her head to dispel the disturbing thoughts. She turned to watch the boy's breakfast preparations.

Pulling the chicken from the fireplace, he inspected it with the critical eye of an experienced cook before handing the spit to Leena. Turning from her as though her opinion of his culinary skills did not matter, he poured the oats from his cap into a cauldron, added water from a bucket, and slung the kettle over the fire.

Where does a boy so young learn to cook? Wouldn't his mother perform that task at home? Maybe his father taught him on their hunting trips. With a mental shrug, Leena moved her burden toward the table. *I need to stop looking for reasons to suspect him.*

"I'm sorry about that bandit gang, m'lady." This was the first time Arvin mentioned the incident since they had left the scene of his massacre four days ago. Leena looked into the bottomless depths of his dark brown eyes. "It's just I was so scared. I knew them men meant to hurt me, then kill me. I know my mind wasn't working right, but I want you to know that I thank you for what you done, and I'll try to do the best I can for you."

His expression was so sincere that Leena's heart reached out to him. He was too young to survive alone in the world. His brash exterior and brutal nature were only the protective defenses of his mind. Maybe he could be a good boy if given a chance. For a moment, she wanted to hold him and tell him it would be all right. *But what if this is just a ploy? Who is he really? Could this little boy wanting to please be an act concealing a dangerous mind?*

"I understand, Arvin. And thank you for your honesty." *I hope that sounded sincere enough.*

He looked at her for several moments as she tried to appear deeply concerned. For a second, she thought she saw a glint of something, perhaps triumph, in his eyes as he spun away and grabbed a long-handled wooden spoon to stir the kettle.

Was that a chuckle? No, I'm sure he was only clearing his throat.

Searching the cupboards, Leena found a platter for the bird and set it in the center of the rough wooden table. The silence between them continued as she searched the cupboards for dishes. Digging through various earthen jars in a cabinet, Leena found a full honey pot among the earthen jars on a spice shelf. Its sweetness would go well with the gruel bubbling in the kettle. Using a rag to protect both hands from the hot wire handle's heat, Arvin placed the steaming cauldron on the table with a smile of success.

"Can you ride, m'lady?" Arvin's words wrestled around a mouthful of roasted chicken.

"I never have. Can you?" Warm, honeyed breath accompanied Leena's words, the sweet taste bringing memories of spring wildflowers' perfume. The flavor pulled her thoughts back to carefree girlhood days as she lost her struggle to concentrate on Arvin's words.

Although she did not realize it until she returned to find her village destroyed, her life in Quillan held nothing but pleasant memories. To Leena, her family was her world. Her town had no school, so her mother taught her hedge witch skills as she instilled the moral code of a good and honest person by example. During their family-togetherness times in the evenings, she and her father regaled each other with outlandish tales of heroism and wonder. But her time with her sister, Riana, formed her most precious memories. As all sisters do, they'd had a few spats while growing up together, but those were soon forgotten, and they remained best friends. Their bond only strengthened as they explored the forests around Quillan, looking for herbs and discussing life.

Everyone in Quillan agreed Riana was beautiful. She stood a hand-span shorter than Leena and was as slender as a willow wand and graceful as a swan. Although their mother assured Leena that she looked just like her sister did two years ago when Riana was sixteen, Leena felt big, awkward, and plain by comparison. But she took comfort in the thought that perhaps she would be as stunning as Riana one day. Overall, Leena's most enduring memories were of laughter. Whenever two or more family members were together, life was fun. Her thoughts wandered toward memories of harvest festivals.

"Of course, m'lady, and I can teach you." Arvin's words rang loud in the still room, dissolving her memories. "We could make a shorter trip of it if we rode. There's plenty of saddles and tack in the barn."

He looked at her, expectation and hope shining in his eyes. She saw no reason not to use the horses. Hay and feed in the barn would soon be gone, and who knew how long the family would be detained? The animals could starve if left there.

"I think it's a splendid idea."

The boy beamed as though she had awarded

him a heartfelt compliment. "I'll go saddle them now." He jumped up and started toward the door.

"No, no, there's no rush. Finish your breakfast. You can saddle them while I clean up in here." She wanted to prolong the pleasure of the meal and revisit the memories that the honey induced.

Arvin looked startled. His gaze slid around the room with an expression that said, "Why should we bother cleaning up?" A slight cloud darkened his face, but he sat back down to finish his meal.

"It's the right thing to do. Especially since we're uninvited guests," she said. His shrug dismissed her explanation as if he accepted the need to humor her but did not understand it. "Now, come on, sit down, and finish your breakfast. It might be some time before we have a hot meal like this again. Let's enjoy it," Leena said as her hand patted his. The hint of confusion left his face as he looked down at her fingers. A flush rose from his neck, reddening his ears.

"Yes, m'lady. It's a good idea." The boy's hanging head did little to hide his bright-red ears. His subdued voice failed to raise above a whisper.

Arvin left to saddle their mounts. Leena cleaned the dishes and restored them to their cupboards, then removed and rolled both used blankets from the beds they slept in. Trying not to notice the two smaller beds in the room where Arvin slept, she lifted their packs, slung the rolled blankets over her shoulder, and pulled her scarf closer around her chin. She found a pair of mounts ready to travel when she reached the barn. A couple of oat-filled sacks roped together at their tops spanned the back of a third horse.

Arvin took their packs from her, tied them together, and secured them over the packhorse's back behind the oats sacks. He bound the blanket rolls with sturdy hemp twine he'd found in the barn, then attached them to their packs and inspected the load to ensure all was secure.

"If you've a mind, m'lady, we could bring the kettle and the honeypot. There's still plenty of room, and we can return them someday when we come back by this way."

Warm surprise flowed over her at discovering the boy had noticed her delight in finding the honey. *He can be thoughtful when he chooses.* She returned to the cottage to fetch them.

After storing the articles on their packhorse, Arvin led his mount and turned the animal so its left side faced her.

"Here's how you mount, m'lady." The boy slid his left foot into the horse's stirrup and, with practiced ease, floated onto the saddle. His heels dug shallow furrows in the mount's side when his rear settled onto the seat. With a small whinny, the horse flew through the snow. Arvin raced the animal around the barnyard for several minutes in intricate patterns, demonstrating his riding skills. After several minutes of showing off, Arvin turned the animal toward Leena, racing at a full gallop. Frozen in place, she debated which way to jump and avoid the beast. At the last possible second, he jerked the reins toward his chest, sending snow flying in sheets over her. *What was that all about?*

"See, m'lady? Nothing to it."

TWELVE

By the time they halted for their midday meal, Leena regretted ever seeing a horse. Her chaffed rear flamed with every step her mount took, and she wondered whether her aching left leg would ever straighten from its sidesaddle bend. Pulling her skirt above her leggings would allow her to ride astride the mount. However, something in the boy's manner warned her this would be far too immodest for these circumstances. She couldn't ride like this until they reached the Great Wizard's castle. She vowed to find a pair of men's trousers that fit her in the next town. *Maybe ladies don't wear pants, but I can't ride like this for the weeks or months it'll take to get to the Great Wizard's castle.*

With the agility of a creaky, older woman, Leena rolled to her stomach and slid from the animal's back. While Arvin rummaged through their packs for food, Leena turned away, touched her hedge witch wand, and used its enhanced healing spell to cure her aches. As she felt the wand beneath her tunic, her hand brushed the Garlan Branch. *How long can I keep it hidden?*

For a moment, Leena wondered whether she should tell Arvin about the Branch. *No, I'm not sure how much I dare trust him.* He could only suspect she had some source of additional power, but he couldn't be sure. Was he hoping to find some way to control her and, therefore, her power source during this trip? If not, why was he on this trip at all? Maybe he just didn't want to live his life alone. Okay, she admitted, she didn't know what Arvin was up to. Even though he was improving a bit, he was still far too unpredictable.

After a quick cold meal, they rode deep into the night, looking for a place to stay. They had passed no towns or cottages since leaving the farmhouse where they secured their mounts. By midnight, they could ride no more. The boy's head bobbed with every step as he nodded in the saddle, and Leena's inner resources were minutes away from being drained. They had to rest, even if it meant sleeping on the road since deep snow covered the forest and fields around them.

"Arvin." The boy continued on unheeding. "Arvin!"

He jerked, lifting his head. "Huh, wha...?"

"We have to stop. We need to rest."

Nodding, the boy pulled the reins to halt his mount.

They slid to the ground. As though sleepwalking, Arvin stumbled to the packhorse, released the blankets, unrolled them, and flopped down on one. He pulled the other over himself and fell into a deep sleep, leaving Leena to unsaddle and groom the horses. He had also left her without a blanket.

Leena watched the boy for several minutes to ensure his light snores were not a ruse. Using the horses to hide her actions, she touched the Garlan Branch. Remembering the raven it called, she removed her hand from its comforting touch.

With her hedge witch wand, Leena cast a warming spell on herself and healing spells on the horses to reduce their fatigue. Edging around the trio of horses, she confirmed Arvin remained asleep. With his snores sawing through the still night, Leena placed oat sacks over the horses' heads to feed them. She looked down at the deep snow.

Oh well, I've been through worse.

Stamping a bed-sized flat area in the snow, Leena spread out her shawl and, knowing the rest would replenish her hedge witch magic energy reserves, she slept in the warming spell's comfort.

FOR SEVERAL DAYS, the riders saw no signs of civilization. The endless forest stretched around them with only the flat path of a pristine, snow-covered road ahead to show people had once traveled here. Few birds remained, but they occasionally spotted game in the distance.

Life settled into a comfortable routine. Rising at dawn, they breakfasted on hot gruel smothered with honey, then rode until the sun was in the afternoon sky, broke for a quick lunch of cheese, rolls, and apples, and continued until darkness made progress impossible.

The journey's monotony stole their will to talk, so they spoke only when necessary. At times, Leena forgot why they were riding. It seemed this trek was all there was, just them, traveling north, now and forever.

"What was your life like in Wedgelin?" Leena's voice was deep and rough from lack of use.

Arvin remained quiet for so long that Leena feared he would not answer. Reining his horse to a stop, he turned it to face her.

"My father was a tinker but wanted more for his son." The last word came out harsh and grating as though a curse. "Somehow, he secured an apprenticeship for me at the manor house as a knight's page. The work was grueling. My days were spent keeping and tending the knight's horses, maintaining a constant shine on his boots, weapons, and armor, cleaning the knight's quarters, and even helping the knight dress. It was menial and demeaning; however, he taught me combat skills in trade. Someday, I'll be the most skillful knight who ever lived. Legends of my power will live for centuries."

Arvin glared at her, his expression daring her to contradict him. Leena sat mute, uncertain whether she wanted him to continue the tale. After several minutes, he jerked the reins, forcing his mount's head to snap back facing the trail, and rode on in unwelcoming silence.

Oh well, so much for a friendly conversation. She'd have to be more watchful to learn what she needed to know about him.

The endless thuds of the horses' hooves in the deep snow played a monotonous backbeat as the day grew cloudy and storm clouds swelled dark on the horizon before them.

Their food supplies had dwindled over the four days since they'd left the farm. When they stopped for a midday meal, Leena found they only had three apples, one roll, and a crumb of cheese remaining. Except for oats, this was their food until they found a village. Even their oat supply was running low because it was all they had to feed the horses.

Arvin stared at the miserable fare she had laid out. He picked up an apple and the roll and started toward his horse. "The rest is yours, m'lady," he said around a mouthful of the bread as he mounted. "Go on and eat, then wait here. I'll be back soon." His boot heels dug deep into his mount's ribs, and it shot away at a gallop.

"Where are you going?" she called to his fading back. If he heard, he did not respond.

The first large snowflakes began falling before she finished lunch. As she repacked, the flakes drifted down in a growing curtain, blotting the hori-zon, sealing Leena in a white world of soundless, vision-limiting snow. In less than an hour, seeing beyond an arm's length became impossible. Black clouds swallowed the afternoon daylight as the snow suppressed all noise. Leena felt trapped in a world where light and sound no longer existed.

Where did Arvine go, and when will he return? As the daylight faded, Leena asked herself these questions more than a dozen times. She had no idea where she was. No one she knew had ever been this far north. Did Arvin even know if there was a town nearby, or would he plow through this endless snow-covered road for uncountable miles until they starved to death? Although she did not trust him enough to reveal her protection spell or admit to possessing a Garlan Branch, a kind of acceptance had developed between them. She had grown used to his company. This cold, desolated loneliness weighed heavy in her breast without his companionship.

The wind rose, and white flakes flew like a meteor storm into her face. The cloud cover and snowfall grew so thick that she could no longer tell the time of day. Head nodding with fatigue, she stood and led the horses up the gentle slope next to the road, hoping to find shelter. More than a hundred yards from the road, a stand of pine trees rose ahead, almost invisible through the heavy snowfall. Relief washed through her as the dim light beneath their sloping green limbs revealed that the lower branches were high enough to provide shelter within the cave formed beneath their thick, protective needles. Lifting the snow-laden branches, she shooed the horses, with light swats on their rumps, into a sanctuary where they could stand hidden and secure. Muscles aching, she unsaddled and groomed the weary mounts.

Leena spread out her shawl on the needle-strewn ground and sat waiting. Her eyes grew heavy. Casting a warming spell on herself, she leaned against the tree trunk. "Mum, Da, Riana...I'm coming to find you," she whispered. She repeated this mantra until her eyelids drifted shut.

Leena's eyes snapped open with no memory of falling asleep. Snow blocked most of the daylight, sealing her pine tree cavern in shadowy dimness. Through the night, a four-foot-deep soft white wall had surrounded the outer branches of her shelter. Moving to the fresh barrier, she clawed a tunnel through the pristine wall with the determination of a dog burying a bone.

Refreshed and recharged, Leena crawled on hands and knees through the trench she created and stood beyond the tree's branches to view a glistening, panoramic landscape. Snow-reflected sunlight drilled into her eyes. Blinking away blinding tears, she scanned the hill down to the road. Above, a cloudless blue sky shined on an endless glittering white blanket, concealing the road and covering the countryside as far as she could see. The graveyard stillness sent a chill shivering up and down her body. Closing her eyes, ignoring the soundless landscape, she sniffed the crisp new air, letting its pleasant icy bite nip inside her nose while she stretched her stiff muscles.

Where's Arvin? He didn't know she had moved into the trees for shelter. Did he pass here in the night? Faint sounds caught her ear, distant clinks of metal on metal. *Maybe that's him. But what if it isn't?*

Smooth, fresh snow had covered all traces of yesterday's travel. The slightest noise carried a far distance in the morning silence. Leena heard the crump of a horse's sneeze and strained her eyes north along the road, hoping to see Arvin.

A banner appeared above the northern horizon, too far away to see the golden symbol on its red background. A midnight-black soldier's helm emerged beneath the fluttering banner, followed by another. Two more appeared, and another two. Finally, a column of thirty ebon-helmed and breast-plated riders drew closer, wearing matching black uniforms beneath their armor. Their shiny boots and pikes glinted bright sparkles from the rising sun. Her heart jumped as she recognized the golden eagle crest of Allivan on the scarlet banner and the riders' breastplates.

Why are they here? This can't be a coincidence. Her heart pounded so loud that she feared they might hear. Leena ducked to hide behind the parapet her tunneling had created. Through the small gap, she watched the soldiers' approach.

The gigantic horses lifted their hooves high to clear the snow. Powerful flank muscles bulged as they plowed steady furrows through the knee-deep powder. Their noisy trappings clinked and clattered, drowning all other sounds. The knights wore helmets like they expected an imminent battle. Closing her eyes, Leena sent a silent prayer, thanking the Spirit that no wizards rode among them.

As the first rider pulled abreast of her pine tree cave, Leena touched the hedge witch wand, feeling its power, debating whether to activate its Branch-enhanced protection spell to hide herself.

Palms sweating, she watched the column pass her shelter without a glance in her direction. Although more than a hundred yards away, they seemed so close she could throw a stone and hit them. Finally, their supply wagon creaked past. A bored teamster clucked as he slapped the reins. Leena did not draw a sigh of relief until the wagon crested a far hill and disappeared.

Were they looking for her? Leena scooted backward on her hands and knees. There was nothing south of here but the towns and villages the Great Wizard's troops had already destroyed. She couldn't stay here. What if they came back?' Grabbing items at random, Leena stuffed them into her backpack as her mind whirled in furious confusion. Every instinct screamed at her to get as far from here as possible, but where could she go? Without Arvin, she was lost and feared she would not last long traveling cross-country alone. Arvin was her guide. He might know a way they could travel and avoid the knights.

I have to do something. Leena wanted to scream with frustration. Where was he? She couldn't leave without him, but staying here might be worse. What if the Great Wizard's soldiers expanded their search? She needed to be far from here before they did.

She lifted the tree limbs to ensure the road was empty before leading the horses out. Her eyes caught a flicker of motion.

Uh oh, someone's coming. I'm trapped. They'll see me if I try to leave now.

Using her shoulder, Leena forced the horses back beneath the branches. Dropping onto her hands and knees, she crawled to her hiding place behind the parapet. With the low-hanging branches as camouflage, she peeked between their needles.

A lone rider approached using the crushed snow path left by the soldiers' passing. Her breath hitched as she clutched her wand. She didn't know how army units operated. Was that a scout performing a more thorough search for Arvin or her after the column passed?

Eyes darting around the landscape, Leena scanned the area for an escape path, but the grove stood a hundred yards from the nearest tree. *Oh, Spirit, I'm trapped.* The rider neared, searching the snow on either side of the road.

Something in his manner looked familiar. *Arvin!* Her relieved sigh sent a fog trail ghosting from her mouth.

Not daring to risk a shout, Leena stood and waved both arms above her head to catch his attention. Arvin's head fixed on her as he spied her flying arms. Turning his mount, he galloped up the hill, heedless of the deep furrow he left in the snow behind him. A slain deer lay across the saddle in front of him, its head lifting and falling as though nodding in agreement with the horse's pace. Behind his saddle, several thick sacks flapped like bird wings lifting in flight.

"No questions now if you please, m'lady. We've got to hurry."

Leena led the horses out and mounted as Arvin spurred his horse up the slope beyond her shelter, farther into the forest. Nearing the hilltop, Leena turned to look back. The road was a half mile behind them. Their tracks left a visible path winding through the scattered trees up the slope. When the knights returned, they could not miss it.

Her hand flexed toward the Garlan Branch and stopped. Nope, it wasn't worth the risk of attracting a raven. But she was unsure whether her hedge witch wand was strong enough to shift this much snow. But she had to try it. She had no choice.

As her hand reached for the wand, a fierce wind sprang up along the face of the hill. A low snow wall lifted and danced a path along the horses' tracks. Its fury died as it reached her, leaving the slope smooth and unmarked like no one had passed this way in decades. Only the soldiers' horse and wagon tracks showed anyone had ever been here.

Who did that? Is another witch, or maybe a wizard, out there watching us? It couldn't be Arvin. He's too young; besides, he's a knight's page, not a wizard. Her eyes studied the road. *But who else is there?*

"M'lady, where are you?"

The distant call came from deep in the woods behind her. Reaching the hilltop, Leena used her hedge witch wand to hide the short portion of her back trail that had not been covered by the strong wind. Turning from the road, she followed the voice toward Arvin. A chill rushed through her when his glare fixed in her direction. As she neared, he reined his horse around and walked it into a section of trees scattered enough to allow them to ride side by side.

He couldn't be mad at her, could he? She waited all night and half the day for him to return, just like he wanted. He should realize she had to hide, and it was a good thing she did. Okay, maybe it's something she didn't know about. For now, she'd just pretend everything was alright.

"What happened? Where were you?" Leena tried to sound calm and concerned.

"I'm sorry I took so long, m'lady." As though embarrassed by his anger, Arvin's face morphed into wide-eyed innocence. "I left yesterday to get some game so's we could eat. About two miles down that road, I came to a crossroads town. I thought maybe I could buy us some food, but the place was full of them Great Wizard's soldiers. There's a permanent garrison in the town.

"Like a fool, I rode right up to their gate. When a sentry called to me, I turned and ran. I knew they'd chase me, and they had fresh mounts. Ours have been hard-used lately, so I couldn't outrun them. As fortune would have it, the snow was gettin' thick enough they couldn't see me, so I raced into the forest. The falling snow covered my tracks, so I waited till they rode past. It was fair dark by then, and they couldn't see no better than me.

"I left the horse and snuck into the town. The place was full of soldiers, so it took a long time 'cause I had to be careful. The snow was coming so hard I couldn't see nor hear nothing, so I had to be extra sure I didn't accidentally run into anyone. Finally, I found a storehouse and loaded some bags full of food.

"It took longer to get back to the horse. The blizzard was blinding, and, with wandering around town, I wasn't sure the direction was right, so it was near morning when I found my mount. The snow stopped falling by then, but it was so deep I left tracks everywhere I went. What I did was lead the horse under trees where there wasn't no snow, then used a branch to brush out our tracks between trees. It took me a bit to get back to the road far enough from town it was safe.

"I was just about to mount when I heard an awful clatter coming along the road behind me. It spooked a stag not a hundred feet away. So I shot it and waited hidden to see what the noise was. It was them knights you saw, galloping on their huge steeds, making all that noise. That took care of the problem with me leaving tracks on the road. So, after they was far enough away, I gathered my deer and followed along. I hoped you'd be smart enough not to let them see you." His eyes shot the unspoken question of her intelligence at her as though not expecting a sensible response.

"When the snow started, I took shelter under some trees. I was about to leave when the soldiers appeared," Leena said.

Arvin stared at her as though waiting for more. After a long pause, he shrugged, accepting her meager response as all he would get. "Well, maybe luck is with us. Anyway, we can't stay on the road no more. There'll be more soldiers the farther north we get. I've heard there's an east-west road through the next town where this road ends. I think it's called Pineton. It's about twenty miles north of here. If we use that road, we can come into the town from an unexpected direction. That way, no one should suspect we're the ones they're looking for. I figure if we travel through the woods at a northeast angle, we have to find that road eventually."

They reached a small clearing, and Arvin pulled up. They had crossed several hills since leaving the road.

"I'm sorry, m'lady, but I didn't sleep last night, and I've got to rest."

Dark half-moons of fatigue painted shadows beneath his eyes. *How could I not notice how tired the boy was?*

"I'm so sorry, Arvin. You must be exhausted. Do you think it's safe to make a fire here?"

"I think we're far enough from anywhere. No one'll see the firelight or our smoke. You think you could build a fire while I dress out our friend here? We have to cook him soon if we mean to keep him."

Arvin left to find a place far enough away to dress the deer so that scavengers feasting on the refuse would not be attracted to their camp. Feeling his fatigue, Leena watched him walk away, lugging the deer on his shoulders.

Leena used her hedge witch wand to empty the clearing of snow. Gathering several fallen branches from beneath trees surrounding the clearing, she built a stack of firewood large enough to keep them warm through the night. A lively fire danced in the center of their clearing when Arvin returned with the stag ready to roast. The boy selected several sturdy limbs from the firewood pile Leena had gathered. He wasted no time suspending the headless, skinned, and gutted animal on a makeshift spit.

"Keep the fire low and roast it slowly," he said, pulling the blankets from the packhorse. "That way, it'll stay fresh longer."

His low snores echoed through the trees within seconds of him rolling into the blankets. Leena looked at Arvin's sleeping face, at peace in childhood innocence as he slept, and a wave of pity flowed over her. The poor lad had lost his parents and now wandered in unfamiliar woods with a girl lacking survival skills. For a boy, he was doing well, but she knew it must be tough on him.

By midnight, the stag was roasted to perfection. Leena's mouth watered, and her stomach rolled and growled in anticipation from the aroma of smoky venison. She had eaten nothing since yesterday. She sliced a chunk using her sword and juggled it from hand to hand until it cooled enough to hold and eat. Feeling like a barbarian with greasy hands and juice dripping from her chin, she tore into the roasted flesh. Leena could not remember a meal tasting so delicious.

As she sliced a second chunk, the boy awoke.

"Smells wonderful, m'lady."

She held the sword out toward him, a hefty hunk of the stag skewered on its point, the juices glistening in the firelight. He tore into the well-cooked meat while she sliced another for herself. She looked at his face as they squatted beside the fire, feasting on roasted flesh. Grease ran in sparkling rivulets down his chin and between his fingers. Despite herself, Leena laughed.

A dark scowl rose on his face as he glared at her. Then, seeing her face and hands, he realized the reason for her amusement. For a second, the boy fought to withhold his laughter and failed. Soon, they were howling together like this was the funniest thing they had ever seen. Leena suspected their laughter was a much-needed relief from the suspicion-bred tension that had festered in their necks and shoulders since they met. For minutes, both rolled on the ground, holding their stomachs as loud, jovial peals of joy rang through the woods.

Eventually, their laughter subsided. Then, one would look at the other, and both would erupt in hysterics until their cackling tapered to a few random chuckles. Silence descended over the campsite as they finished their meal. For the first time, Leena felt comfortable around Arvin.

Warm, fed, and content, Leena curled beneath her shawl, drifting to sleep. *Arvin has a few hard edges, but deep down, I suspect a kind person might be hidden inside the boy. Be careful there, Leena. You still don't know enough about him to make that judgment.*

Beneath the tree-filtered dawn light, Arvin packed the remains of the deer in peaceful silence. Leena scooped handfuls of smothering snow to extinguish the fire. They mounted and rode northeast alone in the endless winter's white blanket.

CHAPTER

THIRTEEN

Pineton looked cozy and welcoming from their perch atop the hill leading into the settlement. The White Horse Inn stood at the town's center like an enticing beacon under its vast, snow-covered roof. After three days of traveling and three nights of sleeping on the hard ground since fleeing the Great Wizard's soldiers, Leena wanted a hot bath and a warm bed. Plus, although Arvin had gathered enough human food for several days at the garrison, their oat supply for the horses had dwindled at every stop, and the snow was too thick for their animals to forage. They needed to buy provisions.

"As you can see, the road north that we left near the garrison town ends here in Pinetown. I've not been around here before, but I think we should be

183

close to the road to the Great Wizard's castle by now. It's probably somewhere not too far west of here." Arvin's voice seemed loud in the winter silence. "I guess it's time we stopped to get directions." A calculating flicker danced in the boy's eyes as he turned to look at her. "It might be better if you stayed here while I go down to scout around and ensure it's safe."

What? Why?

"'Surely, they wouldn't be looking for us to arrive from the east." Leena fought to keep a panicked squeak from her voice while a small whirlwind of doubt tore through her chest and stomach. An undertone in his words shouted a warning within her she could not understand.

Arvin stared at her for several long seconds with an unreadable expression. She sensed he was considering and discarding options, weighing their chances of acceptance in the town.

He shrugged. "You're right, of course, m'lady. I guess I've gotten in the habit of being overcautious. It's time we had a hot meal and soft beds." Without another word, he spurred his horse forward. Leena followed, leading the packhorse.

Throughout the town, hearth smoke columns stretched toward the darkening sky, the gray streamers reaching peaceful fingers across a pink sunset's fading beauty. A lonely pang stirred within Leena while they walked their horses past the welcoming glow of lights shining through the clear glass windows of several houses lining the silent street. Her heart remembered Quillan looking this cheerful before its destruction. Like fireflies greeting the coming night, more lights winked on as they passed. People were arriving home from whatever jobs they labored at during the day. Her homesickness grew as she fought lonely, building tears. More than anything else, she wanted to be a part of a community. It seemed so long ago that she was among people. Shaking off the feeling, Leena wiped her eyes with the edge of her shawl and followed Arvin through the town.

Relief flowed through Leena's being when they neared the inn and noticed that no hoofprint indentations marred the snow-hidden road south that they had avoided with their cross-country trek. However, many tracks broke the snow covering the east-west route. In both directions, foot, hoof, and wheel depressions marked a path on the white ribbon that disappeared into the growing darkness.

At the stable next to the two-story wooden inn, a groom, with hands rubbing his upper arms for warmth, pushed the large doors open and stepped out to take their mounts. For a silver piece, he promised to give the horses a good rubdown, plenty of oats and fresh hay to eat, and clean straw for their bedding. His cold-reddened hand plucked the coin Leena offered and stuffed it into his trouser pocket. His frigid breaths rose in foggy puffs before him as he grabbed the animals' reins, hurried the three mounts into the barn, and shut the doors behind him. Carrying their backpacks, the two travelers trudged toward the inn.

To Leena's overwhelmed senses, the inn's common room was a kaleidoscope of sights, sounds, and activity. So much was happening that Leena did not know where to look first. Throughout the massive room, everything vied for her attention: the clatter of cutlery against pewter dishes, several dozens of voices raised in conversation, bursts of laughter, the enticing aroma of roasting meat and spices, and most of all, the oppressive heat. Shutting the door to keep the bitter cold outside allowed time for her mind to absorb and accept the confusion of noises, colors, and motion throughout the room.

Their arrival went unnoticed. This community was the confluence of three roads, well accustomed to strangers passing through. She followed Arvin as he weaved a path through the mass of people and secured a table near the rear. They stowed their parcels beneath the table.

"You order some food while I see if they have rooms." Arvin raised his voice to penetrate the noisy chaos. Without waiting for a response, he turned and disappeared into the mob.

Leena had never eaten in an inn and didn't know the proper etiquette for ordering food. Should she force her way to the counter? Would their possessions be safe here, unattended? Should she stop the lady carrying heavy-laden trays and ask her?

Anger at her ignorance welled up as red-cheeked embarrassment threatened to bring frustrated tears. She felt like a small girl wishing her da was here to advise her. He had been accustomed to sharing an ale with people at the tavern in Stocksbury during the harvest festival. He had known how to attract a serving maid's attention.

"Is there a problem, miss? Perhaps I can help."

Her eyes scanned past the military shine of calf-length riding boots and over the man's form-fitting black trousers and gray uniform shirt until they looked up into the bluest eyes she had ever seen, watching her beneath hair as coal-black as her own. Red flickered on his right shoulder. Fighting a sudden dizzy spell, Leena struggled to understand the gray patch sporting a scarlet embroidered version of the Garlan Branch. For a moment, she lost track of where she was. Studying the man's guileless expression, she fought to understand why he stood on the other side of the rough wooden table. Who was he? Why does he wear the Garlan Branch on his patch? Was he sent to finish the job the Great Wizard's troops started?

"Huh?" *Oh great! What a dolt I am. I have to say something. Just because the patch has an emblem resembling the Garlan Branch doesn't mean that's what it's supposed to represent or that this guy knows who I am. But he has kind eyes. Besides, what can he do in this crowded place? If things get rough, I can use an immobilization spell and walk away before anyone notices.* She stopped the thought there.

"I don't mean to be forward, miss, but you looked upset, and I can't resist helping a beautiful young lady in distress." His eyes were laughing but not mocking.

She did not know whether to be thrilled or upset. *Beautiful? He called me beautiful! But young? I'm almost seventeen, and he can't be over twenty himself.*

"I, uh...I've never been in an inn. I don't know... er, that is, I want..." His pleasant smile transitioned to confusion with each word she tried to speak. *What's wrong with me? I'm blabbering like a toddler.*

"How in blazes does one order food around here?" she blurted the question loud enough to silence conversations around them. The heat of several dozen staring eyes radiated across her cheeks and flowed along the back of her neck. She hung her head to hide her blush.

"That can be a problem, miss, especially when it's crowded like this." Calmed by his understanding tone, she dared to look back up. "Allow me."

With guilty expressions, the surrounding heads turned back to their conversations as the man scanned the crowd. "Evelyn!" Though not loud, his masculine voice easily penetrated the returning conversational bedlam.

"Yes, m'lord." A serving girl, wearing a bodice far too revealing for Leena's taste, appeared at his side. "What can I get you?"

"The lady would like to order some food."

He's so confident, so at ease. I could never feel that at home in a place like this.

"We've beef stew and bread tonight, m'lady. Can I get you one?"

"Two, please. I'm traveling with a friend. He should be back in a moment."

"As you wish." Evelyn disappeared into the crowd.

The young man pulled out the chair before him, spun it around, and sat at ease facing her, his arms resting across its back, his eyes staring into hers. She had never seen anyone sit this way. *It looks so...dashing. Yeah, that's the perfect word for it.* The thought froze within her as she tried to keep her eyes from the open neck of his form-fitting gray cotton shirt.

"So where are you heading, miss?"

A sick unease rose within her. *Who is this man? I can't tell him the truth. What if he's one of the Great Wizard's troops? I mean, do they always wear their uniforms? They wouldn't wear them on their own time, right? So why's he in his uniform?*

"North," she said. *Oh, Spirit. There's no road north in this town. I better shut up before I utter more stupidity.*

He said nothing, his expression expectant, waiting for her to continue. "Uh-huh," he said when it was apparent she would say nothing more. "That might be a bit of a problem. Most people head either east or west from Pineton since there's no north-bound road here. Some go south, but that road's rarely used in winter since it's hard traveling when there's snow. I'm coming from the Wizard's Highway that meets the west road into Pineton. That road heads north toward Elderon and the Great Wizard's castle. But I doubt you're going that far?" His curious eyes made the statement a question. She let the unspoken query hang in the air.

"Well, I'll leave you to your meal. Maybe we'll

see each other again someday." He hesitated, his expression encouraging her to say more. Perhaps he wanted her to ask him to stay, but she couldn't. He stood, turned the chair back to the table, and lifted his tankard toward her in a salute.

"I'm glad to have been of service. I hope someday I may serve you again."

The disappointment growing in her chest surprised her as she watched his back fade into the crowd. She wanted to call him back to explain that she did not intend to sound rude, but she dared not.

"I've secured us two rooms, m'lady, and they'll prepare baths for us in the morning." She jerked at the sound of Arvin's voice. Lost in thought, she had not seen him approach. He glanced in the direction she had been looking, then back at her with a curious expression.

"Something the matter, m'lady?"

"No," she said. Then, responded more cheerily, "No, I was just waiting for our food to arrive and daydreaming. Do you think we could have the rooms for two nights? It would be nice to have our clothes washed."

His face scrunched in confusion. Again, he glanced in the direction she had been watching when he arrived. Something disturbed him, but his expression said he saw nothing unusual. She could almost see his mental shrug.

"That's not a bad idea, m'lady. The horses could use the rest."

Neither spoke as they ate. Throughout dinner, Arvin shifted in his seat. Something in the room made him uncomfortable. His eyes never stopped darting around as if he feared someone would confront them. *Or perhaps*—the unwelcome thought jumped into Leena's mind before she could stop it—*he's hoping we won't be recognized.*

She shook her head. No, she was just tired. The encounter with the stranger had unsettled her. Now, she was seeing night frights at every turn. She needed to think of something else.

He's so strong, so handsome and self-assured. Who is he? She had not thought to ask the helpful stranger's name. She dared not look around for him. Arvin was nervous and unpredictable at the best of times. She did not want to see his response if he caught her watching the stranger again.

Finally, they concluded their endless meal. With Arvin leading, both gathered their bundles and headed through a hallway at the rear of the common room and up a dim flight of stairs.

"You take the room on the left, and I'll take the

one on the right, m'lady." He motioned toward doors on either side of the wooden hallway.

Sliding a small iron bar from its slot in the door-jamb, she freed the door. On the other side, she found a peg on a string and a hole drilled halfway through the door. With the peg inserted in the hole, the bar could not slide, and the door would not open. She would be safe here.

A cozy fire danced gaily in the small iron-grated fireplace, warming the room. Outside, a new moon cast a dim light through the diamond-shaped panes of the frosted window. Conversation in the common room resonated below the floorboards, muted and soothing, like the pulse of river waves lapping the shore.

She considered lighting the lamp and unpacking for a moment, but the food had been delicious and filling, and she was now so tired. Her discarded outer garments fell to the floor in a confused disarray around her until only her undergarments remained. She no longer noticed the Garlan Branch, now pressed against her stomach, secured by the drawstring around her underskirt's waist. With a smile, she snuggled into the crisp, chilled comfort of linen sheets beneath a mountainous feather quilt. In seconds, her body warmed the space. Although bone-tired, she listened to the room's silence, wondering whether sleeping was safe. No unusual noise broke the common room's background babble as her mind slipped into a dreamless sleep.

It wasn't until later that evening—so late that all noise had ceased in the common room—when a quiet scratching ripped her from the depths of long-needed, healing sleep. All thoughts of descending back into slumber evaporated. Wide awake, Leena strained to hear whether the noise would repeat.

Like a mouse slinking across the floor, a near-silent scritching rose at the door as the bar moved against its prohibiting peg. Once, twice, a hesitation. With more force, the bar clicked against the restraining peg. Silence descended, as if someone listened beyond the portal to determine whether the noise had awakened her.

It has to be Arvin, doesn't it? He's the only one who knows I'm here, except for several dozen people in the common room. I'll have to ask him in the morning? Because if it's not him, it might be someone after the Garlan Branch.

She wanted to sit up and see if the moonlight streaming in was enough to detect whether the would-be invader was straining the bar against the protective peg, hoping to shatter the small wooden locking pin and permit entry for the thief or assassin. She could not budge. The loud pulse in her ears smothered all external noise. She dared not move. Even shifting the heavy down cover might be enough to alert the intruder that she was awake and aware of their intent to penetrate her room. She could not take the chance that any sound might provoke them into violent action.

Her hedge witch wand, beneath a pile of dirty clothes on the floor, might as well be in another country. She reached toward the Garlan Wand at her waist. What good would that do? She could cast a protection spell, a healing spell, and an immobilization spell. Any of those would call a raven to come crashing through the window. How long would she survive trapped in this small room with it?

What about the sword she retrieved from the bandits who captured Arvin? Why did she leave it on the floor by her pack? What good was a weapon if she couldn't get to it quickly? Even if she could, what use would it be to her? She didn't know how to use it. No, her best option was to lie there silent, hoping they would leave when the door refused to open.

The bolt scratched against the peg one more time.

Near silent squeaks in the hallway diminished as noiseless footsteps slipped away. *Did they leave? It sounded like they left. But why? Maybe they thought the risk of waking others by shattering the pin was too great. Or perhaps they plan to return with some quiet way to slide the bolt open.*

Jaws clenched, jumping at every creak, Leena waited, with her fear fighting the fatigue that threatened to drag her into sleep. Blood rushed from her heart, tingling her extremities every time a log in the fireplace settled. An eternity later, the red sunrise found her tired but still wide awake.

FOURTEEN

A bright morning sun streamed warm rays through ice-enclosed window glass. During the night, the fire had burned out while Leena lay unmoving, staring at the darkening ceiling as the flame's light diminished.

What if the intruder had crept back during the night and now stood on the other side of the door, waiting to confirm that she still occupied the room? Even the sound of her covers moving might be enough to alert them she still hid within.

Besides, nestled under the thick comforter, her body heated the bed to perfection. However, it was time to brave the cold floor with her bare feet and start her day.

What did she need to do today? A pair of

trousers was her first order of business. She just couldn't ride sidesaddle another day. Then, she needed to see a blacksmith to ensure her sword had a keen edge. *If I'm lucky, maybe I'll find someone who knows how far it is to the Great Wizard's castle. If I'm really lucky, I might find someone who knows what happened in my village and can explain why it happened. But I guess that's too much to expect.*

Her body jerked, scattering her thoughts as three sharp raps rattled her door.

"Yes?" She doubted the person outside heard her mild, frightened squeak. *What's wrong with me? Arvin said someone would draw baths for us this morning. I suspect my would-be intruder isn't out there chatting with her while waiting to attack me.*

"Yes?" *There, that's better.*

"Is m'lady ready for her bath?"

"Oh yes. Thank you." Leena opened the door, using it to shield her revealing night clothes, peeking only her head around it. A white-haired, plump-faced woman with a crisp, white apron covering her floor-length, blue linen dress stood on the other side. "Where's the bathroom?"

"At the end of the hall on the right." The woman nodded her pink-cheeked face in that direction. "Here's' a towel, and I'll run and have your bath ready quick as a doe. Leave any clothes that need washing in the basket by the bureau."

Leena watched the woman scurry away, then shut the door and tugged clean clothing from her pack. Removing her hedge witch wand, the purse with her share of the dead bandits' coins, and her scabbard belt from the pile, she tossed her soiled clothing into the basket. Leena padded barefoot to the bathroom with an oversized towel wrapped around her, an armload of clean clothes, and the Garlan Branch snuggled into its familiar place behind her waistband. She would have to part with it while she bathed and hoped the thing would understand. *It's probably best. After last night, I can't trust I won't need its protection in this place.*

Although the bath was less than ten yards from her room door, she constantly scanned the hallway to ensure no one peeked through a cracked door to confirm she still occupied the inn. She saw no one.

Oh, this hot water is glorious! She let herself soak in comfortable warmth until her toes and fingers wrinkled. Clean, dressed, and refreshed, she padded back to her room. Opening the door, she stepped back, let her eyes inspect everything within, and found no sign of an intruder. After shutting and locking the door behind her, she donned her sword, purse, and hedge witch wand. *Now, I'm ready to face the day.*

Several people crowded the common room. Their excitement, activity, and anticipation flowed over her. These people had places to go and were eager to move on.

"Sit where you like, m'lady." A plump man behind the counter motioned with a broad arm sweep. He looked enough like the woman who had drawn her bath that they could be bookends. Leena wondered if they were siblings or if time and familiarity had molded them into twins, as it did for some couples who had shared a life together for many years.

"Want a pot of tea?" The man shuffled around the counter and placed a bowl and mug before her.

"Yes, that would be lovely." She felt odd saying that. But his formal greeting made her want to prove she was a lady.

"There's gruel and a ladle by the fire with honey, milk, nuts, and berries on the sideboard. There's also bread, butter, and wild berry jam if you'd like."

"Thank you, sir. Can you tell me whether the young man from room seven has eaten yet?"

"Oh, he's long since gone, m'lady. He was gone before the sun came up. Woke the groom to get his mounts early, he did. Ate cold meat and left. I have to say I don't approve of guests helping themselves to the larder at all hours, miss." His tone was not hostile. However, much of his warmth and friendliness had disappeared. The man turned to go.

Leena's mind spun. *He must be mistaken, or maybe I'm misremembering Arvin's room number.*

"Did he mention where he was going?"

The man's eyes softened as though suspecting she had nothing to do with the raid on his stores. "I'm sure I don't know, miss. The groom told me only that he left early this morning. You might check with the groom, though. I'm sure he could answer that. Now, you'd best have some breakfast. What's done is done, and the next few minutes won't change things." His face brightened with the smile of a kind uncle giving advice.

He was right, of course. Arvin was unpredictable. Her rushing around now would change nothing.

Leena scooped a heaping bowl of gruel and smothered it with nuts, honey, berries, and milk. A sharp knife carved a warm, fragrant bread slice. Soft butter melted into its crevices, and the wild berry jam was unlike anything she had tasted.

After breakfast, she found the groom, but he could add nothing to what the proprietor told her. Arvin arrived at the stable long before sunrise, had the groom saddle his horse while he loaded the packhorse, and then rode west.

So be it. Although a tenuous friendship had grown with Arvin, Leena still found it difficult to trust him. Something about him bothered her—maybe a look in his eyes, his erratic behavior, or both. Besides, he had a disturbing habit of popping up at unexpected times. She suspected they would meet again.

Oh well, he's gone for now, and I have enough other things to worry about.

This town was much livelier than any place she had known. Pineton was a trade town. All around her, merchants talked and made deals over bowls of gruel. Outside, people gathered in the streets and shops while loaded and unloaded carts rolled back and forth along the main road. Business was being conducted everywhere in this town. Half the buildings on the main street were shops. This town was much livelier than any other place she had known.

Leena tried several dress shops before a clerk suggested she try the general store. With a disdainful expression, the harried-looking clerk peered over his wire-rimmed glasses to inform her that the general store was where *men* bought work clothes.

The general store was more extensive than any

shop Leena had ever seen. Foodstuffs, clothing, farm instruments, and hardware crowded tables and shelves in neat stacks. The sheer number of goods assailed her mind.

In a pile of homespun trousers, she found a boy-sized pair that would fit if she used a belt to cinch the waist. Because Arvin had taken most of their foodstuffs, she restocked with dried meats, fruit, and nuts. She also purchased a large bag of oats and paid for its delivery to the hotel's stable. On a whim, Leena bought a dark blue ribbon that contrasted nicely with her black hair. Now, she could tie it back so it would not blow in her face as she rode.

Leena juggled packages, admiring how sunlight glinted on her new satin ribbon as she hurried toward the armorer's shop. Her smile vanished as a shadow darkened the crushed snow before her. She had no time to stop herself from slamming into the man clad in a black and gray uniform when he stepped out of the men's clothing shop as she passed.

With an ungracious thump, she sprawled on the icy street amid the scattering of her packages tangled in her skirt on the uneven street ice. Her angry glare disappeared, and her heart skipped a beat when she looked up into the deep blue eyes of the man from the inn.

"Forgive me, miss. This is my fault entirely." He extended a hand to help her up. "We seem to run into each other under the most peculiar circumstances. I suppose I should introduce myself. My name is Darius."

Darius. What a perfect name. Her mind filled with the soothing resonance of his deep voice and the comfort of his warm hand holding hers.

"I'm Leena," she said without thinking. *Oh Spirit, what have I done? Arvin heard my name from the Great Wizard's troops. What if this man's one of those troops?* Her cheeks burned at the stupidity of spouting out her name. Relief flooded through her when she saw no hint of recognition in his eyes. The name meant nothing to him.

She held his hand a moment longer. Did she feel a slight pressure from him? Was he holding her hand longer than necessary? Did he not want to let go?

Oh, no. What am I doing? Flustered, she jerked her hand away and looked at the disarray around her. Hot embarrassment flamed her ears as she snatched up the ribbon and started gathering packages. Before she could stop him, Darius bent and picked up the pair of trousers peeking from one of the fallen bags.

"Are these for your traveling companion?" He

held them out to her. Irritated to feel her cheeks reddening again, she snatched them from his hand, bunched them, and stuffed them to bulge from a random bag in her unwieldy armload.

Am I doomed to embarrass myself forever in front of this man?

"No, he's gone, and, well, you see...I'm...that is, I don't like riding sidesaddle, and I thought I'd try these." *Why do I have such a difficult time explaining things to this person? And why did I ever tell him Arvin's gone? Stupid, stupid, stupid.*

"Ah," he said, as though the nonsense she spouted was profound. He helped her re-stack the parcels in her arms. His glance drifted to the sword she wore around her waist. "Did your companion leave without his sword?"

Enough! I'll shrink to nothing if I have to suffer one more embarrassment around this man. Why does he do this to me?

"It's mine," she snapped. "Now, if you'll be so kind as to move, I can get to the armorer to sharpen it." Lowering her head, Leena shouldered past him toward the shop with the image of an anvil above a pair of crossed swords burned into its wooden signboard. Unbidden, a tiny thrill rushed through her as she wondered whether he would follow. *Stop it! You have more important things to take care of at the moment.*

The armorer's store room felt oven-hot after the snow-covered world outside. A large bellows wheezed powerful breaths through an open door from a room behind the counter, sending heat into her face as the doorway flared bright red with each compression. The clang and ping of hammers against metal rang in the small enclosure. An assortment of knives, swords, spears, and weapons Leena did not recognize were displayed on the thick wooden surface separating her from the armorer. The noise, the heat, and the activity reminded her of Thomai. She wondered where he was today.

A tall, burly man sporting biceps larger than her thighs stood waiting patiently behind the counter. A stained and soiled leather apron protected his rough woolen shirt and sturdy woolen trousers. He seemed unmindful of the many dark-rimmed holes burned into the unprotected areas of his clothing. Unease rose within her as the man's eyes narrowed into a glare as hard as the steel displayed before her. "Can I help you, miss?" His rough voice and curt words did little to dispel her rising alarm.

"Could you check my blade and see if it needs sharpening?" She placed her parcels on an empty counter section, unbuckled her belt, removed the sheathed sword, and held it out to him. The man's eyes widened for a split second, then constricted again as he drew the short sword and examined its blade.

"It's been years since I've seen an Elven blade and never one so fine." His voice was hushed, reverent. "Would you consider selling it, miss? I'd offer a tidy sum for this."

Whoa, Old Hotchkiss said Elven blades have magic properties and only come to those who deserve one. But I got this one by accident. I don't even know how to use a sword. However, this man's greed tells me that this sword is something special. She looked into the armorer's eyes and saw his impatience growing as she failed to respond. *I have to get out of here now.*

"No, just sharpen it, please. How much will it cost?"

"Well now, I got to say to myself, how would such a pretty and proper lass such as yourself come to possess so fine a blade? Maybe your father or uncle gave it to you. But then, they would have told you this is not a blade you flash around. So maybe you stole it. And if you did, it'd be my duty to take it back and hold it until the proper owner comes looking for it."

The unease within her rose to alarm as she looked into eyes that held no trace of mercy.

"Sir, I've changed my mind. Please return my sword, and I'll be on my way." Her hands rushed around the counter as she talked, filling her arms with reclaimed packages.

"Look, miss, I'm not an unfair man," the armorer continued as though she had not spoken. "Tell you what I'll do. You can pick any short sword from the table here. Made them myself, and they've all got keen blades." He swept his arm over the display. "I'll even throw in a scabbard," he said as he inspected the blade's runes, his eyes shining with greed.

"No, thank you." Leena tried to sound polite. "If you'll return my blade, I must leave now."

Irritation, then anger, flared in the man's eyes as he pointed the sword's tip at her. *What the...Does he intend to run me through and claim I'm a thief?*

If only she could invoke a protection spell now. Her gut clenched as she hesitated. Even if she dropped her armload of packages, she could not reach her hedge witch wand in time. *Oh, Spirit, help me!* She was a stranger in this town, and this man's man was a respected community member. Nobody would believe her word over his. *If I'm dead, everyone will believe whatever tale he tells. What can I do?*

She forced a smile. The entrance door was so far away. *Maybe if I turn and walk out, he'll let me go. What if I agree to his deal?* She knew nothing about

Elven swords. One sword was just as good as another to her. She wasn't even sure she needed one. But she knew enough to know that an ancient Elven sword was something special.

The look in his eyes told her she would not leave here alive. Trying to calm her breathing, she fought her rising panic. *Think, Leena.*

With the fascination of a mouse mesmerized by a snake, Leena's eyes locked on the sword's tip as it inched toward her. The unwavering point crept closer, now less than six inches from her neck's rapid, pulsing vein. He would strike before she could move out of range, and she could do nothing to stop him.

Leena dared not move. The armorer's pitiless eyes told her he waited only for the slightest excuse. Maybe if she screamed or fell over backward. She could not. The Garlan Branch at her waist was calling on her to react, but every muscle was frozen with fear as the blade edged closer.

So this is it. I'm going to die and can do nothing to avoid it. Tears threatened to spill from her eyes. She saw her father's smile, the dimple in his cheeks. She thought of her mother's face turning apple red when she or Riana teased her until she snorted like a pig with laughter.

I'm sorry. Leena's mind sent a silent apology to

her sister—wherever she might be. Waves of guilt and sadness washed over her. On Midwinter night, for the first time, Leena had not told her sister where she was going when she left the house on her lone adventure. That night, she was sure they would share a lifetime together. She had relished thoughts of the thrill Riana would enjoy when she told her of receiving the Garlan Branch. Now, her life would end here. Only two inches now separated the blade and her neck. She would never see her sister again...

The light behind Leena dimmed as a figure filled the doorway. Her heart sped up. *Maybe I can use this distraction to reach my wand.*

"Have you gotten my blade sharpened yet, sis? We have too much to do today for you to be dawdling." The voice was sharp, but she breathed an inner sigh of relief. It was Darius!

Uncertainty grew in the armorer's eyes, and the sword tip wavered. Leena took a step back. The armorer would have to come around the counter to strike her now.

Through the door behind the large man, apprentices hurried about their work. Leena had no doubt that if the blacksmith raised the alarm, they would swarm into the shop like an insect army, each wielding a deadly weapon.

Clutching her packages, she turned to Darius.

"I'm sorry, Dar, but my hands are full. If you want the thing sharpened, why don't you take care of it yourself?"

While she talked, Darius sidled up and rested his hands on the counter in apparent frustration with her. She noticed his right hand sat next to the hilt of a shiny, steel broadsword with a leather-wrapped handle.

"Look, sis, I told you we have too much to do today to lollygag around. Let's get out of here, and I'll sharpen it myself when I can find some spare time." Darius turned to the armorer. "I'm sorry she troubled you, sir. Please return my sword, and we'll be out of your hair." He extended his left hand.

The armorer glanced at Darius's right hand resting near the hilt of the sword lying on the counter, then at his uniform, and up into his hardened stare. Slowly, he sheathed the Elven sword and handed it to Darius.

"Thank you, sir," Darius said. He turned to Leena. "Come on, runt, let's get back to the inn."

Leena followed Daruis's broad back into the street. He set a fast pace while she juggled packages, struggling to keep up. When Darius held the door to the common room open for her, she noticed his casual glance back toward the armorer's shop. With a wave of his arm toward an empty table, he closed the winter's chill outside.

The common room had few customers at this time of day. Travelers and businesspeople had gone their ways, and the midday meal crowd had not yet gathered. Leena stowed her parcels under the table as Darius ordered a pot of tea. They sat silent, each lost in private thoughts, until the waitress deposited their drinks and moved away.

Studying the hot liquid in her cup, Leena tried to dispel thoughts of how this day might have ended if Darius had not arrived when he did. She struggled to ignore the mental vision of her dead body bleeding out on the armorer's dirty wooden floor. *What must this man think of me? My ignorance put our lives in danger.* Her heart thundered as her stomach performed gymnastics. She looked up at him, praying to the Spirit that she would not find hate and anger.

The restful depths of his calm, thought-filled eyes studied her for several moments as though considering what he should say. Like a bright summer sun creeping from behind a thunderous cloud bank, his serious expression melted as a smile twitched at the corners of his lips.

"Dar?" His eyes sparkled with humor.

"Sis?" Leena chuckled as relief flowed through

her despite an internal vow to remain serious. "Runt?" she said in mock dismay. Before they knew it, both were smothering laughter, trying not to disturb the few others in the room. Using the distraction of the serving girl pouring more tea, they struggled to pull themselves together.

"I have to ask," Darius said once they were alone again, "why you were trying to have an armorer sharpen an Elven blade? Humans have neither the tools nor the magic."

"I know very little about weapons," she admitted quietly. "I, uh, found it and figured I should have an armorer sharpen it."

His gaze bored into her as though looking for any sign of deceit in her statement. Finally, he sat back and shook his head in wonderment. "You really don't know what you have here, do you?" He lifted the sheathed sword, drew it partway from its sheath, and studied the carvings on its blade. "I don't read Elven runes, but there's no doubt this is an Elven king's blade. When used correctly, this blade could shatter armies. I've never known a human to possess one of these. Are you sure you want to keep it?"

He held it out to her.

Leena could not help wondering whether the blade had come to her by more than random chance.

She thought nothing of it when she picked it out from the pile on the bandits' wagon. Something about it had felt right in her grip—light and swift. Once again, she felt the hand of someone or something guiding her destiny. She reached to accept it.

"I think I must."

Darius's gaze lingered on her face, searching it. His eyes told her he wondered whether he wanted to assume responsibility for helping her. With a shrug and a nod, he stared into her eyes. "I think there is much we need to talk about, but first, we must get you safely out of town with your blade."

For a moment, she considered telling him she didn't need his help. That she was a hedge witch, and a simple calming spell would prevent anyone from harming her. Her enhanced protection spell would allow her to leave town unseen if the calming spell was not enough. She wanted so much to trust him. He had an air of integrity about him and he had saved her life.

Still, he was a stranger. And a stranger coming from the Great Wizard's castle. The Great Wizard who destroyed her village and took her family hostage. *Could his Mister Nice Guy be an act? Was he sent here to gain my trust and then deliver me and the Garlan Branch to the Great Wizard?*

She dared not trust him until she knew more

about him. "I'm leaving in the morning," she said. "Surely, the armorer would not be brash enough to try something in full daylight."

"It's easy to see you're not used to traveling. Most armorers work for whoever pays them. They do not concern themselves with the good or bad their weapons might do. Undoubtedly, that armorer knows men who would slit your throat for a silver piece. Now that he knows you have the blade, I've no doubt he'll contact those who can retrieve it for him."

Leena paled. "How can you be so certain? I saw how he looked when he saw your hand resting near the sword on his counter."

"Because when we entered the inn, I saw an apprentice hurrying up the road just before I shut the door. By tonight, the armorer will know when you're leaving. It's a fair bet someone will wait for us somewhere along the road when we leave," Darius said.

"Us?"

"I'd never forgive myself if I found out something happened to you because I wasn't there to help. You said your traveling companion is gone. Who else is going to protect you?"

What? Who does he think he is? I may have been a bit clumsy and naïve, but that doesn't give him the right to assume I can't protect myself. And why would I trust him not to hand me over to the Great Wizard when we get to Elderon?

"I'll have you know I'm not without defenses."

"I'm not saying you don't have skills. But, are they enough to defend yourself against a band of bloodthirsty rogues?"

Okay, so maybe he had a point. But she'd just met him last night. How did she know he wasn't here because the Great Wizard sent him to bring her in? Maybe capturing her meant a reward or a promotion for him. She was sure he would find it much easier to have her walk into a trap unsuspecting. No, it would be far better to get away from him now.

"It just so happens that I'm a hedge witch in training," she blurted. Even before she finished the sentence, she wished she could take the words back. Cheeks red with shame, Leena looked down, no longer noticing her teacup. For just a few moments, she wanted to avoid Darius's eyes.

There's no shame in being a hedge witch. In fact, every town and village respects and appreciates their hedge witch's skills because they heal sick and injured people and animals. But now I have one of the most powerful wands in this world.

Everyone knew the legend of how Robart almost

doomed all humans until he discovered how to use the Garlan Branch. They followed him because he was a lord's son. He had the combat skills of a knight. Would anyone follow a half-trained sixteen-year-old girl with no fighting skills into battle? Not a chance. Perhaps the Great Wizard only wanted to prevent her from destroying the entire human race. No, there had to be more to it than that. Wouldn't the Great Wizard summon her to his castle for a chat or go to Quillan to reason with her? He didn't need to slaughter whole towns and villages.

Darius sat silent, thinking over her words, waiting for her to continue. *Okay, I have to face the music sometime.* She looked up into his eyes.

"Alright, granted, that could be helpful." His voice lowered so no one else in the room could hear. "If you can cast a protection spell, it could save you for a while. However, from what I've seen, the drain on a witch is tremendous in battle, and few can maintain the spell for long. Can you cast a protection spell?"

It'd be no problem with the enhanced hedge witch wand protection spell. But I can't tell him that. She watched him as he gauged the play of emotions across her face. *He seems kind and honest, but I dare not trust him.*

"Okay," he said, breaking his silence. "However, I

think it might be a good idea if I help you learn to use that sword. How far are you going?"

The question caught her off guard.

"To the Great Wizard's castle."

"Hmmm," Darius withdrew in silent thought. "I'm headed east. However, I still have two weeks before I'm expected at the coast, and it's only three days back to the Wizard's Highway. If you permit, I can accompany you as far as that. It'll take you north to Elderon. Anyone there can show you how to find the Great Wizard's Castle. It might add a day to your trip if we stop early each evening, and I try to teach you the proper use of a blade."

Try? Does he think I'm too stupid to learn?

With angry speed, she bent and gathered her packages. "Fine, I'll accompany you," she huffed, "because I believe there is danger, and I'll *try* to learn to use the sword. Thank you, sir!"

The confused look on his face only added to her frustration as she stormed to her room to find her clothes clean and folded on the dresser. Still smarting from Darius's implication, she mumbled to herself as she jammed clothes and provisions into her pack. Afterward, she threw herself onto the bed and glared at the open-beam ceiling.

Without warning, as though possessing a life of their own, her hands grabbed the pillow and shoved it against her mouth to muffle the heart-wrenching sobs that followed. Her village was gone, her family had been taken as hostages, and she was alone, not knowing whom she could trust. She cried for the Woodsman couple and all the others she had to send to the fields beyond. She cried for all the towns and villages that were now empty.

But most of all, she cried for her vanished childhood.

FIFTEEN

The common room was crowded with travelers and townspeople gathered for a pint. After her tear-induced nap, the sadness burdening her heart and mind since returning to Quillan from the Garlan Tree was less intense but not lost. She found an empty table near the fire, caught Evelyn's attention, and mimed eating with a spoon. The serving maid nodded and pushed through the crowd toward the counter.

Scanning the horde, Leena found little difference between the well-dressed people packing the room this evening and the scores of strangers, mostly men, at last night's gathering. She froze when she saw the armorer sitting with a thin man whose long, black beard matched his floor-length dark traveling coat. The two men hunched close together over their table in quiet conversation. The bearded man glanced at her, then snapped his eyes back to the armorer. Leena averted her eyes, hoping the bearded man would not warn the armorer of her arrival.

A clay bowl filled with stew, a small loaf of bread sitting on a cutting board, a knife, and a carved wooden spoon clattered to the table before her. Leena turned to thank Evelyn but saw only the departing serving maid's back weaving between well-dressed business people. Leena's stomach growled a greeting to the stew's savory perfume, and she devoured it with gusto.

"I apologize for this morning, miss. I didn't know you were related to a knight of the Academy."

Leena looked up. Uninvited, the armorer pulled out a chair and seated himself across the table from her. Though his words were conciliatory, his angry expression showed no pity.

"Your apology is accepted, sir. Now, if you'll excuse me, I'd like to finish my supper in peace." Her head ducked down to her meal as her mind screamed for this man to leave. She doubted he would try to strong-arm her in the crowded inn. Still, an overwhelming aura of violence surrounded him like a threatening storm cloud.

"My offer still stands. Feel free to name any sum you want for the Elven blade."

"I'm sorry, but it's not for sale."

Before she could jerk her arm back, his hand flashed across the table and grabbed her wrist.

"Listen, miss, that sword's no good to you. I doubt you even know how to use a regular sword, much less an Elven blade." Pain radiated up her arm as his fist clenched and twisted the wrist bones until they threatened to break. "With that blade, no one could stand against me. I advise you to accept my offer now. I'll not offer to pay again, but I will have that sword."

"Hey, sis, it seems you and the armorer are becoming close friends." Darius pulled out a chair and sat down. His right hand lay across his lap, fingers touching his sword's hilt.

The pressure on her wrist eased as the armorer broke his angry stare, withdrew his hand, and turned his attention to Darius. Although Darius's words had been friendly, his eyes were as hard as steel.

The armorer's sleeves bulged with the muscular arms of a man used to hard labor, but he wore no sword. Shrugging acceptance of his weaker position, he stood and looked at Leena. "Remember what I said, miss. The offer stands until tomorrow morning." Without a glance at Darius, the armorer turned and left.

"Where were you?" She did not mean to sound abrasive, but the armorer scared her.

"I was over there,"—he nodded toward the counter—"talking to some travelers when you came in. After we parted, I thought it best to leave you alone for a while. But I knew there'd be trouble when that brute sat at your table. I assume he was after your sword again."

"He didn't come right out and threaten me, but he let me know he intends to get the sword no matter what it takes. He was sitting with another man earlier, and I'm certain they were talking about me."

"Can you describe the other man?" Darius asked.

"He was thin with a black, scraggly beard and wore a black traveling cloak. That's all I noticed."

"I'll wager he's one of a gang of highwaymen plaguing the road west of here. We might consider changing our plans and leaving tonight rather than tomorrow morning. With luck, we'll be past them before they know we're gone."

"Don't you have something to pick up in the morning?"

"The armorer is putting a new point on a dagger of mine with a broken tip," Darius said. "It's been an heirloom in my family for a few hundred years. I'll regret letting it go, but it's not worth our lives." He looked around the room. "Too many people would see us leave now. I suggest we have the stable boy saddle our mounts and load the provisions you bought today after the common room closes. Then we can meet back here and be on our way before anyone notices."

He seemed so calm and self-assured, as if he knew she would accompany him, but doubt crept into her heart. *Could he be plotting with the armorer to get me off by myself so they can steal the sword and maybe the Garlan Branch?* Her body tingled with fear. But what choice did she have? She had to trust him for now...but only up to a point. Until she knew more about him, she'd keep the hedge witch wand protection spell active whenever he was nearby. It wouldn't make her invisible like the Branch-enhanced spell, but it might protect her from a surprise attack long enough to escape.

"Okay, I'll meet you here," she replied.

"There are some people I must talk to before I leave, so I'll see you later." He stood.

"One thing," she said, looking up at him, "why did the armorer call you a knight of the Academy?"

"Because I am. Captain Darius Thornhill at your service." A smile played at the edges of his lips as his fingers tapped the emblem on his right shoulder. "That's the official emblem of the Great Wizard's knights. It's supposed to look like a Garlan Branch. I graduated two years ago as a lieutenant and have finally been promoted to captain and assigned a duty station."

He swept his arm up as though removing an imaginary cap and bowed with a self-deprecating grin. Still smiling, he straightened, winked at her, and turned back into the crowd.

Leena's hunger had vanished. She pushed her bowl aside. *Uh-oh. Knights of the Academy are the Great Wizard's elite troops. They are sworn to protect and defend the realm and to obey the Great Wizard in all things. I'm in trouble if the Great Wizard knows I'm here.*

Darius stopped to chat with several well-dressed business people. With his attention diverted, she slipped away and hurried to her room.

SIXTEEN

Firelight danced across the wall in Leena's room when she entered. She sat on the bed, chin cupped in her palm to think, then rose to pace the confined space.

Everyone knew a Great Wizard's knight must report anything that might threaten the realm. Was all of this—the conflict with the armorer, Arvin's disappearance, and even meeting Darius—part of an elaborate plot to draw her into the Great Wizard's trap, unaware of the danger?

No one knew about the Elven blade when she arrived in Pineton. Even Arvin dismissed it as a toy. Yet, the armorer found it important enough to threaten her twice.

And where did Arvin go? At least he was leading her to the Great Wizard. She suspected he'd betray her when they arrived, but she felt sure she could use the Garlan Branch to escape. Meeting the Great Wizard was the only way she could determine whether he'd sent an army to destroy Quillan and capture her family.

On the other hand, she questioned Darius's motives. After all, he was a Great Wizard's knight. Was he sent to escort her to the Great Wizard's castle? After the armorer's little chat at supper, she suspected Darius was spot on when he said she needed protection from rogues. Was he the rogue she needed protection from? Once again, she felt trapped.

Leena paced and thought, thought and paced, so absorbed that she did not notice the noise downstairs diminishing. A quiet knock on the door sent blood rushing through her veins as she jumped and spun to see the bar sliding open on the door. The locking peg dangled on its string a foot below the latch bar. *How could I get so distracted that I forgot to lock the door? I have to be more careful.* Reaching beneath her tunic, she touched her hedge witch wand just as Darius peered around the door.

"When you didn't show up downstairs, I came to find you," he whispered. "It's time we leave. Are you ready?"

She would have to face the armorer and his

thugs without support if he left without her. Besides, despite his employer, Leena wanted to trust him. She shouldered her pack, dug into her coin sack, and tossed more than enough silver on the bed to cover her and the boy's expenses.

"How did you know which room I'm in?" Her whisper matched his.

"I told the innkeeper you left a package down-stairs, and I wanted to return it. Now I think it best that we hurry. Minutes could be precious."

Every floorboard creak echoed through the hallway like a boom of thunder as they tiptoed through the silent inn and headed outside. A nearby owl called to the moon, a dog barked in the distance, and the cold, crisp snow crunched beneath their feet. Through the stable's open door, pale moonlight cut a thin wedge into the black silence. The lingering odors of past and present horses, fresh hay, and manure surrounded them as they entered the dark interior.

"Can you make a light?" Darius said.

Leena cast an illumination spell with her hedge witch wand. Its dim light provided a misty glow. Something was not right. Her stomach muscles tightened into hard knots. Shivering from more than the cold, she noticed no horses waiting in the stalls. A shadow trailed beyond a lump, its silhouette breaking the hay carpet covering the center aisle floor. Jumping at the sight, she clamped a hand over her mouth, stifling a scream. The stable boy lay face down. An ornate dagger protruded from his back. Dark blood stained his vest in an expanding lake around the wound.

They crouched next to the body.

"It's the dagger I left with the armorer. That's my family crest on the hilt. I guess he's put a new tip on it." Darius touched the stable boy's neck, holding it there for several seconds. "He's alive. There's a pulse, but it's faint. Can you heal him?"

"Remove the dagger," she said. Darius did as he was told.

Leena placed a hand on the wound, touched the hedge witch wand at her waist, and cast a healing spell to stop the red flow and begin healing the lad. Everything in her wished she felt more confident executing a task her mother had just started teaching her. Fighting to blot out memories of earlier failures on pigs destined for slaughter, Leena willed her hedge witch wand to restore the boy's health. She thanked the Spirit when his chest rose with a silent breath, and his heartbeat strengthened. The boy stirred. Darius rolled him over and cradled his head.

"Who did this to you?"

"Bearded man, black cloak," the stable boy's eyes never opened as he croaked the quiet words, then faded into a deep, wand-induced sleep. Leena found a horse blanket and covered the wounded lad. "He must sleep until morning to heal completely. We need to take him inside where it's warm." She looked at Darius.

He did not answer, but stood thinking as he cleaned the blade by stabbing it deep into a firm hay bale several times. Then he slid the dagger into its empty sheath on the right side of his sword belt.

"I think he was supposed to be found with my dagger in him. Then you and I would be arrested."

Leena raised an eyebrow. "Why me?"

"Because you're my sister, remember," Darius said."We'd never have the chance to tell our side of the story. This boy's from the village. Everyone here knows him, but we're a couple of strangers. I'm sure you noticed the empty stalls. With very little urging from the armorer, the townsfolk would see us as horse thieves forced to commit murder when the boy discovered us."

Darius's blue eyes darkened. "I wondered all evening why the armorer risked being seen with the bearded man. It made no sense. They could have met in his shop, and we'd never know. He wanted us to see them together and be panicked into leaving before daybreak. I'll wager the armorer or one of his cutthroats will be along soon to find the body and raise the alarm. If they find the boy here alive, they'll make certain he's dead this time. We have to get him to a place of safety. He's the only one who can identify his attacker. Without him, even if we somehow escape, we'll be branded murderers." Darius lifted the boy into his arms. "Check to make sure no one's about."

After inspecting the straw on the stable floor to ensure it held no blood spots, Leena extinguished her illumination spell. She peered around the open door at the night-hushed street. "You go ahead. I'll use my hedge witch wand to cover our footprints through the snow so they won't know which way we've gone." As they hurried toward the inn's front door, Leena walked in Darius's footprints.

"Now what?" she asked, shutting the entry door behind them. "Do we just leave the poor lad by the hearth and run?"

"No, I've no doubt we're minutes away from an alarm, and you said the stable boy has to sleep until morning. Whoever finds him will try to wake him. We need to put him somewhere he'll not be disturbed. Check outside while I find a safe place."

Carrying the boy like an oversized sleeping baby, Darius mounted the stairs as Leena cracked the door and peeked outside. Quiet footsteps crunched on the icy road. Someone was heading toward the stable.

Oh no. I forgot to hide our prints. Leena touched her hedge witch wand, casting a slight wind over their tracks. *Please settle quickly.* She willed the wind to cease the second the footprints were buried.

Hurry, please hurry. Leena's mind begged Darius to return.

Motion caught her eye. A figure appeared walking west on the road. His man-shaped moon shadow dipped and glided across the uneven ice before him. Leena recognized the armorer's bold strut as he approached the stable.

Her heart jumped as the floorboards creaked behind her. Easing the door shut, she spun to see Darius descending the stairs.

"He's safely snuggled in your bed. I doubt anyone will check there before morning. Have you seen anything?" he whispered.

"The armorer, he's headed to the stable."

"The innkeeper's rooms are in the back. We'd have to go past them to get out the rear door. This place has creaky floors, so it's safer to risk leaving through the front." He opened the door just enough to see the man disappear between the stable's large, open wooden doors. "He's inside. Let's go."

Taking her hand, Darius drew her outside.

Easing the portal shut, he closed it without noise. Staying within the porch shadows, he pulled her along the front wall of the inn. Unmarked snow lay beyond the east porch rail.

"You'll need to hide our tracks on the porch and across this snow as we run?" Trying to ignore his warm breath fanning her cheek, Leena strained to hear Darius's words. Leaning over the rail, she searched the barren snow beyond.

"I think we should stay close to the side of the inn." Leena pointed along the wall. "No one can see our tracks beneath the eaves in this darkness. Then, we can use the merchant's lane back to the main road west. I'll redistribute the snow to hide our tracks as we run. That way, no one should see us or know which way we've gone."

Darius smiled and nodded as he climbed over the rail and jumped to the shadow-hidden snow beyond. Leena followed, dropping beside him.

"Help! Thieves! Murderers!" The armorer's yell shattered the winter night's silence. A clamoring fire bell by the trough in front of the stable accompanied his frantic shouts. The windows in town flared to light like ripples from a pebble thrown into still water as the clanging bell jerked sleeping residents awake. Leena considered immobilizing the armorer to stop the incessant racket from the stable yard. But it would do no good. Doors were opening all along the street.

Staying in the shadows, Leena and Darius ran. In less than five minutes, the merchants' lane brought them to the east-west road several hundred yards west of the hotel. Leena glanced back at the gathering crowd near the stable and increased her pace. Like ethereal specters, men and women dressed in long white nightshirts struggled into jackets, capes, or shawls, grabbed in haste as they stumbled from their homes.

Running away from the gathering crowd, Leena and Darius found the houses were more scattered, with fewer concealing shadows at the edge of the village."It's more open here, but we're far enough away that no one will spot us. However, some people have stables in their backyards. We'll have to run into the woods if they chase us on horseback. We must put as much distance between us and the town as possible."

Soon, they were in the countryside. On either side of the road, snow-capped log fences bordered the broad, white fields beyond. Although their footsteps were undetectable on the well-trampled thoroughfare, Leena felt exposed beneath the bright light of a shining full moon. Far ahead, a thick forest bordered the well-trodden, ice-covered hardness of the lane. They might find a place to hide if they could make it there without being seen.

Racing, now that sneaking would be useless, Leena's breath came in painful heaves, and her legs ached as a stitch grew in her side. She had to rest, but the trees were so far away. She stumbled. Tugging her hand to keep her upright, Darius urged her to run faster until black spots danced in her vision. She could not go on. Her burning lungs and tired legs demanded rest. Pulling her hand free of Darius's grasp, she bent, hands on knees, drawing deep, fiery, gasping breaths.

"As a hedge witch, can't you cast a rejuvenation spell on yourself?" he asked.

She ignored the deep concern radiating from his blue eyes. *How dare he? Who does he think he is? I may have only started training four years ago, but I know more about hedge witch magic than he'll ever know. Of course, I know how to cast a rejuvenation spell. I have half a mind to...*As her hand reached her waist, a flash of clarity drove through her brain. *Of course, a rejuvenation spell. Why didn't I think of that?*

Her mind cast the spell as her hand touched the hedge witch wand. Her panting disappeared as the whirling black spots before her faded. Standing, she glanced back to see faint town lights glowing far in the distance and an empty road behind them.

"I'm sorry. I guess in all the confusion, my brain forgot my training. Thank you." Leena looked toward the sheltering trees, now less than five hundred yards ahead. She lifted her fists, prepared to continue running.

"Let's walk for a while." Darius's fingers squeezed her shoulder. "I think we're safe enough for now. Soon, it'll be light. I'd rather not reach those trees until we can see better."

"Why aren't they chasing us?" Leena huffed between breaths.

"I've been thinking about that. Did you notice the armorer didn't light a lamp when he entered the stable?"

"Yes," Leena said.

"I'm guessing he hid behind the door, watching to ensure no one noticed him walking into the stable. Then, when he was certain it was safe, he ran to the bell in the stable yard and sounded the alarm." Darius laughed. "Can you imagine the look on his face when they find there's no corpse?"

Both chuckled at the image.

"So, for the moment, they have a mystery, no horses, and no stable boy. They'll probably stand around talking for a while, trying to figure out what happened, and eventually decide it's the magistrate's problem. No one in town will get too upset about a bunch of travelers' horses gone missing. They may worry that we kidnapped the boy. However, the armorer might direct them to our rooms to prove we're also missing and probably the culprits."

"And there they'll find the boy who'll tell them about the bearded man," she finished for him.

"So, returning to town in the morning might be safe. However, with our all-night run, we're nearly a third of the way to the Wizard's Highway. I can leave you there and return to Pinetown in plenty of time to get to my ship. The Wizard's Highway will take you to Elderon, and anyone there can direct you to the Great Wizard's castle."

A horse chuffed a sneeze in the distance ahead.

SEVENTEEN

Staying in the shadows, Leean and Darius edged forward through the trees. Yellow campfire light flicked from a grove ahead.

"That could be merchants camped for the night before traveling to Pineton in the morning." Darius lowered his voice to a whisper. "Or, it could be the bandits that stole the horses. Let's find a safe place in the woods, and I'll scout ahead to see who they are."

Darius tugged her hand, and together they ran, crouching under the drooping, snow-laden pine branches. A thick carpet of needles beneath the tree limbs deadened their footsteps as they entered the refuge. Although the hint of a coming dawn peeked over the horizon, little light penetrated to the forest floor.

"Wait here, and I'll see what we're dealing with," Darius instructed over his shoulder, exiting their temporary shelter. Almost silent, the branches swished shut behind him. Within ten feet of the exit, he had blended into his surroundings until only his footprints revealed where he went. Leena settled onto the pine needles beneath the forest-scented branches of her shelter. They couldn't afford to be delayed here. What if the townspeople had formed a posse and were close behind them? *Whatever you're doing, Darius, make it quick.*

How many people could there be in this group? A few? Maybe half a dozen? After confronting the rogues who'd captured Arvin, she knew she'd have no trouble subduing this gang using the Garlan Branch. But a killer raven appeared whenever she activated a spell with the Branch. And this would be a horrible time for one of those to show up. Besides, she couldn't risk alerting Darius that she had the Branch. He seemed wise in the ways of magic and would know that immobilizing a group was well beyond the skills of even a fully trained hedge witch.

Minutes passed as her wait grew to an eternity. Her heart leaped as the branches beside her rustled with more than the wind. Releasing a breath she was unaware of holding, Leena smiled when

Darius's hands parted the thick foliage, and his dawn-misted figure entered through the opening.

"It's the bandits who stole the horses. There are ten of them, counting the bearded man in the black traveling coat, and they're all asleep. From the jugs scattered around them, I think they spent the night celebrating their successful raid on the hotel stable. I didn't even see one of their group awake as a guard.

"So, we can wait here and hope they'll leave when it's light," Darius whispered, "or we can find a way around them in the woods before the sun's fully up. The only other alternative is to try capturing them, and I'd rather not do that. What would we do with them if we're successful?"

"Well, for one thing," Leena cupped her chin on her fist, thinking out loud, "we could return them to town with the stolen horses and clear our names of the horse thief charges. Also, they'll have found the stable boy alive and well by the time we arrive. He can confirm that the bandits had taken the horses and identify the person who attacked him."

"Yeah. That wasn't the part I was worried about." Leena barely saw his slowly nodding head in the dim light. "First, there's the problem of capturing them. In their firelight, I saw that every one of them was armed with a sword and a dagger.

Also, each has a bow and a full quiver of arrows. Even if we somehow overcame them, how do we get ten men and ten horses to town? We don't have any rope to bind them. What stops them from scattering into the woods when they see us? If they did, how safe would we be trying to guard the ones we captured while protecting ourselves from the others? And the stable boy was stabbed in the back. How likely is it he saw his attacker? It's also unlikely the horse thieves had entered the stable until after he was stabbed. It's likely they waited outside until the assassin signaled it was okay to enter without being seen."

"Okay, so what's your recommendation?"

"The horses are tied to trees on the other side of their camp. Fortunately, it seems they were so eager to get to their celebrating they left them saddled. I suggest we recover our horses and lead them away from their camp while everyone's asleep. Then, we mount up and I take you to the Wizard's Highway. With your skills, you should be able to make it to the Great Wizard's castle safely from there. I'm sure the Great Wizard can get the charges against you dropped. Once you're on your way, I'll find a way around Pineton and continue to the coast with plenty of time to spare before my ship sails."

MAKING NO SOUND, Leena and Darius slipped through the woods around the campsite and made their way to the horses. Crouching low and using the animals to hide their actions, they located Leena's packhorse and their mounts. Leena did a quick count of the animals. Something was wrong. There were too many of them.

"Hey. There are eleven saddled horses here." Leena whispered in the direction she had last seen Darius.

"Why, that's right smart of you to notice, little lady." Leena jumped when the rough voice came from so close behind her that she felt the warm breath of his words on the back of her neck. With the first sound, she saw Darius duck out of sight behind the horse next to him.

I swore I'd keep my hedge witch wand protection spell active so Darius couldn't sneak up on me. Why did I let it lapse? Maybe I'm trusting him too much, that's why.

The man grabbed her arms as he turned to call to his companions. "Wake up, fellas," the voice behind her called. "Seems we got us a pretty little intruder."

His grip's too tight. I can't get to my wand.

Her captor marched her into the camp. The morning sun peaked above the hills ahead of her. Its growing light revealed the mess the bandits' drunken revelry had left.

"Why lookee here." Leena almost smiled hearing the black-haired man she'd seen with the armorer. His voice sounded like it came from a ten-year-old girl. *I think I know why he became an outlaw. I wonder how many people he's killed because they laughed at his voice.*

The man's intense black eyes bore into her as he approached. "And she's wearing the very trinket the armorer's been whining about the last coupla days." Reaching to her waist, he withdrew the Elven blade from its sheath.

"Brash," the man said, staring at the runes etched into the sword's blade, "why don't you tie that young filly to a tree while I study on what makes this overgrown pocket knife so valuable?"

"Here ya go, Brash." Another bandit handed her captor a length of rope. "Use this."

Holding her wrists behind her back, Brash took several turns of the rope around them and tied a knot tight enough to prevent blood flow to her hands. Smiling as though he enjoyed her growing fear, he tossed the rope's loose end over a branch three feet above Leena's head. He pulled the line tight with slow patience, forcing her to bend forward at the waist until her feet lifted onto her tiptoes. Tying the loose end around the tree's trunk, Brash dusted his hands together as if completing a well-done job.

Leena's shoulder sockets screamed with pain, and she struggled to breathe in the lung-constricting position. She tried to lift her head to search for some hope of rescue, but she could only raise it high enough from the awkward position to see the black-haired man's knees.

"There ya go, Rimlick," Brash called.. "She's all trussed up like a lamb ready for slaughter."

His name's Rimlick. At least now she could stop thinking of him as the black-haired man.

Leena heard the Elven blade whistling through the air as Rimlick tested it.

"It don't seem so special to me. It's too small and too light to be of much use against a real sword. I wonder what's got the armorer so het up about it. I guess we'll just have to test it and see."

Leena tried to shrink back as Rimlick's footsteps approached. She shuddered, trying to run away. Her toes scraped small dust clouds beneath her, struggling to run with no traction. She could not move, could not resist, as his left hand rubbed a slow and gentle path up her back and separated her hair forward over her shoulders. A slight breeze cooled the fear-generated sweat at the base of her bared neck. Like a cat playing with its prey, his right hand rested the blade's tip at the base of her spine and scratched its sharp point over her waist and up her backbone.

"Well, little darlin', I'm kinda sorry it has to end like this. But..." the blade hissed through the air as Rimlick raised it in a fluid, rapid movement.

Without touching her wrists, something snagged Leena's bindings. She fell forward as the ropes parted. With a dull thud on the pine needles, the Elven blade fell beside her. Although her arms were stiff and sore, she grabbed the blade before rolling onto her back. Touching her hedge witch wand, she cast healing and Branch-enhanced protection spells on herself.

"What the..." Rimlick's voice sounded confused. "Somehow, I accidentally hit the ropes between her hands. Where did she go?"

"You men spread out. Find her and find my new sword. I got some unfinished business with the young lady."

"Hold it, men! I think we've found the answer to our problems."

A bandit eased to the center of the campsite, his knife poised across Darius's throat.

"Seems you weren't alone," Rimlick shouted, looking around, trying to spot a surrendering Leena. "Now I've heard that the Great Wizard's knights are invincible. So, I propose we put this to the test."

Rimlick froze as the approaching racket of a dozen horses' shod hooves, tinkling bridles, and squeaking leather blotted out all other sounds.

"Okay, men," Rimlick's high voice shouted. "Sounds like we got more company coming. Everyone get your bows and take cover. Let's see what else these new riders bring to the party." Removing the bow from his shoulder, Rimlick ran into the trees behind an invisible Leena.

"Whoa!" a loud, deep voice rang out. Leena looked toward the road to see the midnight-black uniforms of a regular army lieutenant and a dozen mounted soldiers. At the commanding shout, the soldiers halted their mounts a hundred yards away, as though suspecting this camp might be a trap. "Okay," he called, "move in and search the camp. But be careful. It looks deserted, but she could be hiding here."

Oh, Spirit, please help me. From her vantage point, Leena saw the bandits notching arrows. *I can't let them shoot the soldiers.* But she wasn't sure her wand's Branch-enhanced immobilization spell was powerful enough to freeze everyone she could see. The Garlan Branch's immobilization spell could do it, but the price was high. *There's no choice. I have to prevent a slaughter.* She cast the Garlan Branch's spell.

A small blood trail leaked from beneath the knife at Darius's throat. Leena removed the immobilization spell from him. "Okay," she called. "You should be able to move now."

With slow, careful motions, Darius pried the hand holding the knife away from his throat.

Leena searched the early morning sky as Darius walked toward her. It remained clear. *Thank you, Spirit.* Her eyes snapped back to Darius as a hiss flew over her shoulder. An arrow scraped across his left arm. Leena searched for the source and saw no one.

"The next one goes in his heart if you don't release your spell, but only from my men. And I do mean my men only." Rimlick's voice rose from the trees behind her.

I forgot Rimlick wasn't in sight when I cast the immobilization spell. She couldn't let Darius be killed. However, removing the Branch's immobilization spell from the bandits, but not the soldiers, would certainly result in the troopers' deaths.

Dark motion flickered high against the light sky. Leena's eyes jerked up toward a tiny shadow approaching behind the soldiers through the eastern sky, growing larger as it flew faster than any natural bird could. She couldn't leave these men defenseless to be slaughtered by the raven. Touching the Branch, Leena removed the immobilization spell from the bandits and the soldiers.

EIGHTEEN

A scattered flight of ten eastbound arrows flew from the bandits as though released unaimed. One pierced an unlucky soldier's right eye, and he flopped from his mount like a child's rag doll. An arrow sprouted from another soldier's chest. His shout went unnoticed when his horse sped west as if chased by a fierce pack of hellhounds.

Leena's instinct was to cast the Branch-enhanced protection spell on her and Darius, then bolt away from the battle. She was reaching for her hedge witch wand when Darius grabbed her right wrist. Torn loose from her shirtwaist by his sudden jerk, the wand tumbled to the ground.

"Darius, wait..." His other hand covered her mouth, silencing her automatic protest.

"Shhhh! Not now." Darius's whisper brushed her ear. "They're all distracted. We might get away if we keep quiet and make it to a hiding place."

He doesn't know the Branch-enhanced protection spell would make us invisible and unable to be heard. Eyes wide with anger and frustration, Leena struggled to make Darius understand that her skills were needed to prevent more death and injury. The bandits and soldiers were not the most dangerous threat in the area. Lifting her left hand, she pointed toward the sky.

Darius's eyes widened as he looked up, but he refused to release his hold on her. Shielding her with his body, Darius dragged her into the shelter of a nearby pine tree.

At this distance, all he sees is an ordinary raven. He doesn't understand how lethal that creature is. These men have no chance if I don't do something soon.

Turning at the entrance, Darius nodded toward the soldiers scrambling from their mounts, grabbing crossbows, and seeking shelter in the surrounding trees. Within seconds, flights of well-aimed crossbow bolts harvested half of the bandits as their return fire dropped three more soldiers. The remaining outlaws fled their hiding places and ran to the frozen road. Scurrying west, they chased their dark-haired leader, hoping he could provide a strategy to ensure their survival.

As crossbow bolts dropped four more bandits, the rushing wind generated by the raven's gigantic midnight-black wings raised a snow curtain, hiding the world for several seconds. When the air cleared enough, Leena saw two bandits racing away and seven soldiers launching crossbow bolts at the newly arrived monster as fast as they could reload. Shifting her eyes from the remaining combatants, Leena stared into the eyes of the evil demon less than fifty yards away.

Darius turned to see what had captured her attention. Like a mouse mesmerized by the swaying head of a cobra, his eyes locked onto the giant black bird. As though forgetting his arms, his hands fell to his sides, releasing her.

Outside their shelter, the air was filled with the continuous hiss of crossbow bolts. Their well-aimed bolts ricocheted off its iron-hard feathers and into the trees. The massive raven rose and swooped down before the soldiers could change their ineffective strategy. Two more soldiers fell. With each dip of the raven's razor-sharp beak, another soldier dropped with a deep cavern dug into his skull.

When every trooper lay motionless, painting the surrounding snow red with their draining lifeblood, the creature turned, eyeing the two remaining bandits. Rimlick's hands struggled to free his horse from the tree where he had tied it before last night's celebration. A hundred yards behind him, the other remaining bandit raced toward the bearded man as he leaped aboard his mount. Ignoring the chaos, Rimlick dug his heels into the animal's sides, spurring it into a furious run from the battle scene. The man's black beard fluttered like a pennant over his shoulders. In his wake, the other bandit survivor chased the fleeing horse, pleading for Rimlick to stop and let him mount. As patient as a saint, the silent raven stalked behind the begging man. Not daring to turn and face his executioner, the hopeless victim fell to his knees, buried his face in his palms, and wept as the bird's talons dug deep furrows into his back.

Leena and Darius pulled their eyes from the gruesome scene as a lone soldier dragged himself from the road toward the trees. An arrow jutting from the sole surviving soldier's back waved like a flagless mast as the prone man crawled toward the roadside, seeking the forest's protection. Leena reached for her hedge witch wand, intending to send a healing spell toward him. It was gone. Lost in the camp when Darius grabbed her wrist. *Oh no. I can't help him.* She froze as the raven turned and looked straight at her.

She needed to cast a protection spell on Darius and herself without her hedge witch wand. However, this was the worst time to test whether casting another spell with the Branch would call a second raven. *What else can I do?*

Darius stared at the nearing monster, his hand drifting toward his sword.

He'll try to fight it, but I can't let him. He'll be killed. I have to do something. It's almost here. I can't protect him and fight two ravens if the Garlan Branch calls another one. I have no choice. She cast the Garlan Branch's protection spell on them.

Closing her eyes, Leena sensed for her wand. She could not call it. But like every hedge witch, she could feel its magic when no other magic was around.

"Wait here," she called over her shoulder as she sped from the pine tree's shelter. Safe inside the Branch's protection spell, Leena raced to the camp.

Where is it? Where is it? Frustrated tears rose in her eyes as she searched in vain. *It has to be here.* She was close. She could feel it. *There! It's half buried in dirt, but that has to be it.*

Grabbing the wand, she ran back to the pine tree's shelter.

"Okay," Darius's voice rose from the dimness beyond the tree's trunk. "What do we do now?"

Touching her hedge witch wand, Leena sent a sleep command. A sad smile flitted across her face when Darius dropped like a sack of potatoes behind her. Now, all she needed to do was attract this creature away to keep it from finding a sleeping Darius, knowing that if she lost her fight with the raven, her spells would die with her.

You can do this. Spirit, please be with me.

Leena exited the pine tree cave with the Branch's protection spell guarding her and Darius. Edging toward the road, she saw the raven, like a dark, unstoppable force, walking toward the injured soldier, still crawling toward the shelter of the trees beyond the road. She needed to attract the bird's attention. After all, it was here for her. If she could draw it close enough, she could drop the protection spell's shield and touch its chest with the Branch. Perhaps another bird wouldn't come. She had to risk fighting this one now. Leena dropped the protection spell. "Hey, stupid bird! Over here!" she shouted.

The raven's head snapped toward her. The creature's wings spread when its eyes met hers, lifting it into a speeding flight toward her. Waiting until the last possible moment, she recast the spell. The bird landed before her, its head darting around, trying to find where she had gone.

Oh Spirit. Her heart sank in her chest when another black dot appeared on the horizon, growing larger by the second, its soaring flight aimed in her direction. *It's suicide to fight two at once.*

Motion beyond the roadside caught her eye. The arrow sticking straight up from a small mound of black leather rose and fell in irregular spurts as if it had a life of its own. The sole surviving soldier was minutes away from death, too weak to protect himself. Touching her hedge witch wand, she cast a healing spell on the injured man.

With a flurry of wings, the second raven landed twenty feet behind her. Fear crawled up her spine. The thing could close the distance in a few seconds. How can I kill the raven in front of me and get the spell back up before the new arrival behind me attacks? How does it even know I'm here? It must assume the first bird thinks I'm in this area.

How long could she maintain the protection spell? Even if she held it for a few days, the spell drain would eventually force her to drop it. And what about the soldier she just healed and any travelers who happened by? How many of them could she protect if she didn't destroy both ravens? She was only putting off the inevitable. *Although I'll probably die fighting them, now is better than when the protection spell is weak, and my death would be certain. But I need to give Darius a chance to escape. Leena removed the sleep spell from him.*

Stepping forward, Leena pushed the Branch's invisible protective shell against the bird's chest in front of her. Behind her, the clicking of the other raven's talons grew louder with remarkable speed, racing towards her as though the beast understood she would have to drop her shield to kill its partner.

Once her shield dropped, she would have no hope of avoiding the lethal beak of the raven racing at her from the rear. All of her spells would die with her. Then, nothing would stand between the last living raven and Darius. *What have I done?*

Accepting the inevitable, hoping the birds would ignore Darius and fly back to their master when she died, Leena raised the Branch, pointing it at the nearby raven's chest. *My death may be the only chance Darius has.* She removed the protection spell from herself and stabbed forward with the Garlan Branch.

The Branch touched the raven's chest, and a slight breeze kissed Leena's cheek as a serpent-like hiss sped past her fear-stiffened neck and shoulders. *What was that noise?* With her back braced against certain death from behind, she prepared to endure the lethal crunch that would end her life.

She did not see the bird in front of her expand. The other bird's large wing slammed against her shoulder from behind, spinning her around and knocking her to the ground. *What hit me?* Lifting her head, she saw the untouched raven speeding toward the road with a crossbow bolt protruding from its eye socket. She lost sight of it when the expanding raven in front of her exploded, covering her with the foul stench of blood and entrails. Fighting to maintain her grip on the Branch with a blood-slimed hand, Leena blinked, then smeared the back of her gore-covered wrist across her eyes, trying to clear the wretched scarlet mass blocking her vision.

Get up. Now! The other raven's going to come back. You need to be ready.

On the far side of the road, the raven with the shaft sticking from its eyes straightened and ruffled its feathers. The soldier she had just healed screamed and writhed as the bird's mighty beak clamped down on his arm. The thing shook him like a soggy rag. With a wet pop, the black leather-clad arm detached from its victim. A crimson stream poured from the open chasm where his arm had been attached, and the soldier fell to the ground, lifeless.

Leena's stomach somersaulted as the beast tilted its head back and swallowed the appendage in deep, jerking bites. Fighting nausea, she struggled to her feet as the bird finished its gruesome meal and turned to charge toward her. A long strip of human skin from the dismembered soldier bobbled beneath its beak as it ran.

Okay, come on. It's just you and me this time. Standing stubborn and unmovable, Leena pointed the Branch at the speeding creature's chest. She held out her arm, gripping the Branch so hard her knuckles turned white. "Come on! I may die, but I'm taking you with me!" Her shout tore through the trees. *Wait! What am I doing?*

Seeming to understand the Branch's danger to it, the raven spread its wings. Its momentum carried it within ten feet of her extended Branch before the creature's broad wings grabbed enough air to enable it to climb toward the sky. The wind of its flight buffeted dirt and debris into her face. She was blind. Blinking, fighting to clear her blurred visions, Leena looked up, trying to follow the Raven's soaring progress.

Its skyward flight stopped. With a graceful bend of its head and shoulders, the dark shadow plunged toward her. *I can't touch its chest from this position. Its beak will drive right through me.* Facing the monster, Leena ran backward, not caring what might be behind her, forcing the bird to change direction. The creature swooped toward her, flying like an arrow five feet above the ground. Less than three feet away, the beast raised its head, preparing to stab its beak through the top of her skull. She had no time to run and no way to escape its lethal strike. *Mum!* Her mind screamed as she raised the Branch in a final defiant gesture.

Her world flared bright red as the bird's iron-hard breast feathers slammed into the Branch, lifting her body and propelling it through the air backward. Leean's heart skipped several beats as the trampled snow flew past yards below her. The raven let out a vicious caw and exploded.

Her mind scrambled to find a spell that would save her from a disastrous landing. The ground came at her fast, and she couldn't catch her breath. With a will of its own, her left arm extended to soften her landing. Flame blazed through her forearm as the bones within it shattered in a rapid series of internal cracks. Her skull slammed against the ground, and darkness closed in.

NINETEEN

Heated agony ripped through Leena's brain, jerking her from a welcome sleep. Something lifted, pulled, and squeezed her wounded arm as though trying to rip it from her body.

Is another raven trying to devour me like the wounded soldier? Did I call a raven again? I don't remember using the Branch to cast another protection spell.

Red-hot pain shot through her arm.

"What are you doing?" The scream was out before she registered the concern in Darius's eyes as he examined her injuries. His warm hand pressed against her shoulder, restraining her when she tried to sit.

"Your arm's broken in several places," he said

softly. Leena stopped struggling at his calm words. "I found some bandages in a soldier's saddlebags." He pointed at the leather bags resting on the ground beneath their pine tree shelter. "I'm wrapping it, then I'll fashion a sling. That should hold until we can get you to a healer." Despite the words' intended soothing effect, his tone had a sharpness that hinted at trouble.

"Don't bother." Leena eased her uninjured right hand to her hedge witch wand. "Just let me lie here for a few minutes, and I'll fix it."

Without a word, Darius stuffed the cloth strips into one of the leather pouches of the saddlebags. *Was that anger in his eyes? Is he mad because I put him to sleep to save his life? I can't worry about that now. I'll explain once I've fixed this arm.*

Leena cast a numbing spell on the injured arm and then, closing her eyes, used her wand to sense the damaged bones within. Minutes passed as her mind aligned the sharp-edged breaks into their proper configuration. After the last one slid into place, a healing spell restored the bones to their uninjured state. She flexed her hand to ensure the damage was repaired and would be as good as new within hours.

Darius was studying a sheet of parchment that

he'd pulled from a saddlebag on one of the soldier's horses.

"What's that? A letter from home?" She walked over to him, trying to keep her words light.

"You might want to explain this." Darius passed her the parchment over his shoulder without looking at her.

A chill crawled up her spine as she unwound the tight roll. Bold print spanned the top of the sheet. Her eyes grew wide as she read.

Reward: 500 Gold Pieces

For information leading to the capture of the hedge witch known as Leena. She is approximately 16–17 years old, with black hair, dark eyes, and is taller than average.

Her hands raced to unfurl the rest of the document.

This person is wanted for questioning in connection with the destruction of the village of Quillan, the town of Stocksbury, the robbery and murder of the Raystack family on their farm north of Stockbury, the theft of several horses, and the murder of a stable boy in Pineton. She is believed to be traveling toward the Great Wizard's castle in Elderon on either the North Road or the Wizard's Highway.

Persons with information leading to her capture should contact their magistrate or the nearest guard post immediately.

What? No, what? This makes no sense. Even the most terrifying murderers and cutthroats have never commanded such a high price. Her mind spun with questions she could not answer.

"As a member of the Great Wizard's forces, I have no choice but to place you under arrest." Darius's stone-cold eyes warned Leena that any protest would be useless. "We'll return to Pineton, where you'll be remanded to the local constable's custody. Now, place your hands behind your head and interlock your fingers."

The world was spinning, threatening to bring Leena to her knees. She was stunned. Her mind floated above her body, looking down at a sad, strange girl in the forest, her eyes wide with fear and blood staining her clothing. She watched herself drop the parchment and place her hands behind her head.

His strong right hand clinched around her intertwined fingers, locking them together like a vise, while his left hand removed her sword from its sheath. Tossing the blade aside, he reached to her skirt's waist and retrieved the hedge witch wand. Flinging it next to the sword, Darius patted the front, back, and sides around her waist.

"Okay, where's the other wand?"

This is moving all too fast. I can't think. I need to explain.

When she failed to answer, his hand rubbed a gentle path around her waist, seeking the Garlan Branch. His hand passed over it, and the pressure forced the Branch's bark into her stomach, but he felt nothing.

"Where did you put it?" Darius's eyes scoured the area, searching for the Branch. "Not telling me won't help you. There's no way I'll give you a chance to retrieve it."

Leena breathed a deep, resigned sigh and let her shoulders slump as much as her awkward position permitted.

"I can't tell you where it is because there's no way you'll believe me without a lengthy explanation. Look, it's been a long night and a longer day. And, although we've had brief naps, we're both tired and hungry. I have plenty of food in my bags. So I suggest I tell you everything I know while I fix a good supper. Okay?"

She could almost hear Darius's forehead wrinkle as he squinted his stern glare, considering the suggestion.

"All right." He released her hands and gathered her hedge witch wand and sword beside him. "I'll listen, but if you even think about retrieving either of these,"—he waved a hand toward the wand and sword—"or your other wand, I'll bind you to a tree so I can sleep safely tonight."

Leena was grateful Darius was amenable, but she couldn't help feeling hurt by his actions. However, she understood why he did it. He didn't know her at all.

Leena talked as she unloaded her pack, cooked dinner, and they ate. Starting with her summer battle against an imaginary staff-wielding giant at the Garlan Tree, Leena told him everything that had happened to her until this afternoon's disastrous fight with the second raven. True to his word, Darius remained silent until she finished her tale. After tossing a few more branches on the fire, he sat alert but unspeaking, gazing into the glowing coals. Leena's stomach churned, ready to spew her dinner while she waited, trying to gauge his thoughts.

"Okay." Darius studied her eyes, searching for any hint of deception. "I'm not saying I believe everything you said. That'll take time. However, your story explains a great deal. The most crucial question is how did the soldiers involved in yesterday's battle receive the poster so soon? It's a two-week journey from Elderon, where the Great Wizard's castle is located, to Weymouth, the nearest regular army garrison to this battle. It's where you said Arvin stole the food and bagged a deer. A courier might make it there in ten days, but only if fresh mounts are available at outposts along the way. If there was a courier, he would have had to bypass the Knights Midden Garrison between here and Elderon. Since it's only six days from Midden Garrison to Elderon, the knights might have checked with the Great Wizard to gain more information about what they were facing before racing off to capture you. That could mean whoever created this"—his finger tapped the rolled scroll—"did not want to risk a poster getting into the Great Wizard's hands. "

Leena nodded, but remained silent.

"So, after Weymouth Garrison's commander received the posters, he'd need time to get his soldiers mounted and assemble provisions to travel and distribute a batch of them. He'd be in no hurry since he has no reason to suspect you're in his area. He'd take at least a day to assess everything and another day to distribute horses, rations, and bedding to the soldiers. Then, he would need to send troops to all the towns in his district. On the third day, he'd send a lieutenant with a mounted squad to his cities and villages, including Stocksbury and Pineton. It can take horses three days to reach Pineton from Weymouth during deep winter snows. Then, once the posters were distributed, I'm sure the poor lieutenant who found himself in Pineton would have a crowd of hopefuls clamoring to be the first to tell him about you, hoping to collect the reward. My best guess is that the lieutenant arrived there yesterday morning. After calming the crowd enough to get some helpful information, he trotted out here.

"No matter how I look at it, the earliest those troops could receive the poster from the Great Wizard's castle and return here for this battle is over two weeks. And yet the poster states the stable boy was killed, and we know the alleged murder took place last night. However, I also know you saved the boy's life. So, how could that murder possibly be mentioned in the poster? Also, if you were that important to the Great Wizard, the story would have been all over his castle. Nothing stays secret long in that place. I left there seventeen days ago. No hard-riding courier passed me on his way to Weymouth during my trip, and I never heard your name until we met in Pineton three days ago."

"I can't explain any of it," Leena said. "This is the first time I've seen anything that says I'm being sought after."

"I'll admit, your invisible stick is a powerful weapon capable of causing significant damage, maybe even destroying Quillan and Stockbury. But why would you? I can see no way that would help you find your parents."

"I was not responsible for the destruction of Quillan and Stockbury," Leena snapped, fighting tears of pain and anger. "Quillan was my home. My family is gone, and I don't know where they are. The only thing that keeps me getting up each day is the hope they're still alive."

"I'm sorry." Darius's eyes softened. "I wasn't insinuating you did. The fact that any part of this poster can't be true tells me that all of it is probably lies. Now, that Arvin boy. From what you told me, he'd have no problem destroying a few towns and villages to get what he wants. Also, how'd he happen to be in your town when you returned from getting the Branch? After hearing how he dealt with the bandits, I wouldn't be surprised if the empty farm you stayed at was the Raystack family farm, and they were home when he arrived."

Darius paused, staring at her. His stern expression warned her he searched for the slightest hint that any part of her story was untrue. *Please, Spirit, I can't be arrested now. I have to find my family before anything worse happens to them.*

He shrugged. "Okay, you're no longer under arrest, and I have to say, that's a relief. I hated going all official on you, but it's a job requirement. We're supposed to intimidate those we arrest to reduce the chance of conflict. However, everything I know about you says you're telling me the truth. So, I suggest we take a long, hard think about what we should do next. Can you use your Branch to protect us from ravenous beasts while we sleep?"

Relief and joy roiled within her.

"Sure," Leena smiled, "if you don't mind being awakened every few minutes when I lower the protection spell to fight the raven it brings and then put another spell on."

"Okay, let's take turns, then." Darius returned her smile. "One sleeps while the other watches and thinks."

"Naw, I think I'll just use my hedge witch wand instead. Then we can both get a good night's sleep."

Leena woke to the rustle of new logs settling on the fire. Sitting, she yawned and stretched into the pale pink aura that promised a new dawn would soon arise. A warm smile rose within her as Darius tossed another log onto the fire, sending glowing crimson sparks dancing up, only to die before touching the pine-scented branches covering their shelter.

"Good morning, Sir Knight. What have you decided?"

"Well, first of all, while you wasted half the day sleeping—"

"What?" She pointed east, where a small, red crescent peeked above the horizon. "Dawn's still half an hour away."

"Okay." Darius raised his hands in mock defense. "So maybe it's not all that late. Anyway, while you slept, I gathered all the horses I could find and recovered most of our supplies." Reaching behind him, Darius retrieved the kettle she'd found at the first farm where she and Arvin slept. A rounded mound of snow rose above its rim. Settling it on the glowing coals, he pulled her oat bag and honey pot forward. "At least we can have a hearty breakfast while we decide where to go next."

"That's easy." Leena leaned toward the fire as though her proximity and intensity would convince Darius they had no choice. "I need to get to the

Great Wizard's castle and find out where my family's been taken."

Darius nodded, contemplating her words. "There are two problems with that. First, we'd have to split up because two ships are waiting for me at the Longport docks, ready to sail in twelve days. I allowed myself fourteen days to get there from Pineton, but this little detour has eaten up two of those. Now, I'll just have time to get there, check-in, and stow the things I need for the trip aboard the ship. There's no way I could return to the castle and get back before then."

"I don't see that as a problem." Leena stared into his eyes, daring him to contradict her. "You said the Wizard's Highway is just a few days ahead. I'm certain I can't miss it. I'll turn north there, and that'll take me to Elderon, where I can ask someone how to get to the castle."

"That brings us to the second problem. What do you do about the hundreds of people looking to turn you in for five hundred gold pieces? That's more than most people will see in a lifetime. I assure you, by now, those posters are displayed in every town and village between Quillan and Midden Garrison. And if that's not enough—"

"No, wait. Let me answer before you go on." Unable to sit any longer, Leena stood and paced a path into the pine-needle floor of the enclosed space.

With a heavy sigh, Darius nodded.

"First," Leena bent a finger back, "I was born and raised in a small village. I know that people in towns and villages care about each other and always do what they can to help strangers. So I don't need your help. I'm sure anyone in the villages and towns I pass through will be more than willing to help me get to the Great Wizard if I tell them why it's necessary."

She bent another finger back. "Second, I have a hedge witch wand to protect me. And, if that's not enough, I have the Garlan Branch. You saw what I did to those bandits. No one would dare try to apprehend me if they knew I could freeze them for hours. And third, only the Great Wizard knows whether he destroyed my village. No one's going to stop me from getting to him, looking him in the eyes, and knowing if he's telling me the truth."

Leena thumped down next to the fire, grabbed a bowl, and ladled a heaping load of steaming oat cereal, followed by a generous amount of honey. Stirring to mix her breakfast, she gave Darius a curt nod, confirming her reasoning was beyond challenge. Saying it all out loud gave her courage.

"You're right." Darius looked into the fire. "In

most towns and villages, people help each other and all strangers who need it. But that changes when you get to larger towns and cities. They exist and grow through trade, and every trade center has a bandit gang that preys on poorly defended caravans. When trade is slow, or they're just bored, bandits will take anyone they can and abuse them for their pleasure. You met one of those gangs when you rescued Arvin; another was here yesterday. What would have happened if you hadn't freed Arvin from the gang that captured him? And even good people from a small town might turn you in if they thought the reward would mean a better life for their family.

His words were making too much sense. Leena struggled within herself to find arguments against them.

"I know you rescued Arvin with the Garlan Branch, but at what price? If you want to fight another raven each time you activate a spell using the Branch, you could freeze hopeful bounty collectors for a while. However, if you freeze them, you'd have to cast a protection spell on them and yourself when the raven arrives. You'd face a second raven if you used the Branch to do that. From what you said, you were lucky the soldier's crossbow bolt hit the raven's eye. Otherwise, you would have died. Also, once word got out about your ability to freeze people, many would try to ambush you and bash you over the head or use knockout drops in your food or drink so they could bring you in incapacitated rather than have you freeze them and get away."

Leena gulped. In a weak voice, she said, "I can handle it." But could she?

"Also, with a high price on your head, how many bandits will try to capture you and extract the information the Great Wizard wants rather than kill you outright? They'll figure that if the Great Wizard's desperate for your information, he'll pay far more than five hundred gold pieces to the bounty collectors if you're no longer alive to provide it. Can you keep your hedge witch wand's Branch-enhanced protection spell active for days or weeks?"

She shook her head.

"Even if you could," Darius continued, "what happens to anyone who tries to help you? You saw what happened to that unfortunate soldier who survived the ambush. If you're forced to use the Garlan Branch protection spell, what will the raven do to get you to drop your shield? Or what would happen if whoever controls the birds sends two or three ravens at a time? How many lives will be lost before you can save a crowd of people who are trying to help you?"

Slow tears trailed down Leena's cheeks, dropping into her bowl unnoticed.

"Last, what makes you think the Great Wizard has anything to do with those posters? What if someone else created them to stop you from getting to the Great Wizard? What better way to ensure you die along the way than to put such a high price on your head that everyone thinks you are extremely dangerous? Who's going to risk trying to take you alive if they believe the attempt might prove fatal to them? How well can you protect yourself from an arrow in the back?"

"But what can I do? The Great Wizard is the only person who knows where my family's been taken."

"Does he? How do you know that's true?"

"Arvin told m..." She stopped, dazed by the realization that every assumption that drove her to make this trip was based on Arvin's tale. Her heart sank. *I'm a stupid, stupid girl.*

"Okay, let's talk about Arvin for a bit," Darius said. "He told you he came from Wedgelin, a village in the north. I was born and raised in the north, and I've never heard of that village. I admit, it could be a small village off the beaten path. But he also told you he followed the soldiers' path from Wedgelin to Quillan."

"Yes." Leena struggled to see where he was taking this line of reasoning.

"How long did he say he followed the soldiers?"

"He didn't say exactly. He just said they attacked his village over three weeks earlier." *I'm getting tired of this verbal dancing. Why doesn't he get to the point?*

"And when did you get the Garlan Branch?"

"Midwinter Night, the night before I met him." *How could he have followed the soldiers for three weeks and know they were looking for a hedge witch named Leena before I received the Branch?* "Are you saying Arvin was responsible for destroying Quillan and hauling the villagers away to slavery? How is that possible?" she asked.

Darius nodded. "I would not be surprised if he was an experienced sorcerer enchanted to appear as a lad."

Leena gasped. "No...I..."

"Don't beat yourself up. I'm sure Arvin depended on the all-consuming emotions of finding your village destroyed and your family gone to override your logic long enough to carry out whatever plan he has for you." Darius reached a consoling hand to pat hers.

"But the bandits captured him. Surely, someone who destroyed two towns would have little trouble overcoming a few bandits." Confusion washed through her. *How could I be so blind?*

"True. Unless Arvin wanted to get caught. My guess is he hired them. What better way to earn your trust and dispel any suspicions you might have that he's not the small, helpless boy he wanted you to see? If we go on that assumption, killing them would be necessary from his perspective. They saw you immobilize their entire group. Even uneducated bandits would know that ability is far beyond ordinary hedge witch skills. I think he wanted to keep that knowledge just between you and him."

From a distance, Leena felt her mouth opening and closing, but no words came out. Her mind refused to slow enough to capture and review a single thought.

"But...but how did he know I would get the Branch?"

Darius pulled a twig from the fire and blew on the ashen tip until it glowed. "I can only guess." He shoved the stick back into the fire and watched flames lick its surface, dancing like a small orange curtain rising along its length. "I'm sure he's not what he appears. His actions are far too sophisticated for a young boy. That's why I believe he's a wizard. If it's true, he probably warded the area around the Garlan Tree to alert him when it gave another Branch. And didn't you say a mysterious blizzard hid your tracks from the Weymouth Garrison soldiers when you started your cross-country ride? You also said the column didn't have a wizard, so who else was there to create the powerful wind? Arvin is the most likely candidate. I think those are reasonable assumptions."

Everything was starting to make sense, even if she didn't want to believe it.

"So, let's say this boy, or whatever he is, sends a raven to discover who has the Branch. How long was the first raven around before you shielded yourself?"

"I didn't shield myself then. I didn't know how. But I accidentally set a tree on fire with the Branch." Flame crept into her cheeks. "Then the raven found me, even though I hid in a snow mound." Darius strained to hear her soft voice.

"So it seems each activation of the Branch calls a raven. Then, let's assume whatever the raven saw, heard, or sensed, its master knew instantly. It explains how Arvin homed in on you. Why else would he have remained in your village once the alleged soldiers moved on? If they were his mission, wouldn't he continue following them? When you destroyed his raven, it confirmed you had the Branch, but it also made him more cautious. Other-wise, he would have tried to take it from you then.

After all, it took Robart months to master it. You're a hedge witch, which gives you some advantages Robart didn't have. However, you're still only half-trained. From Arvin's perspective, that should give him plenty of time to discover how to relieve you of the Branch."

Lifting his eyes from the fire, Darius stared at her. "Would you be willing to show me the Branch?"

Their eyes met. Wanting, needing to believe, she sank into his warm, trusting gaze. *I have to trust someone. So far, I haven't done so well on my own.*

Her hand reached beneath her shirt and closed around the familiar rough surface. Praying Darius was as honest as he seemed, she drew the Branch and extended it toward him.

"Where is it?" Darius's soft, confused voice resonated in the enclosed space. "I think it must be invisible to everyone except you. Can I touch it?"

Everything inside of her screamed, *No, no, no. Run. Now!*

"Yes." Although she willed the branch to remain steady, she could not stop her hand from vibrating with the strength of her tension.

Darius lifted a slow and deliberate hand. Inches short of the Branch, his hand deflected aside. As he reached again, his hand rose above the Branch to close on empty air. He tried waving his hand from right to left above Leena's thumb. His palm rose over the Branch inches from its surface.

"I feel nothing. My hand passes less than an inch above yours through empty air."

Leena smiled. The protective field concealing the Garlan Tree must also exist in this Branch, and it deflects sight and touch by others without her mental control. That was good to know.

"Okay then," Darius said, watching Leena tuck the invisible Branch beneath her shirt. "Getting back to Arvin, although he believes you have the Garlan Branch, probably because a raven alerts him when it's used, it seems he's no more capable of seeing or touching it than I am. Otherwise, I don't doubt he would have murdered you in your sleep and claimed it for his own."

"You have a point," she said. "There were plenty of opportunities for him to have taken it."

"I think it's safe to assume he controls the ravens. So first, he sent one, hoping to confirm the Garlan Tree had granted another branch. When that didn't work out, he needed to get you to reveal whether you received a Branch and, if so, whether you still had it. For all he knew, you could have hidden it or thrown it away in fear after your fight with the raven. So, he destroys your village and shows up as an innocent child to gain your trust.

When you do nothing to reveal the existence of the Branch, he runs away from you to trash Stocksbury so you'd believe his story about following the army.

"Once he's sure you're following his trail north to find your family, he runs off to find a convenient bandit gang willing to appear to have captured him. The coincidence of them stopping right in front of you to torture him was a bit much. I'm guessing he sensed the Garlan Branch's aura. So, knowing you were near, he signaled the group to stop and enact their little play, causing you to use the Branch's immobilization spell. The raven's appearance confirmed what his senses told him, removing all doubt. Once he knew you still had the Branch, he no longer needed his merry band of men. But then he had a problem. How can he get his hands on something he cannot see or feel? I'm sure he searched you several times while you slept. I imagine it was Arvin trying to get into your room at the inn in Pineton for one last try before he disappeared."

Leena's skin crawled at the thought of the little monster's hands roaming over her body as she slept.

Darius continued. "So maybe, if he gets you in a jail cell where you can't hide the Branch, he can search you less gently. So he goes to Weymouth, the first crossroads town near you, and alerts the garrison there that the destroyer of Quillan and

Stocksbury is wandering up the road toward them. However, you avoid being seen by the soldiers through your hedge witch skills, making it hard to know where you're hiding. Then the little scoundrel stays with you for a while, hoping for another opportunity. Again, his luck runs out when I show up. So he slithers away to plan anew.

"So, what would I do if I were an unscrupulous little louse who wanted the Garlan Branch's power? Well, that jail idea still seems pretty good. But how can I do that? Why not make up a massive batch of wanted posters and get them accepted for distribution through the armed forces courier system? I'd ensure they're sent to every garrison and fort you must travel past with instructions to post them in all towns and villages along your path. That should be a simple task for a wizard as powerful as this one seems to be. But he'd only have them disbursed along your route. That way, there's little chance of the Great Wizard seeing them and spoiling Arvin's plans until it's too late. Why would anyone show the Great Wizard a poster since they believe he's the one who issued them?

"But what if our trusty heroine sees the posters at some point? What does she do? Well, she'd have to run, but which way?

"South? No, she's just come from that direction

and knows there are no answers about her family that way. As far as she knows, that would take her away from any chance of rescuing them.

"West? Probably not. There are very few towns and villages in that direction. From her perspective, the Great Wizard's entire army is out looking for her. Even if she made it beyond the vast forests of Allivan, she'd be facing the Impassable Desert and, somewhere out there, the orc mines. She could spend the rest of her life wandering those vast expanses, trying to locate her family. Besides, she still believes he sent her family north. Possibly, somewhere beyond Elderon. She wouldn't expect to find answers in the West.

"East? Again, probably not. She's never been so far from home before, doesn't know how to read a map, and doesn't know whether there's another route to Elderon in the east.

"North? It's the only direction that makes sense. After all, that's probably where the Great Wizard took her parents. She might not want to go that way directly, but from her point of view, it's the only way to get to the Great Wizard. Even knowing it's a trap, you'd have no choice. After all, you'd still believe he's the only one with the answers you need.

"It's a neat setup. Arvin knows where you must go and that you only know one route to get there.

The chances of someone capturing you before you get to Elderon are excellent. I don't doubt he's alerted every outpost and town official of a way to contact him for the reward if they catch you."

Leena's mind tumbled, unable to fix on a single thought. As though confirming a decision, he nodded and looked at her.

"Which is actually good for us. Every day, the chance of someone asking the Great Wizard about the reward and spoiling the little rat's plans grows. If Arvin thought he could defeat the Great Wizard without the power of the Garlan Branch, none of this would have happened. I'm certain he thinks this plan will give him the power he needs. After all, isn't it nearly foolproof? So the best way we can beat him is to outwait him."

"We?" A small hope rose in Leena's chest. "But you said you must be at the coast in twelve days."

"That's true. But for those twelve days, we can stick together and hopefully devise a viable plan before I sail. At the very least, we'll be away from the areas Arvin's flooded with posters, and maybe we can figure a way to discover where your family's been taken."

"What would happen if you failed to arrive in Longport before the ship sails?"

"Besides ruining my career, risking a court

marshal, and leaving a rescue expedition without a Great Wizard's representative to negotiate a peace settlement, if necessary?"

Can't he see I'm serious? Leena's jaw muscles bulged beneath her glaring eyes. *We're talking about my family's lives here.*

"Okay, peace." Darius held up pacifying palms toward her. "I was just trying to lighten the mood.

"Last fall, a heavy gale on the Eastern Sea blew an Allivanian merchant ship far off course. When the weather cleared, the merchants and sailors aboard found seawater leaking through the storm-damaged ship's hull. Fortunately, they were within sight of a previously undiscovered city on the far shore. They needed to repair the ship and restock enough food and water to return to Allivan, so they landed at an empty city dock. Within minutes, dozens of local people gathered to watch the Allivanian merchants offload their goods, enabling the sailors to access and repair the leaking hull. The crowd gathered around the merchants' trade goods, oohing and aahing as each new load was deposited. One well-dressed man approached and addressed the ship's company in a foreign language. The ship's wizard had a basic translation spell that allowed him to communicate with the people to a limited extent. As the wizard understood it, the sailors and their vessel could leave once repairs were complete. However, the merchants and their goods would be held in the new land until the ship returned with more goods as a ransom for the merchants.

"So I have been chosen as the Great Wizard's ambassador to negotiate a peaceful settlement with the new nation, rescue the merchants, and perhaps establish a mutually beneficial relationship."

"Okay, so what are we waiting for?" With feverish energy, Leena tossed her half-eaten meal toward the back of their shelter and used the empty bowl to fill the cauldron with snow. As the chilled white mass sank into the pine needles and the water heated, her hands flew to the few articles she had removed from her pack and started stuffing them back in.

"Why are you just sitting there?" She glared at Darius, who sat finishing the remains of his breakfast. "There's no time to waste. Get moving!"

"Whoa, get moving where? I think we need a bit more planning before rushing off."

"We have to hurry to the coast, and you said we can plan on the way."

"You're right, but I wasn't finished. Please sit down and relax."

There's no time for this. For several moments, Leena squinted anger into his patient eyes. *Okay, I can see he won't move until he's had his say. But it better be quick.* She let herself drop to sit by the fire, maintaining her impatient gaze.

"Where do you think those soldiers came from?" Darius looked toward the scattered bodies on the road.

"Didn't you just say they came from the garrison in Weymouth?"

"Yes," Darius nodded in agreement, "but what town did the soldiers visit yesterday that's between here and the coast?"

Oh, Spirit. Where is my brain? "Pineton." The word came out in a harsh whisper.

"I think it's safe to assume they left a bunch of those posters there, and several townspeople would just love to have us ride peacefully in. I believe the armorer would be overjoyed to see you.

"And what about the bodies scattered all over the road? Leaving them there is inhuman, but what else can we do? Everything within me wants to go to the nearest town and report their deaths so they can get a proper burial, but we can't do that either. Nor can we return these horses. We can only release them so they can forage for food. Perhaps they'll wander back to Pineton." His hand waved toward the soldiers' mounts, grouped with those the bandits stole. For several minutes, he stared at the carnage on the road.

Seeing anguished lines aging Darius's face, Leena's heart melted. Her hand reached out and patted his shoulder. He heaved a near-silent sigh.

"There's nothing we can do for them now. Hopefully, we can explain later." With a shrug, Darius shook his head. "It looks like the aftermath of a clash between soldiers and bandits. As long as we leave none of our belongings behind, there should be no reason for anyone to suspect we were involved. Anyway, we're out of options."

His deep voice rose quiet in the winter silence. "We can only head south through the forest for a few miles, then turn east toward the coast. We can return to this road when we're far beyond Pineton. Hopefully, no overachieving soldier has distributed any posters beyond Pineton.

"One other thing. I suggest you avoid using the Branch until this mess is cleared up. I'm sure Arvin cast a spell on or near the Garlan Tree that alerts him when and in which direction from the tree the Branch has activated a spell. Then he sends a raven."

Out of arguments, Leena nodded.

Okay, there's no other choice right now. But the minute he boards his ship, I'll find a way to get to the

Great Wizard's castle. Then, no one will stop me from finding my family.

TWENTY

Crimson sunset bathed the woods with pink streaks, highlighting dusk-darkened gray trees along the trail of hoofprints behind them. Although bright sunshine and blue skies accompanied them on this first day away from the West Road, the air remained frigid. As tree shadows lengthened, temperatures plummeted, and their horses breathed rapid white vapor plumes into the twilight.

"I think we've had enough travel for one day." Darius nodded toward a large pine with sloping branches broad enough to hide and shelter them and their mounts through the night. "The horses need rest, and I'm in dire need of food."

Darius dismounted and paced to the tree. His

sword tip rang like a small bell against the scabbard's metal throat as he unsheathed the blade. With two deft strokes, he opened a cave-like entrance into the empty area beneath the giant tree's branches.

Leena swung her numb right leg over her horse's rear using slow, deliberate movements. Her knee buckled, refusing to hold her weight when her foot touched the ground. Clutching her saddle horn with white-knuckled hands to remain upright, she bit her lower lip as tiny invisible needles jabbed into the overused lower half of her body. Releasing her grip on the saddle, she forced herself to stand straight, trying to keep Darius from seeing how much her tailbone burned.

Hot anger flashed through her as he turned his back and removed his horse's saddle. His upper body shook in tiny spasms for several seconds, struggling to hide his chuckles as he worked. When his jerking shoulders calmed, he looked at her over the saddle cradled in his arms, his face struggling to maintain a forced concern. "Riding like a man can be difficult at first, my lady, but you'll quickly get used to it."

"Thank you for that information, Your Knightship," she growled.

With her left hand still gripping the saddle horn,

she performed a mocking bow as her right hand slid beneath her tunic and touched the hedge witch wand. Relief pushed a silent sigh from her lungs as the healing spell relieved her aching muscles. Glancing at Darius to ensure he no longer watched, she pulled her jacket tighter against the growing chill, removed her mount's saddle with renewed strength, and lugged it into the shelter.

Neither of them spoke as they scrubbed the white foam lather from the animals' backs and between their forelegs, using folded burlap pads to absorb the moisture. Leena returned beneath the pine's high branches to fill three bags with oats and returned to hang them over the horses' heads.

The clink of steel against stone broke the forest silence as Leena returned to the shelter. Darius had cleared a space in the pine needle carpet beneath the branches. He crouched next to a pyramid of small logs, striking a flint wedge against his dagger, watching the bright sparks fly into the structure, fade, and die.

"The wood's wet. Lighting the fire may take a few minutes," he said.

"Allow me." With a touch to her hedge witch wand, fire bloomed within the well-laid pile. The lively flames sent shadows dancing up through the branches within the enclosure.

"That's an impressive trick. Someday, you'll have to teach it to me."

"I wish I could. However, since you were not born a hedge witch, I'm afraid I'd have little luck."

"You're right. I wouldn't want to be reborn as a hedge witch. That price is too high. Besides, I prefer to stay a knight. I'd better hobble the horses and gather enough wood to see us through the night." He withdrew three lengths of leather thong from his pack. Outside, he squatted to tie a strip between the forelegs of each mount. Thus hobbled, they would not stray far.

While Darius wandered through the surrounding pine trees gathering firewood, Leena pulled two earthenware bowls from her pack and loaded the kettle with fresh snow. Settling the pot at the fire's edge, she watched it come to a boil. She stirred in two bowls full of oats with a stick, then added nuts and honey. Dumping his last load of thick branches by the fire, Darius sat on soft pine needles and filled his bowl. Both ate in contented silence as a gleaming silver moon rose large on the horizon.

With dinner complete, Leena felt content and sleepy. Wasting no time, eager to snuggle beneath her blanket, she cleaned and repacked their bowls. Darius brought their mounts in and tethered them within the fire-warmed protection of their tree-branch sanctuary. As Leena reached toward her pack, hoping to lay out a pallet and dive into a deep, restful sleep, Darius turned to her.

"I think it's time you learned to use that Elven blade."

"You have got to be kidding. It's late, and I'm tired."

"That's the point. You rarely need a blade when you're most prepared. The best time to train is when you're at your worst."

Leena grumbled and followed him to an area he'd cleared outside their pine tree haven. He stood behind Leena and grasped her wrists, showing her how to hold the Elven blade correctly, then taught her several simple exercises. Standing back, he coached her as she stumbled through her sword-wielding tasks. Within minutes, sweat poured from her forehead.

"Hmm," he said, "I'll admit you have a bit of stamina but not much strength. We'll have to fix that."

In an instant, the forest came alive with the whistling hiss of his much larger sword, reflecting golden sparks from the shelter's fire as he demonstrated several exercises.

"I'll help you perform these exercises every

night, and within weeks, you'll be as strong as a man."

"I hope I'll remain smarter than one," she mumbled, not caring if he'd heard her. Smiling and shaking his head, Darius left her to exercise while he retreated under the tree to lay out their sleeping pallets.

Completing the exercise program, Leena let the Elven blade sag to her side. Panting, her shoulders, arms, and chest were on fire. Her muscles jumped and twitched with fatigue. Sheathing the weapon, Leena reached for her wand.

"I wouldn't do that if I were you," his disembodied voice floated out to her from deep within the tree branch shadows. "Much of the strength building comes during the rest between training periods. If you remove the fatigue, you defeat the purpose of the exercises."

"Is it okay if I lie down and sleep now? You don't want me to hack down a tree or anything, do you?"

He remained silent for a few seconds. "No, I don't think that'll be necessary. You may come in and sleep."

Before she could think of a reason not to, Leena gathered a large handful of snow, crunched it into a hard ball, and hurled it toward the voice despite her sore arms.

"Ouch!"

She could almost hear his smile as she curled up on her pallet to sleep. Drifting into slumber, she could not help noticing that, unlike Arvin, Darius had given them each a blanket.

TWENTY-ONE

Leena reined her horse to a stop and cast a spell to hide their fresh tracks beneath a layer of snow. Facing forward to start their trek again, her eyes locked on Darius's face. His body remained statue still as his jaw muscles pulsed with the rhythm of his clenching teeth.

"Can you cast a spell to leave a wind behind us that will hide our tracks as we travel instead of having to stop every few minutes?"

"If one exists, I don't know it." Leena shared his frustration. The same thought ran through her mind each time they had stopped to hide their horses' deep hoofprints.

Darius scanned the sky above the forest's scattered leafless oak tree branches. "Dark clouds are gathering on the western horizon. I'm guessing they'll be over us in another hour. I hope they'll drop just enough snow so you won't have to continue stopping to cover our tracks. It's been three days since we left the road, and we've barely made sixty miles. I can't afford any further delay if I'm to make my ship."

What? Her eyes narrowed. He stared at her, anger and frustration fighting for supremacy on his face. Was he saying that she was keeping him from going faster? How dare he! He'd said they couldn't use the road. He'd told her not to use the Branch. Didn't he realize every hedge witch spell sapped a bit more of her energy? It wasn't like she had an endless supply. It'd be okay if they could get a good night's sleep, but he kept pushing them forward as much as possible, or he would miss his bloody ship. She woke up every morning after spending half the night training, barely half the night asleep, and growing more tired every day. She didn't know how long she could keep up this casting level, and now he wanted her to do more.

Unthinking, Leena's heels dug deep into her mount's ribs. Startled, the horse leaped forward in hunching lunges, trying to make faster progress through the deep snow.

"Wait! Leena! Stop!"

Ignoring his shouts, Leena fought to increase her

mount's speed. The overused animal's scream sounded like a child's panicked cry. Tugging the reins, she brought the poor beast to a huffing stop. Huge fog-laden clouds blew from its nostrils as its flanks quivered with fatigue.

What am I doing? She cast a healing spell on her exhausted mount, using a bit more of her diminishing energy. Letting her head hang, she closed her eyes. *I need rest, but there's no time.*

Darius's mount rustled to a stop next to her.

"I'm sorry, Leena. I know you're doing the best you can." His hand touched her shoulder. He turned his head to the darkening sky to avoid her glare and let the hand drop to his lap. "Those clouds have me worried. We can't afford another six inches of snow. It's over three feet deep now, and our mounts are having trouble enough as it is. But what's worse is that it's been warming all day. If those clouds bring rain, we could be mired in deep mud and stuck here for days. I suggest we turn back to the road. With luck, it'll be hard-packed enough to be useable."

Not daring to speak, uncertain whether she would say something she could not take back later, Leena nodded. She hoped it would rain and hide the frustrated tears trickling down her cheeks.

❧

AFTER TWO RAIN-FILLED days of riding through downpours that melted snow during the day and froze into thin stone ice slabs at night, the bright morning sunlight polished the icy road with a light water sheen. Yesterday's blinding rain drove them into an early shelter. So, today, despite muscles still aching from her exercises last night, Leena yawned and stretched as she rode, enjoying the sensual pleasure of her body refreshed by an uninterrupted night's sleep for the first time in a week.

Her horse stumbled with a loud snort, and she grabbed the reins. She looked back to see what caused the horse to falter.

Brown mud patches peeked through the road's glistening ice surface in regular patterns behind them. With the weight of their riders and packs, the horses struggled, lifting forelegs coated with thick mud boots. Melting snow sent water streaming from the endless branches arcing over their thoroughfare, splattering drops onto the glittering icy road with the frequency of a mild summer rainstorm. Wet dirt and fresh-washed pine branches perfumed the air.

After riding for several hours, the noon sun hung like a yellow globe in a sea of blue, increasing the snowmelt from the trees and spattering the road in an escalating downpour around the two riders.

Thinning ice plates cracked and shattered beneath their horses' hooves. The horses' necks arched with heads down and bodies leaning forward. Exertion-generated whistles ruffled their nostrils as they labored to make headway.

"This is no good." Darius held up a hand, signaling the small procession to stop. "The mounts are working too hard. Their hearts will give out if we push them any further."

He walked his animal to the side of the road and dismounted. The horse's shoulder muscles jerked in spasms as though pestered by horse flies. Lather spotted the winter fur along its neck. The scent of warm horseflesh rose around them. Selecting a pine-bough retreat, Darius unsaddled and unpacked his horse. Although he tried to hide it, the worry lines around his mouth deepened at every stop.

He's thinking of time lost that he can't afford.

Leena dismounted and looked back along their trail. Deep holes filled with muddy water were all that remained of the horses' hoofprints. On either side of the lane, mud-brown snowmelt rivers danced in ice-lined channels.

At least we're the only ones stupid enough to be on the road in this weather. Leena understood Darius's impatience, but she could do nothing to help him travel faster. *And what happens when we get to the coast? Why am I even going east? If the Great Wizard had nothing to do with my family's disappearance, I have no idea where to look for them, so I have no destination. Maybe the Great Wizard could help me defeat Arvin and discover what he's done with my family.*

Her eyes focused on the road without seeing its turbulent flow or hearing its hushed babble.

This road was a mirrored reflection of her life. The part of her that went searching for the Garlan Branch was so innocent. But now, her life had been turned upside down by the dark pools and hidden depths created by schemes of dishonest people. The streams on either side represented people and events rushing by, unaware of her desperate quest. Without direction, there was no choice but to keep moving, keeping the hope alive that she would one day find her family. It didn't matter how many roads she'd travel, how many false leads she'd chase, or how her actions would affect her life or the lives of those she cared about. She vowed to never stop searching.

She shook her head to dispel the morbid thoughts. With a shrug of acceptance, she lifted the saddle from her mount and carried it into their new shelter.

～

"Iᴛ ʟᴏᴏᴋs like we'll be here for a while, probably until the temperature drops again," Darius said after checking the sky for the fourth time in the hour since they'd stopped. "After sunset, the road should harden with the nighttime chill."

Sighing, he eased to a seat on the pine needle floor. Worry lines furrowed his forehead. Leena's heart hurt to see his concern. With a gentle touch, she rested her fingertips on his arm, hoping to assure him she understood his churning emotions. His eyes found hers, and their stares locked, only for a moment, but in that instant, a thrill rushed through her chest unlike anything she had known. She jerked her eyes away.

What was that? Gazing into the fire, she searched for answers. *What did he do to me?* Her heart thundered in her chest, sending a heated rush to her cheeks. *No, I'm a silly little girl letting my imagination run wild. I'm sure he felt nothing.*

Edging her eyes up again, she was surprised to see her shock and wonder reflected in his deep-blue eyes. Again, an electric charge raced from her brain through her limbs and heart. Her hand jerked from his arm as they broke their stare. Like a dense fog, the silent awareness of the emotion that passed between them hung in the air, enveloping them.

"I suppose I should start dinner," her voice rasped.

"I need to check how the weather's doing," Darius croaked. As though needing to be somewhere else, he stood and stepped just outside the opening, staring at the cloud-covered sky. Leena dug the pot and bowls from their packs. Kneeling, her hands filled with dishes, she watched Darius, his eyes fixed on the sky, his posture ramrod straight and unmoving.

She knew he wasn't studying the clouds. She wondered what was going through his mind. *No, I can't think of that now. I'm sure it's just road fatigue and our enforced closeness that set my stomach churning and my fingers tingling. Stop it! I'm sure he'll return and be his usual bossy self again in a few minutes.*

As though her thoughts precipitated his actions, Darius entered the shelter.

"I think, m'lady, you should perform your exercises while I fix us something to eat."

It was just my imagination. That's a relief. Now we can return to normal, and he'll never know...whatever happened within me, if anything did.

"Wait a moment. That's not fair. I'm the cook here," Leena said, wanting to remain by the fire rather than fight the weather outside. Trying to look fierce, she jammed her fists against her sides, elbows spread wide, and glared at him.

Darius avoided looking at her. "One of the first things a knight learns is how to fend for himself. That includes cooking. I'm hungry. So, while you practice, I'll cook." The words were emotionless as he stepped past her and rummaged through their packs.

Leena waited, hoping for more. Darius remained silent, thoughtful. Although she relaxed her arms and angry stare, a frustrated growl rose from her throat as she stomped from the shelter and into the slushy, pine needle-covered snow. Drawing the Elven blade, she began her exercises. Frenzied whistling slashed through the air with a strength that could slay ten ogres with a single stroke. As stiff, sore muscles warmed, her anger faded, and she found joy in the flow of movement for the first time since beginning her training with the Elven blade.

Finished training, skin glistening with the sweat of pleasant fatigue, Leena wandered back into the shelter and sat on a log near the fire. In silence, Darius handed her a hot bowl of boiled oats mixed with dried fruit and topped with honey. Her tummy growled in anticipation. She dug into the meal, her spoon flying from bowl to mouth like she had not eaten in days. Darius's serious expression transformed into a smile.

"What is your problem? Haven't you ever seen a woman eat before?" Leena's forehead grooved as she glared at him.

His grin broadened. "Except for a few mother wolves, I've seen no creature attack food quite like that."

Her hand clenched around the bowl as she considered hurling it at him, but its cargo was too precious to waste. His smile diminished when he gazed at the fire, although a ghost of it remained.

"I think the exercises that gave you such trouble a few days ago have already become too easy. It's surprising how quickly you've mastered them. Tomorrow, we'll add a few new ones."

After cleaning their dishes, Leena stepped outside. The temperature dropped as the cloud-hidden sun settled behind the western horizon. She rubbed her arms to increase their warmth. Father Winter thickened the ice skins on the puddles in the road. She shivered as she removed the leather-thong hobbles and led the horses toward the shelter.

Darius had everything packed when she returned. Leena placed oat-filled feeding bags over her horse's ears while Darius stacked their packs and provisions, ready to load them when the icy road solidified enough to leave.

Darius studied the road when dusk settled into darkness."I know it'll be tough traveling without sleep tonight. But we have no choice. Try to nap in your saddle if you can."

They set out on their journey. A chill northern wind intensified with every passing minute, biting into every gap in their clothing as winter's cold returned with a vengeance. The only sound they could hear above the howling wind was the ring of iron horseshoes on the frozen road surface.

Hours passed. Leena guessed it was midnight. Clouds covered the sky like a dark blanket hiding the moon and stars. With every step, the horses stumbled over the uneven ice, unable to see the road. *We can't travel like this. It's only a matter of time before a horse breaks an ankle.*

Leena touched her hedge witch wand and added an illumination spell to the full-time warming spells they needed. As warm as their outer garments were, their clothing did little to combat the deadly cold. She was grateful for the afternoon rest, which helped restore some of her energy reserves. These three spells weren't a significant energy drain, but their demand was constant. If the temperature remained steady, she could make it until morning.

Hour after hour, the temperature dropped, increasing the drain on her energy reserves. With loud snaps, the ice cracked beneath the horse's hooves. Ahead, Darius rode hunched over, his dark blue cape wrapped around him in a tight cocoon. A thick black scarf hid his chin and nose. Only his half-closed eyes remained visible. The intense cold was using up the warming spells' energy too rapidly. With a shivering shrug, he burrowed deeper into his bulky clothing nest.

Maybe we should seek shelter. How much longer can we ride without risking frostbite? It'd be no problem to heal us, but it'll be another energy drain. It could deplete her reserves long before morning. But they might not make it till morning if she didn't do something.

With gentle heels digging into her mount's sides, Leena increased her speed to ride beside Darius. She removed her glove with her teeth, struggled the bare hand beneath her thick coat, touched her hedge witch wand, and sent the mental command to renew his warming spell. As though rising from a daydream, his head lifted. He sat straighter and turned to look at her.

He nodded his head. "Thanks."

It was a simple word, but she could not miss the appreciation in his eyes.

"I can't keep these spells active much longer. We need to stop and rest soon." She wrestled her shivering hand back into the glove.

A nervous stomach, the first sign of spell drain, tingled within her. Insufficient sleep for several nights, plus maintaining the illumination and two warming spells, was taking its toll. *Please, Spirit, let my magic reserves hold out until morning.*

"The town of Lovell is about twenty miles ahead." Leena struggled to understand Darius's scarf-muffled words. "There's an inn there. We should arrive by dawn. It'll be a good place to hold up. We need some time off the road."

"That sounds so wonderful. There's little I wouldn't do for a hot bath about now." A smile rose on her face at the thought. The smile fled, replaced by a flaming blush rising on her cheeks as the sparkle in his eyes alerted her to the implications of her words.

"But some things are strictly done in private," she huffed, turning to look ahead.

Leena needed to conserve energy. Darius would not survive if she passed into a spell-drain coma. She allowed the illumination spell to dissipate. *I have no choice.* If she held this reduced drain level, she could maintain their warming spells for another three hours, with luck, maybe four.

As the light from her spell faded, a wisp of dawn painted the crest of faraway hills with a mild pink aura.

A sudden icy wind engulfed the two riders, plunging them into terrible, blinding darkness within the frigid blizzard whirling around them. Trees lining the road waved ghostlike branches like phantom arms. The ever-increasing cold drained her inner reserves as Leena fought to maintain the two warming spells.

Ten miles of glacial road still separated them from the town of Lovell. The cold grated chilled tendrils against Leena's cheeks. She needed more warmth. Closing her eyes, she willed her warming spell to increase its strength. Nothing changed.

Darius remained silent. Leena could not tell whether he was deep in thought or resented her silence. She wished he would say something. Although she needed the comfort of his voice, she had no strength to start a conversation.

With slow, regular precision, the horses dared not stop. The temperature was well below that necessary to freeze water. If they remained stationary, the horses would freeze.

Leena's head hung in fatigue. *Maybe dawn will bring warmth.* She lifted her eyes with immense effort and let them drift toward the trees to her right. *The sun should appear in less than half an hour. I have to maintain my spells until then. With luck, the sun's warmth will ease my burden.*

Her horse stumbled. She pulled its head up using the reins but had no reserves to reduce the animal's fatigue with magic. Time crept past. Landmarks mocked her by remaining hidden. Only by the road passing beneath them could she see any progress. They could not be traveling over three miles an hour.

With the slow caution of a shy turtle venturing its nose into the world, the sun peeked above the horizon. The surrounding snow grew pink, lined with gray tree shadows as their horses' plodding hooves clattered them forward.

Leena's stomach rolled, and a wave of dizziness washed over her. It seemed years since her mum had warned her about the life-threatening dangers of depleting her magic reserves. *I can't maintain two warming spells any longer. Darius won't survive without one.* She removed the warming spell from herself. *I'll keep his spell active as long as I can.*

The dawn now provided enough light for Darius to see her. *I can't let him see me weakening.* Her mind spiraled into dizzying blackness. She grabbed the pommel. Supported by her grip, Leena straightened herself in the saddle. The dizziness passed. *Another wave will return in minutes, and the dizziness will increase until I can ride no longer. But I can't let Darius freeze to death.*

Through the red dawn haze, a break in the forest appeared ahead. It might be a natural clearing, and Leena hoped they were close enough to town that it could be a farmer's field.

An all-consuming black wave threatened her vision. With no warming spell, the icy winter air bit through her clothing, working its way into the tender, unprotected flesh beneath. The bitter cold flowed into muscles and blood, draining all remaining reserves.

The pommel seemed miles away as her hand reached to snag it and missed. Her world tilted. She had no strength left to stop it. An arm grabbed her from nowhere and lifted her back into the saddle.

"Leena," Darius's voice floated over her from far away. A pleasant warmth replaced the chill within her at the sound. "Leena? Are you okay..."

The voice faded. Darkness pulled her into its embrace.

TWENTY-TWO

Leena drifted on a sea of memories: her da teaching her how to make patterns and sew without pricking her fingers; her mum walking with her through summer forests alive with chittering insects and varied birdcalls; her mum showing her and Riana how to approach nervous animals, to sense their health and heal them; she and Riana lying in dappled sunlight by a laughing summer brook calling butterflies and making grand plans for the future; the family in a wagon returning from the harvest festival in Stocksbury; the four of them around the hearth laughing together, loving one another with no restraint as they relived joy-filled events and mild embarrassments.

A gentle hand nudged her shoulder. Something out here in the waking world was pulling at her from a distance, trying to separate her from pleasant memories of her past, something fighting to draw her into a world she did not want to re-enter.

"Leena." Darius's low, soothing voice beckoned.

It's too much, too soon. I can't answer. Not yet. Her mind fled from his concerned tone, racing like a panicked spirit into memories of a safe, warm, and loving world.

"Leena, you must try to come back."

How dare he? I've been through enough! My life and everyone I love have been ripped away from me. Every-thing within me screams I must find my family, but even that hope has been dashed. I have no starting point or hint of a direction that offers even a slight hope of locating them. I've earned the right to a few moments of peace.

Wood clattered against a ceramic bowl beside her cheek. As though happening to someone else, a muscular arm burrowed beneath her shoulders, lifting her head. The familiar warmth of a soup-filled carved wooden spoon touched her lips. The mouth-watering aroma of boiled tomato, garden vegetables, and herbs flooded Leena's nostrils. *It smells like Mum's prize-winning vegetable soup. It can't be. She can't be here. What if this is just a dream? Maybe if I let myself slip deeper into sleep, the smell will disappear.*

With intrusive insistence, the spoon forced itself between her lips. Without allowing her mind to wake, Leena parted her lips and let the liquid's healing goodness ease down her parched throat. A smile rose in her mind. Her resistance to the meal faded as her exhausted body gathered strength from the warm flow. Her mind relaxed, and her internal heat increased with each touch of the spoon against her lips.

A growing thickness beneath her tongue warned that her stomach could hold no more. The excellent meal had provided enough for the moment. She would need much more food to replace her energy reserves. However, she also required restorative strength, which only sleep could provide. Eyes still closed, unable to maintain her meager grip on the world, Leena let her mind float into a dreamless sleep.

Something disturbing approached. A cold, not of air but of soul, drew near, searching for her. An inner voice screamed at her to wake. She had to protect herself now. Alert, she let her dreams tatter and float away. *First, I must know where I am and who else is here.* Keeping her eyes closed in case anyone watched, waiting for her to awaken, she listened to the room.

The heavy breathing of someone deep in exhausted sleep joined the gay crackling of a nearby fire. Opening her eyes, Leena scanned a room illuminated only by the flickering glow of dancing flames in a fireplace to the left of her bed. She lay warm and cozy beneath a thick comforter, allowing her nose to enjoy the soothing scent of a pine log fire.

Where am I?

Except for the fire and the lack of a window, this could be the bedroom she shared with Riana in Quillan. *No, don't go there.* She needed to find out where she was and what caused the horrible feeling that woke her.

Muted rustling beneath her as she shifted her weight told Leena she was lying on a cornhusk-stuffed mattress. Next to the bed, Darius slept in a straight-back wooden chair, still wearing his traveling clothes, head drooped forward with his chin resting against his chest. *Ouch. He'll pay for that position with a sore neck when he wakes. Wait, he's still dressed. Am I?*

Alarmed, her hands fled beneath the covers to find she still wore her riding clothes. Her toes rasping against the thick down comforter told her she was barefoot. Her boots sat next to the bed stuffed with muddy gray socks.

Did we make it to the inn in Lovell? And who fed me? Did Darius go to the kitchen and get me a bowl of soup? If so, where are the bowl and spoon? Did someone come into the room to collect them before putting the lights out?

Eyes darting from corner to corner as she scanned the small space, Leena searched for any signs of danger hidden in the flickering firelight. To her left, three feet behind the unforgiving chair where Darius slept, tidy stacks of quilts and pillows rested on a pine shelf mounted to the log wall. Unfamiliar shirts, jackets, and trousers hung on pegs embedded in the wall beneath the shelf. Beyond the foot of her bed, two quilts hung from a rod, like curtains, centered on the far wall, creating a cozy focal point. Several straw shafts waited to aid in lighting the unlit lantern atop a compact three-drawer dresser against the right wall. Her and Darius's packs lay in an untidy pile in the rippling shadows next to the dresser.

What woke me?

Another wave of dread and fear flowed over her. Something evil, bent on her destruction, grew closer to the room where she slept. Even without seeing it, Leena's mind screamed a warning that a raven neared, searching for her. She trembled with fear, remembering the towering creatures at the Garlan Tree and her two encounters with bandits.

How many ravens does Arvin have? How does this bird know I'm here? I haven't used the Branch. There's no time for that now. I have to run. I need to get away before it kills anyone else while trying to find me. Uncontrolled terror raced through her mind, freezing her limbs as it erased logical thought. *No! This is no time for panic. I have to think.*

Leena stopped breathing, waiting as her thoughts slowed. Was it possible the bird could sense the Branch? If so, how long did she have before the Garlan Branch revealed her? Each heartbeat thundered louder as the distance between her and the monster narrowed. With slow movements, hesitating with every rustle from the corn-shuck mattress, Leena reached beneath her tunic. Relief fought fear when her fingers slid toward the Garlan Branch. With every second, the creature's dreaded aura grew.

No! Every time she used the Garlan Branch, a raven appeared. But not until after she used it. Why was this bird here now? Arvin must have realized they were not on the Wizard's Highway by now. So his next logical move would be to send a fleet of birds searching for her in every direction, hoping she would panic and use the Branch to destroy one.

Her hand froze an inch away from the Branch.

An even more horrifying thought threatened her sanity. What if she didn't use the Branch and the raven still found her? How many people would die before Arvin sent more ravens? She and Darius would be dead if that unfortunate soldier hadn't diverted one raven while she fought the other at the bandit's ambush. It would be suicidal to expect that kind of luck again. She was too weak to run, but she couldn't stay here. Darius was powerless against this magic and would die trying to protect her. She had to face the bird alone.

Slow and cautious, she crept off the bed, careful not to wake Darius with the rustling mattress. *Spirit, help me. What can I do?* Her heart crashed against her ribs, drowning all external sound with its ocean wave drumbeat pounding in her ears. Deep in her soul, she knew the creature was close. Leena struggled to remain conscious as dark spots danced before her eyes.

Like an ebbing tide, the dreaded shivering within her diminished as she sensed the creature passing away from her. A whispered sigh eased from her lips when the threat subsided. Leena cast a healing spell over herself with her hedge witch wand. At the speed of thought, her strength returned. Along with the spell drain that afflicted her on the road, the crippling fear was gone. Her mind leaped to crystal sharpness.

Oh no! Again, the shadow of evil intent approached. The creature didn't find her on its last pass, but she feared it would narrow its search with each flyby. She couldn't use the Garlan Branch's protection spell, but she could use the hedge witch wand's Branch-enhanced protection spell. With a silent prayer, Leena closed her eyes and touched her hedge witch wand, letting the spell flow from her mind and through her fingers.

She looked toward Darius. Shuddering anxiety flowed over his sleeping face. Sweat glistened on his brow in the flickering ruby light as a grimace painted his face. His head rose in the first sign of waking. He, too, felt the presence. Unthinking, Leena expanded the protection spell to include him. A peaceful smile settled over him, confirming the spell worked. With a small snort, he sank back into peaceful dreams.

The released tension in her chest also told Leena that the bird had passed again. It no longer scanned this area. *But I must find out if it's leaving is a ploy to lure me into the open. But what if someone comes in while I'm away? I can't leave Darius here invisible. That might bring on too many questions.* Hoping Darius would not sink back into disturbing dreams, Leena reduced the spell's protective area to cover only herself.

Making as little noise as possible, Leena lifted the comforter and swung her trouser-clad legs over the edge of the bed. Digging the wadded socks from her boots, she threw the wool balls on the floor and slid her bare feet into the supple leather footgear. There was no time for socks. She needed to be outside before the raven returned in case it sensed whoever else was in this building and used them to draw her out.

Her steps made no noise on the packed-earth floor as she glided between the hanging quilts in the doorway. In the room beyond, the firelight revealed a large older man and an equally substantial woman sleeping under a blanket, rolled together before a fireplace's heat on a makeshift pallet of corn husks. The woman's head rested on the man's barrel chest. His arm draped over her shoulder in a comfortable embrace. Their weatherworn faces smiled, lost in peaceful dreams like overage cherubs in sleep.

Nope, this is definitely not a hotel. I wonder what Darius has gotten us into this time.

With careful footsteps, Leena navigated beyond the couple snuggled near the fire, past two well-worn rocking chairs and a sturdy oak table with four solid chairs, to the front door. Lifting the bolt, she slipped through, easing the door shut behind her to reduce the rush of cold outside air invading the room. Beyond the covered porch, a pale moon lit the silent winter landscape. Somewhere in that sky, an evil bird searched, but the snow-covered yard before her was quiet and at rest.

Snow slid down her ankles and into her boots when Leena plodded through the eighteen-inch deep snow between the house and a large, weathered, wood-plank barn. *Maybe leaving my socks off was not the best idea. My feet will freeze before I make it to the barn.* Thoughts of her feet fled when a shadow rippled across the unbroken snow in front of her. Her eyes snapped toward the moonlit sky. *Oh, Spirit. I may be invisible, but what if it sees the fresh tracks behind me?* In the distance, a giant raven with outstretched wings glided toward her. *Please, please don't look this way.* With a tilt of its wings, the immense bird turned aside, tracing a methodical pattern as it hunted farther away.

It's lost me. The Branch-enhanced protection spell worked.

The coast was clear. Leena ran toward the barn. Inside, she leaned against the door, closed her eyes, and breathed deeply to slow her racing heart. Using her light spell, Leena surveyed the interior. Their three horses huddled with two other horses, sharing their body warmth with six milk cows. She cast a warming spell on the animals that would last until morning. As she did, she noticed no significant drain on her inner resources. Somehow, the Branch's protection spell fed her hedge witch wand additional power. She reminded herself that she must explore the potential and limits of this sharing soon.

Relying on her four years of training, Leena examined the animals. The cattle were healthy but slim because of meager winter rations, which reduced their milk output. She sent a hedge witch healing spell to fatten and strengthen them to summer production levels. Three of them would calf this spring, so she expanded the healing spell to include the calves. With no further misfortune, the calves would be born fat and healthy.

Once warm, the horses wandered from their grouping and buried their noses in feeding troughs along the wall. As their contented munching filled the air, Leena checked them to ensure they suffered no permanent damage from the cold. All were well.

Retracing her footprints, Leena returned to the house. Slipping back beneath her comforter in the bedroom, she debated whether to remove the protection spell. Even extended to their extreme limit, her senses could no longer feel the raven. Having her invisible when the farmer and his wife awoke would not do. She removed the spell, trusting that her senses would alert her to danger.

It's time to consider what I should do next. Darius said we'll have a plan by the time we get to the coast. But aside from teaching me how to use my sword, he's come up with nothing useful.

With hands clasped behind her head, staring at the pale red firelight flickering over the dark ceiling, Leena wished she knew enough to plan her future.

TWENTY-THREE

"Once the milking's done, I'll go to town and fetch the hedge witch." A deep masculine voice floated through the makeshift doorway, pulling Leena from her reverie. Darius opened his eyes, rubbing them with twisting fists like a child awakening from a nap.

"That won't be necessary," Leena called as she slipped from the bed, paced across the small room, parted the quilt curtains, and stepped through. Beyond, the burly man tugged his wide, leather belt tighter beneath his homespun cotton shirt as though dressing to suit company.

Why did I say that? I don't know these people. After the condition I arrived in last night, he'll have to wonder what I mean, and I can't tell him. For all I know, these people might hate or fear hedge witches. Maybe he didn't hear what I said.

"Morning, m'lady. How're you feeling?" A cautious smile rose on the man's weatherworn face, his words uncertain as though unsure how to address this stranger. As he waited for her answer, his gray eyebrows rose in an expression that asked for more explanation than the question required. Despite his severe appearance—short-cropped gray hair and two-day beard stubble—he had a kind face and weather-crinkled smile lines at the corners of his eyes.

Yes. I don't think he noticed my statement.

"Famished. Would you have another bowl of that soup you could spare? It was delicious."

"Of course, m'lady. I kept it warm in case you woke up so famished you couldn't wait for break-fast." the woman said in a gentle voice. She stood and brushed sleep wrinkles from her floor-length, dark-blue cotton dress. Skirt neatened, the woman lifted farm-worn hands to smooth stray hairs into the gray bun on the back of her head with practiced effort. She folded their pallet and blankets with rapid, deft movements and stacked the neat pile in the room's corner. Her dress swishing, the woman bustled to the fireplace, grabbed a bowl from the mantle above, and ladled steaming soup.

The pair looked so similar, with pale blue eyes and solid, work-hardened bodies, that they could be brother and sister. Watching them, how they flowed around each other, and their instant trust and comfort with these strangers reminded Leena of the honest, hard-working farmers she knew in Quillan. Her heart told her they could be instant friends. She hoped they felt the same.

Darius stepped through the curtained doorway. "You seem quite chipper for a person who nearly froze to death. Seriously, how are you?"

"I feel great." Darius's eyes scanned her face as though waiting for more. With a finger to her lips, Leena whispered, "It was just a touch of spell drain. My mother often warned me about it, but I'd never suffered it before. I guess I'll know my limits better next time."

Darius raised a comforting hand to squeeze her shoulder, but hesitated. The moment passed as the farmwife brushed by them, carrying a large steaming bowl. His hand dropped.

Setting the bowl on the table, the woman lifted a spoon filled with the hearty soup and nodded Leena toward a chair. Laughing, Leena held up a hand. "Thank you, m'lady, but I'm quite well enough to feed myself."

The couple studied Leena's face, worry lines creasing their foreheads.

"So, from your morning greeting, I guess you'd be some sort of a hedge witch." The man's low, soothing voice resonated through the comfortable room.

Drat, he heard me. Oh well, I'll have to own up and hope for the best.

"I'm only half-trained so far, but I intend to become a full-fledged hedge witch someday."

"Well, now you eat, dearie. We can talk about all that other stuff later." The woman smiled and pushed the bowl in front of Leena. The soup was as good as she remembered.

The farmer's wife bustled about, starting breakfast for the rest of them as the men walked out the front door. "We're the Gundersons, m'lady. I'm Elke, and the big oaf that's just gone out with your husband to milk the cows is Gunnar."

Something in Leena's chest leaped at the word *husband*. With an effort, she pulled herself from the inner confusion it created.

"I'm Leena, and my...associate is Darius. He's not my husband, only a traveling companion who rescued me from a difficult situation. I believe he's a good man, but I hardly know him. Sometimes, I'm not at all sure I want to. But..." she stopped, then said, "sometimes he seems pretty nice."

She knew she was babbling and felt helpless to stop. Her cheeks reddened under Elke's raised eyebrows.

"I think he is not your husband... yet," Elke said, turning to her chores. "So, what brings you two out on the road in this weather? A person could freeze at night out there. Are you running from someone?"

More heat infused Leena's face. Although Elke's tone remained casual, Leena sensed its seriousness. *How could she know? What can I say? These are simple folk who want no trouble from the authorities. I need time to think.*

Leena scanned the meager furnishings. A tin wash tub sat on the kitchen counter for washing dishes. Many sacks and bottles sat in neat rows on shelves above the sideboard. No art graced the walls.

They weren't wealthy farm folk, and it was a poor farm, yet they kept their small house warm and comfortable. They had so few cows, and those were bone-thin. She was happy to have plumped them up with her spell. This place wasn't as large or well-furnished as her home in Quillan, but it had the same warm and loving feel. *I can't risk bringing harm to them.*

Elke sat silent, her patient eyes waiting. Tension grew within Leena the longer she hesitated to respond. *I need to tell her something.*

"There was some trouble in Quillan, my hometown. I met a young boy there who suggested we try to find someone to help fix it, so we headed north. We got as far as Pineton before the lad ran off. Without him, I didn't know where to go to get help. So there I was, stuck without knowing how to reach my destination or anyone who could guide me. Fortunately, I met Darius at the hotel, and when he told me he was a Great Wizard's knight, I felt I could trust him."

Interest and concern grew on Elke's face when Leena described how the wretched road conditions during the daytime warmth had forced them to travel at night. By the time they discovered the error of that logic, it was too late to do anything but continue.

Under the woman's comfortable gaze, Leena's trust and understanding of this big woman's heart grew. With every word, Leena felt them drawing closer. The feeling blossoming within her reflected the love she and her family shared. Leena stared into Elke's tender eyes and found the same feelings growing in the older woman, connecting them. A slight touch on Leena's hand drew her eyes to the table, where Elke's hand now rested soft on hers. Leena sank into the warm comfort of another soul who was nurturing and motherly.

"I've never seen the like of it," Gunnar rumbled when he burst through the front door, interrupting the bond growing between the two women. Darius came in behind him. "The three cows who calved last year are producing like it's mid-growing season. I had to pull the summer buckets out of the loft, and I thought they'd not hold enough! We've filled the skimming vat." He turned to Leena. "I guess you had a busy night."

Leena's cheeks flared. "I...uh...woke up in a strange place and wanted to see where I was. So, I wandered outside, saw the barn, and decided to check the horses. They were okay, so I sent them a warming spell and tended to the cows while I was there." She needed to change the subject. She did not want any speculation on the extent of a hedge witch's powers. Gunnar must have realized the animals had spent the night warm. "How did I end up here?" Leena asked.

"Oh, that's a tale to tell," Gunnar's loud voice rumbled through the room. "Early yesterday morning, it was. This gentleman came running down the road carrying you like you were a baby, yelling, 'Where's Lovell? We need a healer.' I was just out the door to do the milking when I seen him loping along like a startled rabbit. He runs up to me, telling me I've got to help him. I looked down at you and had to admit you were a mess, thin as a fence post and flopping like a wee one's cloth doll. I told him you must of passed clean through Lovell in the snow-blinding dark a few miles back. The look in his eyes near broke my heart.

"I could see you'd probably never make it back to town alive, so I called Elke, and we tucked you in while your mister went running back for your mounts. That man was in nearly as bad a shape as you when he returned. So, I turned him over to the missus to deal with while I took the horses out to the barn, rubbed them down, and fed them some oats and hay.

"By the time I got back, he's sitting in there calling your name like he's trying to wake the dead and rubbing your hands hard enough to start a fire. Your eyes tried to open for a moment, so Elke rushed to get you some hot soup. Although you were fast asleep and your eyes never opened, this man of yours sat there and spoon-fed you soup until it started dribbling down your chin. Then he sat there all yesterday and last night.

"I tell you, miss, you're a lucky one. A regular

woman wouldn't be here to tell the tale. Yet here you are, fit as a spring day."

Gunnar's face was animated when he spoke. His voice held pride, and his eyes glowed with glee. The growing kinship for this couple deepened within her.

"If you gentlemen will get out of them heavy coats, breakfast is about ready." Elke set the bubbling pot on the table atop a worn, charred board. Leena smelled oats with a hint of apple. Although she had just finished a bowl of soup, her stomach leaped at the delicious odor.

"There's more than enough if you'd care to join us." Elke's eyes locked with Leena's. Leena fought the urge to jump up and hug the older woman. With no warning, her teeth clamped on her lower lip as a ledge of tears blurred her vision. She struggled to smile through them for a moment and failed. Without warning, Leena burst from the table, ran through the blanket door, pitched herself on the cornhusk mattress, and cried like her world was ending.

THROUGH THE SILENCE beyond the quilt-covered

portal, wooden chair legs scraped across the hard-packed floor in the other room.

"You gentlemen, just sit and have your breakfast." Elke's command held the powerful ring of maternal authority.

Leena sensed, rather than heard, the blanket lift. She tried but was helpless to slow the sensitive emotions boiling within her. Memories of mother-comforted trauma flooded through her as two muscular arms lifted and nestled her head into the woman's gentle, comforting embrace. Through rough linen, Elke's strong heartbeat calmed her with the steady pulse of a distant drum.

"There, there now. You just let it all out." The farmwife's comforting tone reached deep within her, releasing a new flood of tears. Gentle, loving pats soothed her back.

"I know. Sometimes, a woman goes along, holding her hurts and emotions, until she gets so pent up that she don't know how to let them out anymore. Then one day, without warning, it all bubbles up, and the dam breaks."

The soft, singsong voice rolled through Leena, touching places locked away since discovering her family's disappearance. Fighting her tears, she tried to say everything was all right. The words came out in an indecipherable mumble.

"There, there, child." Elke's hand rubbed large, soothing circles between her shoulder blades. "Hush now. We'll have plenty of time to talk later."

Accompanying the back rub, Elke hummed a soft lullaby, filling the room with its calming melody. Its magic worked. The pain, fear, hurt from loss, and loneliness ebbed. This place, this woman, radiated the love, care, and concern her family had shared. She felt safe, trusted, and valuable for the first time since this nightmare began.

Within minutes, her cries dwindled to sniffles, then occasional hitches. Gradually, Leena's breathing returned to normal. With a last tight squeeze, Elke pushed her back and looked into her eyes. The older woman wiped the tears from Leena's face using gentle thumbs. Her sturdy face glowed with concern, acceptance, and understanding.

"Well," Elke stood and straightened her apron, "I think it's time we finish breakfast before it gets cold."

Leena leaped up and pulled the big woman into a firm embrace. "Thank you," she whispered.

"Believe me, child,"—Elke stared at her, joy mixed with sorrow in her eyes—"I needed that as much as you."

Darius sat telling Gunnar about their travels when Leena returned to the table and scooped a bowlful of steaming oats. She sat, tired and ravenous, her emotions raw but cleansed within. She thanked the Spirit that neither man appeared to notice her outburst.

Gunnar looked at her. A big, honest grin wrinkled the corners of his eyes and bulged his cold-reddened cheeks. "Darius here was telling me about your adventures with the bandits. He tried to sound like he was the hero, but it seems to me you done most of the heavy lifting." The man's loud voice matched the mischievous glint in his eyes.

"That's not fair," she replied lightly, hoping her tone would assure the men that everything was all right. "He's been a good deal of help."

Darius's eyes widened with surprise as he sputtered a mouth full of food in protest and started choking. Rumbling a deep laugh, Gunnar slapped Darius on the back with enough force to send him leaning forward over the table.

"I see what you mean. This young man requires a bit of care, doesn't he?"

Darius sat back and cleared his throat. "I'm grateful m'lady found my humble support useful."

Although his expression was serious, his eyes smiled into hers. Touched, Leena reached over and brushed her fingers against the back of his hand. From the corner of her eyes, she noticed a knowing nod exchanged between the older couple. Flustered, she jerked her hand back.

Elke gathered bowls and moved to the wash-basin to scrub them.

"So, my young travelers," Gunnar said, "what are your plans for today? Although it's bright and sunny, the cold's still got a grip of iron. If you're in no rush, I suggest you wait a day or so to see if it starts warming up a bit. These late winter cold snaps don't usually last long. I'd be surprised if this one doesn't signal the start of spring."

Gunnar and Elke both struggled to hide hopeful expressions. Having been raised in a rural community, Leena understood the mind-numbing boredom brought on by winter. Once mending and fixing were completed, they had little to do except care for their animals. No matter how deeply a couple cared for each other, with long days of inactivity and only each other's company, winter conversations became repetitive.

But we can't stay. Darius has a schedule to keep.

"How many days' riding is the coast from here?" she asked.

Matching disappointment on the older couple's faces told Leena how much they hoped she and Darius would not leave soon.

"Well, that'd be nearly two days of travel on

good roads, and these aren't so good right now." Gunnar looked down, shaking his head. "How soon do you have to be there?"

Darius's jaw muscles clenched. "My ship sails in three days. I'm supposed to be there no later than two days from now to draw my gear for the trip."

"I'm sorry, Darius. But there are nearly thirty miles between here and the coast. You could maybe make fifteen miles a day in the muddy daytime. You might do a little better at night on the ice, but I think you've seen the problems with that. Won't they hold the ship for you if you don't arrive on time?"

"No, it's not just me. There'll also be a company of soldiers aboard the military ship. A few months ago, a merchant vessel stumbled across a new land to the east and requested military protection for their trading venture. The Great Wizard agreed to provide support ships and troops. I've been dispatched as the Great Wizard's representative for negotiations."

Studying the table as if it held deep secrets, Gunnar rubbed work-roughened palms together, lost in thought. Then he said, "So, where are these protection troops coming from?" He raised his head and stared at Darius.

"They'd have to come from Weymouth. It's the

only garrison this side of Elderon with enough troops to supply the hundred soldiers needed." Darius's brow creased.

"Uh-huh." Gunnar nodded. "And that'd mean they have to pass here on the same road you just traveled. Well, I guess that's not a problem then. You two are the first travelers who have passed here in more than a week."

Darius nodded, considering the older man's words. He smiled. "I guess there's not such a hurry then. The merchant ship won't sail away without a military ship to protect it. We can join the troops as they pass, and it would be nice to let the weather warm a little. Looking at the road, that may still be a day or two if we're lucky. So, if Leena would like to stay here until then..." Darius looked at her, his face neutral.

Leena raised her brow. Darius would leave with her now and take her to the coast if she felt pressured to continue. She needed to resume her quest, but what good would it be to rush off without direction? The North Road was the only way to Elderon and was likely covered with those posters by now. As Darius pointed out, she had little chance of making it there alone, and there was no one else she could trust. What was her plan if she arrived at the Great Wizard's castle? Walk in and demand an audience? She was one young girl among the herd of petitioners the Great Wizard saw daily. And what if their conjectures about Arvin were mistaken, and the Great Wizard had issued the posters? *No, I can't think of that now. I need more time to decide which direction to go. A day or two here might give me that.*

Leena nodded. Darius turned to Gunnar.

"We'll stay until we can join the soldiers, but on the condition that I be allowed to help with the heavy chores around here."

Gunnar smiled. "Now that's a bargain I can't pass up, young man. But I don't think you know what you're letting yourself in for. This winter's been colder than most, so we're running low on firewood. As it just happens, there's a large forest out back."

Darius shrugged as Gunnar shoved his huge paw toward him to seal the bargain.

"Well, with a few extra mouths around here, I think I'll go into Lovell and pick up enough provisions to feed us for the next few days." Elke stood and headed into the bedroom to grab a wrap from the wall pegs. "I could use some company, dear, if you'd care to come along?"

"I'd like that," Leena said. "I should also grab a few things to replenish our stores." Her glance fell to Elke's threadbare shawl. "You don't need to worry. I have a spell to keep us warm long enough to get there and back."

I know we've only just met, but I feel safe with Elke. Many villagers suspected strangers until they were given a reason not to. At least in Elke's company, Leena would have an ally if needed.

The two stepped through the front door with elbows interlocked like schoolgirl friends.

TWENTY-FOUR

After the smoke-laden fragrance of cottage air, Leena inhaled a deep breath, filling her lungs with the crisp, clean bite of the outside breeze. Chilled sunlight glinted and sparkled on the snow-covered ground beneath a cloudless blue sky. Their footsteps, sinking through a thin, icy layer atop the soft snow, crunched in the snowy wonderland. Pine trees faded into the distance, providing a colorful backdrop to the summer-shading oaks lining the road edges. The oaks' sturdy, leafless branches arched over the unblemished road ahead, their breeze-driven movement dancing thin-lined shadows over the track's smooth snow covering. Leena's spirit soared, alive and buoyant for the first time since the tragedy in Quillan.

"I reckon spell-casting's a handy trait." Elke looked down at her ungloved hands, marveling that they were not frozen.

"It has its uses," Leena admitted with a smile.

The women walked arm in arm without speaking for a few minutes, each thinking private thoughts.

"Gunnar and I have been married for over thirty years." Elke's muted tone rose above their snow-crushing footsteps. "You should have seen him when he was a handsome young man. Ladies from everywhere came to festivals just to see him. Not that he's not still handsome, mind you, but at eighteen, he made your insides melt. We've known each other since we were babies. I supposed we always knew we'd be together. There's never been a day I don't wake up loving him. And, oh, the plans we had. At least a dozen children, all happy and bright. A strong, loving family that would grow together, healthy and prosperous."

Elke lapsed into thoughtful silence. Leena waited, not wanting to intrude on the older woman's thoughts.

"We had a daughter once. Tisa, we called her. The birthing was hard, and the midwife said I'd likely not have another. Tisa was beautiful, but the poor wee thing was sickly and didn't survive her first winter."

"Oh, Elke, I am so sorry," Leena said.

"Mostly, I don't think about it much anymore. However, Tisa left us on a day like this. I remember the sound of Gunnar chopping wood outside as I sewed her a new dress for the pyre. Gunnar swears it was the prettiest thing I ever made, but I know he's just being kind. My hands shook, and my eyes watered so much I couldn't see what I was doing. The Holy from town came out and said the words as we watched the fire help my poor baby start her journey to the fields beyond."

Elke stopped and looked into Leena's eyes. "This morning, holding you, I realized all the precious moments Tisa and I never shared, and everything within me wanted those moments so very much." Her eyes glistened with reflected sunlight. "My heart was so heavy I couldn't stay and hear the men chopping. That's the real reason I had to get away. I just wanted to..."

Leena's arms slid around the woman's shoulders, and she embraced her friend as overwhelming sadness washed over them. Elke made no loud wails of anguish, but her massive shoulders shuddered as Leena patted her back.

Eyes lowered as an apology for being an old fool,

Elke retreated a step, smoothed her apron, and resettled her shawl. With a shake of her head, Elke straightened her shoulders.

They started toward town again, side by side, arms locked at the elbows.

"We've not spoken of Tisa since that day. We put her in a special little treasure box in our hearts and went on with life. I just wanted to tell you that if she were here today, I'd want her to be just like you."

"Thank you," Leena's husky voice expressed her gratitude for the profound honor the older woman bestowed.

Both walked in silence, wrapped in private thoughts.

"So," Elke's tone was again lighthearted, "what do we have to get in town?"

"Well, the first thing I want to do is to find some pretty cloth and make you tieback curtains for the bedroom doorway so we don't have to keep ducking through those blankets."

In the distance, gray smoke tendrils rose from several chimneys above the inn at Lovell's western end, giving the building a welcoming, cozy look. On either street side, thick, sharp-edged snow blankets hid the thatch roofs of several dozen stone shops and houses.

Nothing moved on the town's street. Uneasiness

churned in Leena's stomach. Although countless boot and hoof tracks marred the road's center, the intense cold made venturing outside hazardous for humans and animals. A sudden breeze set the mercantile sign swinging with an eerie squeaking cadence. Its rhythmic screech set the women's nerves on edge with its hopeless siren's call, inviting nonexistent shoppers to enter.

"This is where we'll find most of what we need." Elke's voice rang loud as she turned toward the mercantile.

When they stepped inside, Leena was grateful there were no other customers. Under the watchful eye of the shop owner, the pair discussed and compared several lively patterns for the door curtains before selecting one they both liked. Grabbing a burlap sack, Leena stuffed it with provisions. Together, they gathered staples to restock the food they would consume while she and Darius stayed at the Gundersons' house. Balancing parcels and sacks, they turned toward the shop door. Leena cast her warming spell over them as they stepped into the cold, sharp air.

"If you don't mind," Elke's voice rose from behind the stacks in her arms, "I'd like a cup of hot tea before we begin our trip home. Us old folks get a bit tired from walking now and then."

Leena removed the warming spell when they entered the inn so they could enjoy the fireplace-generated heat within. Loud conversations hummed in the common room. Elke scanned the room and then forged a path through the crowd. Business-people and travelers occupied the tables surrounding the hearth, so they selected a small, cozy table near a window where they could enjoy viewing the town square as they relaxed.

Warming their hands around steaming mugs, Leena described the curtains she intended to make. Her eyes wandered over the tranquil town through the frost-rimmed window, her mind far away, imagining how new curtains would beautify Elke's house and maybe, one day, her own house.

Only rising chimney smoke moved beyond the window. The street remained empty and so peaceful that it seemed like a painting of perfect small-town life. Her mind and body relaxed in comforting visions of finding a welcoming community like Lovell in the future. *Someday, I'll settle in a place like this and enjoy life.*

"Where did you learn to make tie-back curtains? I've never heard of such a thing. It sounds beautiful," Elke said.

"My da is a tailor. He made curtains for all our doors

and windows." Her voice froze. Beyond the window, a dozen mounted soldiers paced their horses toward the town square from the west behind their leader. Leena's heartbeat increased as the hoofbeats drew closer. Unhurried, the riders grouped into the town square.

Something about these guys looks familiar. A rider dismounted. As he entered the town hall, the winter sun reflected ruby from the emblem on his shoulder patch. *Oh, Spirit, they're wearing black and gray uniforms. They're Great Wizard's knights.*

All too soon, the knight exited the town hall and approached the town's notice board, pulling a hammer from his belt. Sinking lower in her seat, Leena watched as he posted a notice, pounding tacks into the board with his hammer, the faint clacking sound muted by the window glass.

"Is something wrong?"

Leena wanted to assure Elke that everything was fine, but her stomach argued that everything was not. *Stay calm. That notice might have nothing to do with me.*

Leena pulled her eyes from the soldiers and looked at Elke with what she hoped was a cheerful expression. She leaned in close and whispered in her most desperate tone, "Where's the privy?" The urgency in her voice was real, though the tightening in her gut told her she could not use a privy now if she had to.

"Oh," Elke smiled as though this explained everything, "it's out back, through that door."

Leena eased the inn door shut behind her while reaching beneath her shirtwaist for her hedge witch wand. She restored her warming spell, invoked the invisibility of the wand's Branch-enhanced protection spell, and crept toward the town's main street. Her heart jumped as booted footsteps thumped less than five feet away on the wooden walkway in front of the mercantile where she and Elke bought their supplies. Shivering, the store's merchant stepped from the walkway onto the street's jumbled ice and snow. Without a jacket, bending at the waist and rubbing his upper arms for warmth, he scuttled across the road in short, rapid steps. Steam billowed from his nose as he read the notice and ran back toward his store, grinning. The man paused before entering and turned to the knights. Trembling from head to foot, he called to a soldier. The trooper approached. Smoke plumed from the merchant's mouth as he spoke in a low, indecipherable rumble.

Careful to make no noise, Leena crept near the elevated walkway to hear their conversation.

"I don't actually have to catch her to get the money,

right? I get paid the same if I just tell you where she is?" The merchant's cunning eyes searched the soldier's face with the sly subtlety of a natural bargainer.

"That's right, sir. However, if you know and don't tell us, you could be found an accessory. I don't think you want that, do you?" The soldier's tone warned the merchant he had patience for neither bargaining nor delay.

"I don't want no trouble. I'm just making sure of my rights."

"Okay, mister." Using a thumb and middle finger, the soldier massaged his temples as he shook his head. "Look, why don't you run in and think about what I said? Then grab your jacket, come back out, and tell us what we need to know before you freeze. You'll get your money if the information's good. And I suggest you do that immediately to save yourself some trouble."

"Okay, okay, I'll tell you. I just wanted to ensure I get what's due to me."

Leena gritted her teeth as the man hurried into his store. *What a snake.* She turned to look at the noticeboard across the street. She paled when she saw the flier.

Reward 500 Gold Pieces

For information leading to the capture of the hedge witch known as Leena. She is approximately 16–17 years old, with black hair, dark eyes, and is taller than average.

This person is wanted for questioning in connection with the ambush and murder of ten innocent merchants and the twelve Allivan regular army soldiers protecting them.

Persons with information leading to her capture should contact their magistrate or the nearest guard post immediately.

Oh no, this just gets worse and worse. Do these guys really think a half-trained hedge witch can murder twenty-two people? These men are Knights of the Academy, Darius's people.

Her gut wrenched, threatening to spill its contents on the street. *Will Darius believe his fellow knights and lead me like a sheep into a hangman's noose?* He did not hesitate to arrest her before.

Maybe she should run away. She still had most of the money Arvin had given her. She could get to somewhere no one knew she existed. *What can I do? What should I do? Mum, Da, where are you? I need you.*

Cool wetness flowed down her cheeks. *I can't do this alone.*

Straightening, she threw her shoulders back and wiped the freezing tears from her cheeks. She had to get Elke and leave this town. But first, she wanted to hear what the despicable store owner said about her.

Leena turned back toward the store. Although the shuffling of men and horses hid her crunching footsteps, she picked a cautious path over the uneven snow and ice-covered road.

"Sir!" the soldier standing six feet before her yelled into the mercantile. "Sir, I suggest you tell me what you know now. I don't think you want to find out what happens to you if she escapes because of your delay. I guarantee you will not like it."

"Okay, okay." The merchant reappeared, shoving his arms through the sleeves of a sheepskin-lined leather jacket. "But all that money won't do me no good if I freeze to death before I get it."

An insincere grin crept over the merchant's face as if he held all the cards in a one-sided agreement. "Less than an hour ago, Elke, an old farmwife from east of here, came into the store with a pretty, dark-haired girl in tow. The girl's a stranger. She was tall, maybe six feet, but couldna been more than sixteen. It was peculiar on two accounts. First, I rarely see farm folk here over the winter unless they've run out of necessaries. But these ladies were looking at the cloth and talking about curtains. They come all the way to town for that on a day like this? I tell you, it was odd."

He must have forgotten all the food we bought.

"Now, as I was saying," the merchant continued, "the second strange thing is these two ladies were wearing only light shawls like they were out for a summer evening stroll, and both looked just as warm as toast. I think that'd take a witch's spell, don't you?" He paused, directing a penetrating stare at the soldier's eyes. The soldier twirled an impatient hand, urging the man to continue. "They were so wrapped up in each other they didn't pay no attention to me. They were like a mother and daughter. Now, I've known Elke since before she was married, and the only child she ever had died at birth. I don't remember if it was a boy or girl, but I know this lass wasn't her. Now that I think about it, I guess that's a third weird thing."

Lena looked toward the inn where Elke sat, drinking her tea and waiting for Leena to return. The urge to cry and scream at the injustice of this situation rolled over Leena. She wanted to run over, hit, kick, and pound on the merchant until he shut up.

"Sir," the soldier's exasperated voice rose, "if you have any *useful* information, I strongly recommend you tell me now. Otherwise, I'll have to arrest you for obstructing the Great Wizard's justice and find someone else with the information. This is your last chance."

"Okay, okay. You don't have to get all huffy. I was just about to tell you. When they left here, they headed for the inn. I'm sure they're still there." His finger pointed toward the window where Elke sat.

The soldier turned and called to his men. "Search the place, find this Elke woman, and make sure she does not escape."

Spreading out to cover the street, they walked toward the building. Three soldiers separated from the group and rushed behind the building to cover the rear entrance as the others moved toward the front door.

Panic flooded through Leena's veins. *I have to do something. I can't let them take her.* She scanned the street, looking for anything that might provide answers. *All of this because Arvin wants the Garlan Branch? Mum said the tree grants a Branch only to the person it designates. No one else can see, touch, or use it. If he's a wizard, he should know that.*

"Don't you forget where the information came from," the merchant shouted at the soldiers' retreating backs. Waiting, his anxious eyes fixed on the inn, the merchant received no response. Removing his hands from under his armpits, he cupped them over his ears as he entered the store and shut the door.

Alone in the street, Leena's knees turned liquid. Trembling, she stood helpless as the soldiers crowded through the inn door.

I need to run. That's what I'll do. I don't care where I go. I'll be safe. So will Gunnar and Elke if I'm not around and no one knows where I've gone. But who was she kidding? That soldier threatening the merchant proved Gunnar and Elke would be tortured, maybe even killed, for not giving information they didn't have.

Oh Spirit, I can't run, and I can't stay. What can I do?

Voices rose as two soldiers dragged Elke through the inn's door with firm grips on her arms. Icy fear shivered through Leena's body as they frog-marched the older woman into the street. Slight bell tones clinked from the swinging manacle chain connecting a pair of iron cuffs around her wrists.

With brutal jerks on Elke's arms, the soldiers forced her to stop at the center of the road, less than fifteen feet from Leena. In response to the rough treatment, fear fled Elke's face, and she held her head high in anger and resistance. Leena admired how Elke stood tall even as her teeth clacked and her body trembled from the cold. *At least I can fix that.* Touching her wand, Leena cast a warming spell. Only a slight rise in Elke's eyebrows showed her pleased surprise for a second before settling back into stern resolution. Only Leena saw the subtle movement of Elke's lips in a "thank you."

She knows I'm here watching her. That's good. Leena chastised herself for wasting time listening to the merchant's story. She should have run to the inn and grabbed Elke after she saw the poster. The soldiers wouldn't have been able to find them with the protection spell's invisibility.

Stop it! There's no time for that now. With luck, there'll be time to feel guilty later. She needed to do something. *Think, Leena!*

She moved closer to the soldiers and Elke.

Merchants and travelers flowed from the inn, crowding behind a shoulder-to-shoulder guard wall restraining them from contact with the prisoner. Spirited laughter and loud, indecipherable conversation flooded the street with a holiday air. At the commotion, doors along the street flew open, discharging merchants and townspeople to crowd the road, forcing Leena to retreat several steps.

Is there anyone I can turn to for help?

A thought struck her. Maybe she should reveal herself and let them capture her. Then they'd take her to the Great Wizard, and he would clear up this whole mess. But could she trust him? He was a wizard, after all, with the near-limitless power of a Garlan Branch.

Leena looked around. Motion flickered in the shop where they'd bought their provisions. The merchant stepped outside onto the boardwalk and scanned the crowd. The satisfied smile on his face showed more than greed. His grin held the smirk of a man finally paying off an old debt.

Beyond the merchant, a flash of midnight black caught Leena's eye. A wide-brimmed dark hat pulled low over a shadowed face disappeared into an alley beyond the mercantile. Something—the posture, the rapid retreat—seemed familiar. *I'm sure I've seen that person before, but where?* She could make it behind the mercantile and catch a better look at him if she hurried. The thought fled as a clinking chain brought her attention back to Elke's plight.

Stepping forward, a soldier removed a chain looped over his shoulder and locked one end of its six-foot length to the center of Elke's manacles. He snapped a hard jerk on the other end of the chain to ensure the lock remained secure. Turning to the crowd, he shouted above the gleeful chaos. "Can anyone tell me where this woman lives?"

Crowd chatter grew fevered as each tried to out-shout the others. A dozen people pointed east. Holding his hands high, the soldier struggled to silence the mob. The chain whipped back and forth with his motions as his words disappeared beneath the racket. The soldier lowered his hands, crossed his arms over his chest, and glared the crowd into silence.

"Now you, sir." The soldier pointed to a man in a thick cloth jacket. "Can you tell me where this woman lives?"

The man pointed east. "It's about three miles out on the left side of the road. It's the house with the split log fence. You can't miss it. If you want, I'll come along to show you."

"That won't be necessary." The soldier studied the crowd. "I'd appreciate it if you all stayed here in town. We are looking for a dangerous criminal and don't know how many accomplices she has. If any of you tag along, I'll have to assume you are part of her gang, and my men will take appropriate action. Believe me, if you survive your capture, you will not like the questioning that follows."

He let the words trail in the frigid air. The crowd's hush took on new depth. No sound rose from the small cloud breaths rising before every face. After a minute, the mass drifted away, mumbling about people they needed to see or chores that needed doing. Within minutes, the assembly disappeared. The soldier tugged Elke's chain as the last person vanished into a building.

"You, you, and you"—he pointed to three soldiers—"bring the horses. Without waiting to see whether the soldiers obeyed his orders, he started east on the road as his troops walked behind, and the three men led their horses at the rear of their column.

"Come on, you," he growled, tugging Elke's chain like a horse's lead rope, "it's time we see whether the witch has returned to your home. With luck, we'll catch her before she escapes. But it won't matter if she does. These posters are spread all over Allivan. She won't stay free for long."

Slowed by the need to remain quiet, her tracks hidden within the mass of soldiers' footprints, Leena passed the men leading the soldiers' horses. Careful to stay far enough away from the troops to avoid contact, she crept forward until she was close enough to the leader to hear everything he said.

"I'm going to warn you only this once, Madam. Refusal to tell us what you know is abetting a criminal. If the rumors are true, this young girl could be the nastiest character Allivan's had since Mad Halsey. I'm sure you don't want any part of that. So, telling me where to find her could spare you quite a bit of pain, possibly even save your life."

Elke remained silent as she plodded behind the soldier with her head held high.

What must she think of me? Why would she protect a stranger she met only a few days ago? Deep inside, Leena knew the answer. Elke's expression had said it all when they talked on the road into town. *She trusts me. No matter what she hears, she'll reserve an opinion until she speaks to me and looks into my eyes. Then she'll see and know the truth.* Leena's heart melted at the depth of the woman's faith in her.

Through the trees ahead, snow glinted off the top rails on the first stile of Elke and Gunnar's fence.

It would take ten minutes to reach the gate. Leena had to figure out some way to end this nightmare. She could immobilize the group like she did the bandits when they'd captured Arvin, but that would bring at least one raven and make Elke an escaped criminal. She and Gunnar would lose everything. By law, their farm would be confiscated, their reputations lost, and both would most likely end their days in prison, separated from each other. That was far too much to inflict on a couple who'd only shown her kindness.

The gate stood less than fifty yards ahead. In the distance, the familiar chunk of axes chopping tree trunks brought memories of domestic harmony on the farms Leena visited outside Quillan.

What would Darius think when he saw Elke shackled by his fellow knights? They would show him the new poster. He knew what happened to the bandits and soldiers, but would they believe him? Would he even tell the truth, or would he turn on her?

As the seconds passed, Leena only saw one way out of this mess where no one else would get hurt. She would reveal herself to the soldiers and let them capture her. Then, they would take her to the Great Wizard.

The axes fell silent. Only the chuff of a horse, the crunching of boots on ice, and the jingle of chains disturbed the farm's peace. Far across the snow-covered field, Gunnar and Darius stepped from the forest, axes resting over their shoulders as they stared at the approaching crowd. After a quick conversation, both men hurried across the field toward the column. At the sight of them, the soldiers drew their swords. Five soldiers stepped between Elke and the approaching pair. The man holding Elke's chain scanned the area as though watching for more men to approach.

TWENTY-FIVE

"You men, halt and drop your weapons," the soldier holding Elke's chain shouted. Gunnar and Darius skidded to a stop in the shin-deep snow twenty yards away. "Drop your weapons." The soldier shouted in their direction.

Confusion wrinkled both men's faces as they looked at each other, hoping for clarification. Then they realized the soldier meant their axes. In silent agreement, Darius and Gunnar lowered the axes to the snow.

"Now, step forward with your hands held over your heads," the soldier said gruffly.

Raising their hands above their shoulders, Gunnar and Darius, looking down as they approached, lifted their boots high to clear the deep snow and prevent a sudden fall that might bring a violent reaction from the troops. The lead soldier ordered them to halt when they were within five feet.

"Do either of you gentlemen know this woman?"

"She's my wife, sir, and I demand to know why you've got her shackled like a common criminal."

"She is impeding the Great Wizard's business, sir, and I suggest you be a bit more respectful if you want to avoid sharing her fate. We are looking for a young hedge witch named Leena. We learned in town that this woman and a young girl were shopping together, and we believe that young girl is the witch we're looking for."

"And I'll wager it was Rawley, the shopkeeper, who told you she was with this girl, right?" Gunnar's complexion, reddened by the cold and his rushed trip to the front yard, deepened with anger.

The soldier hesitated. "I'm not free to say who provided the information that led us to this woman."

"Her name is Elke, and she's a gentlewoman despite being a farmwife. But never mind that." Gunnar's chest swelled as his voice rose in outrage. "Your refusal's enough proof for me that my arrow struck true. Old Rawley's been waiting these thirty years for a chance to pay Elke back for the audacity of choosing me over him. And you, a representative of the Great Wizard, blindly took the word of a jilted suitor and trussed her up like a hog to slaughter."

Using Gunnar's tirade to conceal her movements, Leena crept to Elke's side and touched her shoulder. The older woman's slight smile assured her that Elke knew she was there.

"Sir, she's been arrested for refusing to cooperate."

At these words, Gunnar's face flamed red with rage. Everything in his voice and attitude screamed that he was preparing to act. The soldiers tensed, ready to respond.

I can't let him attack these soldiers. He'll be killed before he takes a step. Leena reached for her wand, but Darius's hand on Gunnar's chest stopped him before he could take a step.

"Lieutenant, may I have a word with you?" Darius's voice was calm, almost conversational.

The soldier's brow furrowed. "Darius?"

"Hello, Arstead, it's been a while." The soldier rushed forward to grasp Darius's hand and pump it in mighty jerks as though meeting a lost friend for the first time in years.

"It's great to see you again." A grin split Lieutenant Arstead's face. "It's been what, at least two years? Last I heard, you were cooling your heels at the Great Wizard's castle, awaiting an assignment."

"And I finally got one, along with a promotion to captain. But we can catch up later." Darius's grin sobered. "Right now, you and I need to have a private chat. Why don't you have a few of your men take this couple into their house and have the others go to the barn and take care of your mounts while we take a walk? But before we take our walk, I want your assurance that these people will be treated with respect, not as prisoners, while we're gone. I assure you they have done nothing wrong."

Arstead stared at Darius for several seconds, then at Gunnar and Elke. Pulling keys from his belt, Arstead removed Elke's shackles and chain. "My men will treat them as guests since you vouch for them."

"Great." Darius laid a reassuring hand on his friend's shoulder. "These people are friends. You say she's refused to cooperate. Have you considered the possibility that she has no information to give you? As Gunnar said, you might have been duped by a man with ulterior motives."

Darius held up a silencing hand before Arstead could respond. "I'll explain it all to you as we walk. But first, there's a paper I need to retrieve from my bag in the house."

Leena waited on the porch as Darius fetched the poster he retrieved from the soldier's saddlebag at the ambush site west of Pineton. As the two men walked toward the road, Leena used Darius's footprints to hide her own. Careful to make no noise, she stayed close behind Darius as the two knights talked.

"First, under whose authority are you looking for this girl, and for what crime?" Darius's voice remained neutral as though trying not to put his friend on the defensive.

"It's not just me, Darius. All the Great Wizard's troops are on alert." Arstead's tone was apologetic as he reached into his shirt and removed one of the new Wanted posters. He passed it to Darius.

After scanning Arstead's document, Darius held out the one he had just secured from the farmhouse. "Perhaps you should see this one." He passed it to his friend.

"Where did you get this?" Arstead's words were almost a whisper as he passed the poster back.

"I was at the battle your poster describes, and it was not Leena against innocent merchants and army regulars. Both sides wanted to capture her for different reasons, and neither wanted the other to have her. In the end, they slaughtered each other." Leena noted Darius omitted the ravens. "I pulled this from one of the dead soldier's saddlebags. That skirmish happened nine days ago.

When did you receive your posters from the Great Wizard?"

"Nine days ago. Our colonel told us to take this road since other troops would catch her if she went north toward Elderon, and the Weymouth garrison would cover the roads between Pinetown and Stocksbury."

"So you received the poster on the day the battle happened?" Darius asked. "And how long would it take to get those posters from the Great Wizard to your garrison at Midden?"

"An excellent rider could make it in a week." Arstead's eyes widened as his voice softened. "So, these did not come from the Great Wizard."

"Also, both posters say the hedge witch is wanted for questioning. It does not accuse her of any crime. There is no mention of accomplices, nor does it grant authority to detain anyone else. What did Elke do that caused you to arrest her?"

"She refused to answer any of my questions."

"I'm not surprised. From how you approached Gunnar and me, it's a fair guess that you liberally laced your questions with threats and accusations." The reddening of the lieutenant's face was all the confirmation Darius needed. "Aside from this merchant, has anyone else in Lovell accused her?"

"Several men in the inn said they saw Elke with a young, dark-haired girl they did not know."

"This early, most people in an inn are traveling merchants. How likely are they to know who's a stranger here and who isn't?"

"I'll admit it is not likely, but the merchant—"

"Who has an ax to grind, plus the lure of five hundred gold coins probably helped loosen his tongue."

Arstead stiffened. "I'll grant you that, but five hundred gold pieces are more reward than ever offered before. Wouldn't that prove the girl is highly dangerous?"

"Or it could show the Great Wizard's urgent need to question her. Have you ever heard of a hedge witch that could destroy a town, let alone several?"

"No, but something happened at those places. The posters indicate the girl's at the heart of it somehow, and it seems this Elke knows something. Look, Darius, I'm just doing my job."

"I know that." Darius smiled at his friend. "But I'd wager the thought of how capturing the girl could enhance your career has crossed your mind." Again, Arstead flushed. "Okay, so the question is,"—Darius patted the lieutenant's shoulder—"what do we do from here?"

"It wouldn't hurt if I could talk to this Leena. It's

not that I distrust you, Darius. You've always had a brilliant head on your shoulders. But your information is secondhand. If I could ask her a few questions while watching her face when she answers, we could probably clear this whole mess up."

Leena touched her hedge witch wand and removed the protection spell and, with it, her invisibility. "I believe you're right."

Arstead spun around, reaching for his sword hilt faster than she would have thought possible.

"Hold on, friend." Darius grabbed the soldier's wrist, preventing him from fully drawing his weapon. "You said you wanted to ask her some questions, not skewer her like a hog on a spit."

The trio stood motionless while Arstead considered his options. "Okay." With a sigh, he let his weapon drop back into its sheath. "Tell me what happened from your perspective. I suggest you stick to the truth. I'll be watching your face, and I'll know if you lie."

Without mentioning the Garlan Branch, Leena told Arstead how she found her village destroyed and met Arvin. Within minutes, she outlined their trip from Quillan to meeting Darius in Pineton, their escape, and the bandit's ambush without mentioning the ravens. As she talked, Darius added information about the ambush and their travels.

Silence settled over the group as Leena wondered whether Arstead would accept any part of the tale as accurate.

Arstead nodded. "I admit, even if distributing these posters within the time frames we discussed wasn't impossible, your tale sounds far more plausible than the crimes the posters outline. I'd heard about your assignment to the far eastern shores, Darius. So, I guess we'll wait here with you until the troops from Weymouth, scheduled to accompany you on your journey, show up, and you can join them. And since I doubt your farm friends could provide any more information than you've given me, they will not be bothered by my men any further. There is one more thing, though."

Leena stiffened. *Is this where he tells me he still has to arrest and deliver me to the Great Wizard as a wanted criminal?*

"What is Leena supposed to do after you board your ship? These posters are everywhere, and I doubt most people will wait to discover they're fake. Alone, she could be killed or captured and tortured by bandits trying to get information that could be ransomed for far more than five hundred gold."

"If the reward even exists." Darius shook his head. "But I can't take her with me even if she wanted to go."

Leena straightened her spine. This was it, the moment of truth. She needed to end this somehow. "There's only one solution," Leena said. "I must go to see the Great Wizard. Your men can take me there."

Staring at the ground, his hand rubbing his chin, Darius remained silent for a moment. "Are you sure?"

Leena nodded. "It's the only way."

"Okay then." Darius looked back at the road east. "I suggest we return to the farm." He looked down at the work shirt he had donned for woodcutting. "I'll get in full uniform, then we can wait for the regular army troops to arrive."

TWENTY-SIX

Leena trudged up the road toward the house, shivering in the cold. She didn't bother to use a warming spell. Darius and Arstead walked ahead of her, chatting. Her heart felt heavy, and she was scared.

Am I doing the right thing? So much had happened since Midwinter's Night. She had been a silly girl with silly dreams of being a hero. Now, she needed to trust that she was doing what she could to save her friends and find her family.

"Shhh!" Darius suddenly held up a hand. "I hear horses, and they're moving fast. They could be the regular army troops I've been waiting for, heading for the ships, or they could be bounty hunters looking for Leena. Let's get off the road. We're close enough to the farm to see who they are before we reveal ourselves." He turned to Leena. "You'll be safer invisible until we know who we're dealing with."

"I might do better than that." Touching her hedge witch wand, Leena cast the Branch-enhanced protection spell she'd used to hide from the raven. From within its protection, the spell shimmered the air around all three with its power.

Like rolling thunder, the rumble of approaching riders pushing their mounts at full speed grew more ominous. "Whoa!" The leader lifted a hand high. Behind him, a hundred riders leaned back against their reins, forcing the beasts to a stop half a mile from the Gundersons' farm.

Leena gasped. Those are black army uniforms. These must be the soldiers crossing the Eastern Sea with Darius. But the men dressed in mismatched outfits at the back of their column were definitely not soldiers.

"Rimlick! Is this the farm you told us about?" the leader shouted over his shoulder.

A rider with a long black beard, wearing a black, wide-brimmed floppy hat and a shin-length black cloak, walked his horse forward and stopped beside the man who shouted the question.

Leena's heart sped up. It was the bearded man the armorer was talking to in Pineton. The same bearded man who'd prepared the ambush that killed the soldiers and the bandits. The man who'd escaped on his horse before being killed. She also recognized him as the figure she'd seen disappear into the shadows in Lovell when Elke was captured.

"Yes, yer lieutenantship. And you remember our agreement." The bearded man's voice had the oily sincerity of a practiced liar. "We get any information you extract from these people, and we get to deliver it to the Great Wizard."

"Yes, yes." The Lieutenant waved a hand like he was swatting an annoying fly. "I just want to ensure that the person responsible for slaughtering twelve of my men gets the slow and painful death she so richly deserves."

The bearded man smiled, revealing crooked teeth.

"Now, I want you and your men in those woods in case anyone on the farm tries to escape. And, if they do, I want them taken alive and unharmed. A corpse or someone so damaged they cannot be questioned is useless to me. Do you understand?"

"Yes, yer Lieutenantship."

"And send the wizard up here that the captain assigned to us in Weymouth. There's a chance we might need him if the hedge witch is here."

Turning his horse, the bearded man disappeared

beyond the mass of soldiers. Within minutes, a dozen scruffy bandits galloped north through the snow-covered fields and faded into the forest beyond.

A man rode forward on his horse past the halted column. His pale-gray, floor-length robe had bunched around his thighs, squashed into a ball between his abdomen and the saddle horn. His wispy, shoulder-length hair matched the robe's color as its strands rose and fell with the horse's gentle rhythm. He halted next to the lieutenant.

A wizard. This cannot be good.

"Okay, Wizard, I think it's time you proved you're more powerful than a hedge witch. First, can you tell me how many people are here and where they are?"

A gentle, trilling hum rose from the wizard's throat as he closed his eyes, lowered his head, and placed his index and middle fingers against his temples. His aged, cracked voice replaced the eerie hum.

"I sense the farmer, his wife, and nine knights in the house. Three more knights are in the barn, tending the group's mounts. I also sense twelve bandits creeping up behind the barn. They're tensed as though preparing for battle."

The lieutenant hissed through clenched teeth, "I

should have expected the only reason those bandits joined our group was to capture the witch and collect the Great Wizard's ransom. First, let's see if we can't rid the world of them. Then we'll see why those knights are here and how we can get the information the Great Wizard needs. After the bandits are gone, our priority is capturing the farmwife. If all these people are here, the witch must be nearby, and I'm sure the farmwife knows where she is."

Leena glanced at Darius and Arstead. They looked worried, which did little to boost her confidence.

"That witch caused the death of twelve of my soldiers. If the knights are protecting this farmwife, they are doing so against the Great Wizard's orders and should be considered his enemies. As such, I authorize using maximum force against them if necessary." The lieutenant closed his eyes for several seconds, his face neutral. "Wizard, do you sense any sign the witch is here?"

"No, m'lord." The wizard's voice rumbled and broke over the words.

Leena let out a relieved sigh. *Knowing the wizard's senses can't penetrate my Branch-enhanced protection spell is good.*

"Okay, she'll likely hide and run west if she catches sight of us, figuring we'll continue east if we don't find her at the farm. You stay here and continue sensing while we capture and question the farmwife. I assume you can disable the witch if she appears?"

"Yes, m'lord."

"Good. But remember, capturing the witch is our job. Believe me when I say you would not want to be responsible for letting her escape. Lock a red wizard's fire signal over her head to track her movements if you locate her. Then we'll follow its light and take her into custody."

The lieutenant turned away as though the wizard meant no more to him than a pesky insect. After a few minutes of futile waiting, the wizard walked his mount back to the column's rear.

"We need to get Elke and Gunnar out before these guys arrive," Darius whispered. Leena jumped when his breath warmed the side of her neck.

Darius tapped Arstead's arm, and the small group started toward the farmhouse, carefully stepping only in the footprints of the Great Wizard's knights earlier.

"Okay, men," the lieutenant shouted, "our wizard says nine of the Great Wizard's knights are in that farmhouse, and we need to know why they're here. Sargent Winslow, take a dozen men and surround the place. You four stay here and guard their horses. We don't want the witch stealing one and getting away while we tend to the house's occupants."

The lieutenant glared at the wizard. "Sargent Colton, take two squads and remove those bandits behind the barn. I don't know why our wizard suggested we bring them along anyway..."

The lieutenant's words faded behind them as Leena, Darius, and Arstead entered the farmhouse.

TWENTY-SEVEN

"Listen up, men," Arstead shouted as he shut the door. "A dozen or more soldiers will burst in here in a few minutes..." He stopped. No one appeared to hear his words, although chairs had crashed to the floor when every man jumped up as the door opened and closed. He turned to Leena. "Is this because of your spell?"

"Oh yes. I'm sorry." Touching her hedge witch wand, Leena released the protection spell, and their group reappeared. Every knight's hand dropped to their sword, drawing them as they stared at the newcomers in alarm.

"Men," Darius called out, "Several soldiers will break in here in a few minutes. They mean to capture and torture the farmer and his wife, and probably the rest of us, if they don't get the answers they want. There are too many to fight. This hedge witch,"—he nodded toward Leena—"has a protection spell that will make us invisible and unable to be felt or heard. We need to get out of here as fast as we can.

"Elke, Gunnar," Darius's voice rang loud over the shuffle of men re-sheathing their swords and righting toppled furniture, "grab what you might need to survive a few days on the road. You have less than two minutes before the soldiers arrive, so choose wisely. Leena, let's get our packs."

"But..." Before Leena could start spouting reasons they should stay, Darius held up a hand. " We're out of time. We have to move. Now!"

Ignoring the shocked expressions still painting the knights' faces from the new arrivals' sudden appearance, Leena grabbed her pack, opened the door a crack, and peered out. Six crouching soldiers, spread ten feet apart, crept toward the house. The front of their line would be at the door before the knights inside could exit. They were trapped.

Leena shut the door and cast the protection spell over herself, Darius, Ellke, Gunnar, and the surrounding knights."Okay, the protection spell will keep us safe. But we need to get to the road and the remaining soldiers. Then it'll be up to Darius and Arstead to convince the army lieutenant that the bandits are a much more significant threat than I am, and together, they can develop a plan to eliminate them. So, is everybody with me?"

A small sea of nodding heads confirmed they understood her plan.

"One last thing, only step into existing footprints. While we're invisible and they can't feel or hear us, I doubt they'll miss any new tracks appearing in the snow. For now, it's best they think we're still in the house."

Leena stepped onto the porch to see a deadly rain of arrows appearing like feathered porcupine quills in the chest of every visible soldier sneaking toward the house. In less than a second, another lethal shower sped beyond her vision north of the house. The flump of falling bodies attested to the bandits' murderous accuracy.

Leena studied the six prone soldiers in the front and another six in the sideyard as they passed. None showed any signs of life.

"If the army lieutenant sends any more soldiers, we must get between them and the ambush before the bandits fire another volley. Our protection spell will deflect any arrows fired at the troops. Line up shoulder to shoulder and walk forward, keeping between any soldiers and the bandits until we're back on the road and out of the range." Leena spread

Elke, Gunnar, and the knights apart using hand motions and walked them toward the road beyond the farmhouse.

No arrows flew from the forest as the group stepped onto the road and walked toward the mounted soldiers outside the achers' range. Leena examined the road beyond the regular army's column. The gray wizard sat on his mount a mile east, half-visible within the tree shadows covering the road. He was studying the soldiers, no doubt trying to sense whether she was with them.

"Darius, Arnstead," Leena said. Although the mounted troops beside them could not hear her, Leena's voice rang loud within the bubble of her protection spell. "You and your knights hide in the trees at the roadside. I'll remove the protection spell from all of you. Then you two can step out and convince these soldiers that the posters are fake and none of us represent a threat to them or the Great Wizard. While you do that, I'll wander down the road and have a chat with their wizard."

"Are you sure that's a good idea?" Darius asked.

"Do you trust me?" Leena stared into his eyes.

Darius placed a hand on her shoulder. "Yes, always. It's their wizard I don't trust."

"But he's with the army. What could possibly go wrong?" Leena chuckled. "But it should be alright as long as I'm hidden by the protection spell. She looked around to ensure the group was hidden within the trees and removed the protection spell from all but herself. As she picked her way across the hoof-trodden snow and ice-covered road east, Darius's and Arstead's whispering voices faded behind her.

What am I doing? I'm a partially trained hedge witch, and this guy's an experienced wizard. Have I lost my mind?

Leena knew she hadn't thought this through thoroughly. But after the bandit's attack on the soldiers and her group being trapped in the house, she had to do something. They were all in this mess because of her. She suspected they wouldn't leave this place alive if she didn't confront the wizard.

She touched the Garlan Branch at her waist. *With the ravens around, I don't dare use it. It's not fair. Wizards are trained to use combat magic, while hedge witches know only healing magic.*

"Well, well, well, Leena. We meet again."

How can he see me through the protection spell? Leena's thoughts swirled in confusion as the wizard spoke. Gone were the croaks of his conversation with the regular army lieutenant. Although the man sitting atop his horse looked ancient, his words came out in the pleasant, youthful baritone of a man born for public speaking. *How does he know I'm here? He said he didn't sense me when the army lieutenant asked if he could. I have been such a fool, and I may have just walked into a trap.*

"Oh, dear. Have I upset you? Maybe you'd prefer this." Too fast for Leena to see the transition, Arvin now sat in the saddle, smiling down at her. "If you'll be so good as to turn the Garlan Branch over to me, I might be inclined to spare these people you've become so fond of." His small, boy-sized arm, no longer matching the young man's voice, swept toward the road east of them.

Leena took a deep breath. Just because he knew she was here didn't mean the protection spell wasn't working. Maybe he had a sensing spell that alerted him when a magic caster was near. Her hand drifted toward the Garlan Branch tucked into her trousers.

"And, if you're considering casting a spell on me," a mocking grin lit his face, "I assure you, I've faced and defeated many far more powerful wizards' spells than you can imagine."

Leena's lips curled into a smile. If that were true, why was he frozen when she'd cast the spell on the bandits that captured him? *Arvin, I think you just made a booboo.* Touching her hedge witch wand, she cast an immobilization spell.

For several seconds, Arvin sat immobilized. Then, as if waking from a dream, his body shook as he laughed.

Uh-oh. This time, he analyzed the spell and over-came it.

"You see? You are a simple country hedge witch. You have no chance."

Arvin's hands lifted, rolling in the air as though kneading bread, and shot forward, launching a crackling, orange fireball that roared toward her head, growing as it approached. Forgetting about the surrounding protection spell, Leena ducked. The fire spread, covering her barrier's outline as it contacted the invisible protective shell. Above her, the raging fire grew, sending heat waves rippling toward the sky, melting snow and ice for several feet around her protective sheath. The unbearable heat grew as her protection shell glowed red. Leena stood straight, staring at the disintegrating barrier as holes appeared throughout the structure, turning it into a fiery lace doily. Like melting candle wax, the holes grew, and their crimson edges dripped in thick, elongated streams. Trails of red liquid swelled around her. Small, glistening puddles of the disintegrating enclosure crept across the ground, liquefying the road's surface and burning the ground as they crept toward her boots.

What's happening? How can he destroy my protection spell? Even with the Garlan Branch-improved shield, her spell wasn't enough. The Garlan Branch vibrated on her hip, calling to her. But, if she used the Branch, it would call another raven. She couldn't fight Arvin and the raven at the same time.

Spirit, please help me. What should I do?

"You know," Arvin's voice rose above the fire's crackling thunder, "you have only seconds left to live. If it were me, I'd give up the Branch. But the choice is yours. I can take it from the ashes of your corpse just as easily."

He's right. I have no choice.

Reaching beneath her shirt, Leena's hand slid toward the Branch.

"No, you don't." Arvin raised a hand, curled it into a tight fist, and twisted it like snapping a chicken's neck. Against her will, Leena's arms and legs flew out, locking her body in an excruciating position. Her wrists and ankles were bound and outstretched to the breaking point as if tied between two far-separated trees. Agony screamed through her elbows, shoulders, and groin as the invisible force pulled tighter, threatening to separate her joints. Her breath stopped when the immense pressure of her outstretched arms prevented her chest from expanding. *Oh, Spirit, please help me.*

His triumphant shout rose above the dying flames. "Now that I know where it's hidden, I don't need you." Dismounting, Arvin transformed back into the gray wizard. "It's time you saw a real wizard at work." He raised a hand and waved it across his body like a man sowing seeds as far as he could.

Too tired, too defeated to respond to his taunts, Leena struggled against the immovable bonds. Following his arm motion, an icy wall flowed across the molten, glowing lake surrounding her, transforming the ground from liquid red to shiny black glass. Arvin stalked toward her, smiling, taking his time to prolong the suspense and make securing the ultimate prize more joyous. His smile turned to surprise when he lifted her shirt and plucked the hedge witch wand from her waist.

"This is it?" He glared into her eyes. "I expected something more. A Garlan Branch should be gold-plated with diamond inlays. It should not look like an ordinary hedge witch wand." He stopped, his eyes going wide. "And that's because it is an ordinary hedge witch wand, isn't it? You tricked me, didn't you? That's not very nice. In fact, it could prove quite lethal."

Arvin's right fist crashed into her stomach before she saw him move. Fire flared in her gut as breath burst from her mouth, emptying her lungs. Stars floated in her vision as she fought to take an indrawn breath. With her throbbing arms and legs over-stretched from her sides, she had no defence. Unable to see through her blackening vision and with no air in her lungs to cry out, his left fist caught her unprepared. Right, left, right, left; his merciless fists pounded her defenseless stomach.

Mum, I need you. Leena's world faded.

As her surroundings eased back into consciousness, Leena opened her eyes to find her head hanging with her face pointed toward the ground. The fiery pain in her joints told her that Arvin's invisible bonds still secured her limbs, holding her upright, suspended two feet above the ground, and stretching her to the breaking point. The black curtains of her hair limited vision to either side. Memory flooded back, and she wished the darkness would return. She needed time to heal.

With every passing second, the roaring fire of her stomach muscles grew as they swelled from the abuse of Arvin's fists. *There will be some serious bruises if I don't heal them soon.* Her hedge witch wand was not in its accustomed place, but the Branch's rough bark pressed against her tender stomach. *He didn't find it. That's good. The Branch must be invisible to even the most powerful wizard. But that does me no good since I can't direct its energy without my fingers touching it.* She wondered if it was just her fingers. Leena closed her eyes and sent her hedge witch healing spell command to the Branch. The spell did nothing. Her head thundered with pain from hanging toward the ground, making it difficult to keep her thoughts straight. At the moment, the Branch was just a useless stick. She'd hate to think about what would happen if a raven appeared now.

Distant shouts rose in the east, far behind her. *Where's Arvin?* Was he standing silent in front of her, ready to start his boxing exercises again? Or did those shouts mean he was in a heated battle with the soldiers back at the farm? With infinite slowness, Leena raised a head that weighed a thousand pounds.

"Ah, so you're awake." Arvin paused for a few moments, listening to the chaos. "I suppose you're wondering what all the fuss is back there. While you were napping, I sensed the soldiers hunting my men. Even though I have only twelve bandits, and they have over a hundred soldiers and knights, it would probably be a fairly even fight. Soldiers like large, open fields to fight on. They're not much of a threat in the forest. But bandits thrive in the woods, preferring to sneak up on their foes and shoot them in the back if possible. It's much safer that way. However, just to make the fight more interesting, I cast a healing spell over the bandits. Any injury short of death will heal instantly for the next hour. That should keep everyone over there busy,"—he nodded toward the farm behind her—"until you and I can conclude our business."

She forced herself to look toward his eyes, but that did not stop her world from spinning.

"I got a little too emotional during our last conversation. I won't make that mistake again." Arvin raised his hands, displaying their swollen knuckles.

She knew he could heal his hands if he wanted to. Leena glanced up into the suppressed glee in his eyes. *But he wants to savor his pain. He's using it to increase his anger and contrive more effective tortures.* Her heart sank.

Rubbing his red, puffy-knuckled hands together produced the sound of rasping waves against a gravel shore as he strolled toward her. Lifting a friction-warmed hand, he trailed a soft fingertip down her cheek. Unbearable heat raged along her tender skin like a white-hot branding iron, obliterating all other considerations.

Leena bit her lip to prevent screaming. *There's no way I'm going to give him that pleasure.*

"Can you imagine what it would feel like to have that in your eye? Oh, wait, you don't have to imagine it." He pointed his index finger toward her right eye. His smile grew as he eased the maiming digit closer. Less than an inch remained before Leena lost half of her sight forever.

No, no, no. Her mind screamed the endless litany as the last of her resistance crumbled. Leena tilted her head back, fighting to keep as much distance as possible between his dirt-encrusted nail and her precious eye.

Arvin's eyes gleamed with delight at the escalating panic contorting her features. The air hung heavy with silent tension broken only by the hissing rush of her quickening breaths. The faint scent of her fear-generated sweat perfumed the still air. She could tilt her head back no more. Less than a quarter inch remained until his touch destroyed her vision.

Thwack, thwack.

As if by magic, two arrows sprouted from the center of Arvin's chest, breaking his imprisoning spell. Leena's arms and legs fell slack as Arvin collapsed. Before Leena could find her balance, she tumbled, loose-limbed, onto the shiny black glass roadway next to his lifeless body.

TWENTY-EIGHT

"Leena, are you all right?" Darius and Arstead shouted as they ran from the roadside trees.

"Not quite." Leena sat up, shaking her arms to get the blood flowing. She freed her hedge witch wand from behind Arvin's belt. "But I will be in a moment." Her aches faded as she cast a healing spell over herself. She stared down at the wizard's body, letting the pain and fear subside as her anger grew.

It's not enough. Her jaw clenched as a fire grew within her. *It's too easy. He died without suffering. No, no, no!* With every inner shout, her fists rained like blacksmith hammers on Arvin's inert stomach. *He needs to know what it feels like. He needs to suffer the fear of a slow, painful, inevitable death.* Her wide-mouthed sobs tore through the silent forest as tears rushed down her cheeks. She forcefully grabbed his face and pried his eyelid wide with her fingers. Deep inside, a voice pleaded for her to stop before she did something she might regret forever. She shrugged it away like an annoying insect. With the speed of a striking snake, her fingernail dived toward the defenseless orb.

"Leena, no!" A firm hand grasped her wrist, stopping her finger less than an inch from its target. As though waking from a nightmare, Leena raised her head and looked into Darius's kind eyes. "Revenge might feel good for a moment, but the shame of it lasts forever," he said.

"Arstead," Darius glanced over his shoulder to his friend, "can you run and tell everyone what's happened here and why we must get away now?"

"You betcha, boss." Arstead rushed toward the farmstead.

Leena jerked her arm free of Darius's grasp. "What took you so long?" The harsh words rasped out between sobs.

"It took a while to convince the army lieutenant that the posters are fakes." Her anger and fear subsided at Darius's gentle words. "It didn't help our cause that twelve of his men lay dead in the farmyard. He was angry and wanted someone to pay. Once we were sure he understood the posters were fakes and his wizard was most likely the person who created them, we suggested he gather his troops and forget the bandits in the woods for now. We must continue to the ships while the army lieutenant still has enough men to rescue the merchants when we arrive in the new country. While he sent riders into the forest to find the troops chasing the bandits, Arstead and I sneaked here as fast as we could without alerting the wizard."

Standing, Leena dusted loose snow from her trousers and looked down at the impaled sorcerer. "That's Arvin. He must have assumed his wizard's appearance after he fled Pineton, infiltrated the regular army system, and traveled with the soldiers when they left Weymouth. He obviously spent his time convincing the lieutenant that torturing and killing me would be fitting revenge for the loss of his troops at the bandit's ambush. I'm guessing this body is Arvin's natural state. While taunting me before starting his torture, he shifted from his wizard's body into the boy's body that traveled with me from Stocksbury to Pineton to prove that he and the boy were the same person. Is he dead?"

"If only it were that easy," Darius said. "Putting a wizard down takes a lot more than a few arrows. It takes a stake through the heart, a bunch of firewood, and sometimes a few other wizards. No, the spells that wizards keep active on themselves ensure few things can kill them."

Darius placed his hand on her shoulder. "He'll be as good as new by tomorrow, and we have nothing we can use to control him then. We don't even have enchanted shackles to bind him. Therefore, we must get out of here and as far away as possible before he wakes up." Darius glanced at the sky. "It'll be sunset in less than four hours, and we have a lot of ground to cover before morning. So, if you're up to it, we need to get packed and on the road in less than an hour to have any hope of escaping before he can catch us."

Air puffed Leena's lips as a deep sigh rushed from her mouth. "We should return to the farmhouse and let Gunnar and Elke know they must escape with us," she said.

"Why would they have to escape?"

"Because Arvin is addicted to revenge. He'll take out his anger on anyone available when we're gone."

"Okay," Darius nodded, "let's get to it."

TWENTY-NINE

Elke looked around the main room of the farmhouse as though deciding what to pack. "How much time do we have?"

"None, I suspect." Darius threw his pack over his shoulder as he halted at the door. "Even now, Arvin's body is repairing itself. We learned in training that complete renewal takes at least twelve hours. By that time, we must be far from here. Gunnar, would you help me load the horses?"

Darius and Gunnar left to tend to the animals as the women grabbed sacks and filled them with food stocks and cooking utensils. Then Leena and Elke gathered items the older woman could not bear to leave. Elke looked at the small room as they turned to the door.

"I would've liked to see those curtains." Tears

rimmed her lower eyelids. She buttoned her heavy coat with a sad headshake and a resigned shrug.

Leena suppressed her sadness at Elke and Gunnar's loss. She hoped there would be time later to help the couple accept the need to escape now. She exited the house to find Darius waiting with two saddled horses tied to the porch rail beside their heavy-laden packhorse. A deceased soldier's horse stood next to the waiting trio, ready to assume its new profession as another packhorse. As a line of soldiers walked their saddled horses from the barn toward the road, Leena positioned a blanket on the new packhorse's back, then helped Elke secure several bundles.

Darius and Gunnar emerged from the barn, leading a pair of mounts for Gunnar and Elke and two more deceased soldiers' horses laden with bales of hay and bags of grain. Leena smiled, hearing their deep voices discussing where they would go and what they would need to meet the group's uncertain future.

"Sweetheart," Gunnar smiled at Elke, "I think riding in that dress could be a bit bothersome. I'm sure you'd fit a pair of my trousers. I suggest you change."

Elke reappeared minutes later, cinching a piece of twine around her waist. "I never realized just how big around you are." Chuckling, she stowed her dress and apron on the packhorse.

Gunnar and Elke paused at the gate, looking back at the farmhouse as the soldiers rode past. "This farm's been in my family for as long as anyone can remember," Gunnar said. Shaking his head to dispel the uncomfortable thoughts, he asked Darius, "Any ideas on how long we'll be away or where we should go until it's safe to return?"

Grabbing the packhorses' lead ropes, Darius rode after the departing soldier column as if he had not heard.

AN HOUR PASSED, and no one spoke as the column rode east.

The soldiers' tense expressions told Leena that everyone knew the danger they faced. The bandit archers were somewhere nearby. How long would it be until they started picking off the soldiers one by one? Only an occasional cough from a human or snort from a horse broke the endless clopping from the soldier's mounts ahead of them.

I've cost Elke and Gunnar so much. They've lost a lifetime's work. Perhaps someday they'll return? But if they returned, how would the townspeople feel about them? The last time they saw Elke, she was being led away, chained like a common criminal. Then she and Gunnar fled. Their escape would confirm guilt in the minds of many. Those people would always suspect the couple, regardless of how this ended.

Leena pulled her mount to a stop.

They've sacrificed everything for me, and what have I given them in return? They're now criminals and fugitives. She felt helpless. She wished she could return to Midwinter's Night and stay home with her family. She missed her mum and da. And her heart ached for her sister. When they were girls, they would lie in bed at night and talk until sunrise.

A crazy thought teetered at the edge of her mind. Perhaps she should return to Arvin and prove to him that only the person the Garlan Tree chooses can see, feel, or use the Branch. Wouldn't he have to leave her alone then, since he couldn't use it anyway?

Elke proceeded a few paces ahead. Stopping when she realized Leena was no longer beside her. The two men leading the pack animals behind them stopped a few paces away from Leena. Both sat patient, waiting.

"I can't ask you people to do this for me," Leena spoke loud enough to be heard by all three.

Darius handed his packhorse's lead rope to Gunnar and rode up beside her.

"First, you did not ask us. Each of us made this decision independently. Second, I'm guessing you're wondering if going back to talk to the wizard would keep him from taking revenge on us if he gets the chance. Do you think anything you say will convince Arvin that he can never use the Branch? Do you think he would hesitate to kill you if he thought the Branch might transfer to him when you die? And, even if you could convince him it wouldn't happen, do you think it would stop him from seeking revenge on all of us for killing him? For better or for worse, we're stuck with one another until we can get this mess turned around. Now, let's get moving. We're easy targets for the bandits when we're standing still." Darius slapped her mount's rump and rode back to retrieve his lead rope from Gunnar.

"He's right, you know." Elke looked ahead as they rode on. "Besides, me and Gunnar's been getting too settled in our old age. For the past several years, we've only been passing the days, waiting till we depart to the fields beyond. It's about time we see something more than our little corner of the world. We've been needing a bit of excitement."

Leena smiled inside at the woman's attempt to soften her pangs of conscience. She looked behind.

Somewhere, there was an answer. Her inner smile grew on seeing Darius's calm and complacent expression and Gunnar's eager, almost cheerful grin.

Then her smile faded as if wiped away by an invisible hand. Beyond the group, a tendril of black smoke rose like an enticing finger, beckoning them back to the Gundersons' farm. Leena stopped her mount. Following her lead, the other three halted their horses and turned to see what she was staring at.

They had traveled over four miles. The smoke from the fireplace would not be visible at this distance. As they watched, the base of the smoke broadened and was joined by another thin tendril to its left. The two merged to form a thick black column rising into the clear blue of the winter sky.

Now, she knew why the bandits had not picked them off as they rode. *They stayed to torch the Gundersons' farm. I don't doubt they first looted every valuable thing left there.*

Leena could not stop the tears of rage and frustration blurring her vision. Elke rode up beside her and stared at the condemning smoke. *If we're lucky, the bandits will sleep near the burning buildings to stay warm for the night and not start after us until Arvin revives.*

"It's time we move on," Elke patted Leena's

hand and gently squeezed it. Her eyes held no accusation, only understanding of shared pain. Leena's heart went out to the woman she met just a few days before. She turned her mount east with a final sniff and rubbed a coat sleeve across her nose.

THIRTY

The mounted soldier swaying in front of Leena slumped in his saddle, his head nodding with every step, his bobbing silhouette black against the rising pink sun ahead. Not for the first time, she envied the regular army riders' ability to hang their heads and sleep while allowing their horses to continue walking through the night. Her attempts to follow their example ended with her jerking the reins to stop her mount to prevent a limb-threatening slide to the icy road below.

"Okay, men," a loud shout came from the lieutenant at the front of the column, "at a gallop forward!" The clatter of clinking bridles and creaking saddles grew louder, spreading back through the column as the pace increased. The noise rolled over Elke and Leena and drifted back over Darius and Gunnar behind them.

"Why are we speeding up now?" Leena called back to Darius. Rather than fight the noise of their increased pace, Darius rode up beside her to explain.

"We did well to make twenty miles yesterday evening and last night. However, there are no clouds in the sky to hinder the sunlight. Once the sun is up, this road will become a mud pit, and we'll slow to a crawl. Arvin will wake from his death state within the next few hours. Then it will take him a bit to finish healing, gather his bandits, and come after us.

"The problem is, we still have ten miles to go on tired mounts. The lieutenant wants to cover as many miles as possible before the road gets too muddy to move at more than a walk. If the sun isn't too hot, we can travel another three or four miles over the next hour before we're forced to slow down."

"But won't Arvin also be hindered by the muddy road?" Leena noticed the worry lines on Darius's face.

"A talented wizard can dry the road before him and have it last long enough to allow him and his men to pass safely over it at five miles an hour. That means he'll get to the coast in six hours from when he starts if he's willing to push his mounts that hard. If we get slowed to two miles an hour when we hit the mud, it will still take us another three hours to slog through it to get to the shore. So it's a race to see whether we can get to the coast, load up, and get far enough out to sea before he arrives."

They continued onward.

Every horse huffed large fog-laden plumes as they struggled to draw deeper breaths and take yet another step through the hoof-churned surrounding mud. Watching their efforts, feeling their fatigue, Leena's mind searched through every spell her mum had taught her, seeking anything that could make the road before them more passable. She found nothing.

Her horse struggled with every step to lift its mud-caked hooves. Leena touched her hedge witch wand and cast a healing spell on the laboring mount. *That'll help, but I don't have anywhere near enough power to heal all the horses.*

Once again, she looked at the bright blue sky above before scanning the brush-covered coastal plains surrounding them since the forest ended five miles back. How much farther did they have to go? It was almost evening. Surely, they must be close. Arvin and his bandits couldn't be far behind now. A bell tolled crisp and sharp through the still air as if in answer to her thoughts. *That can't be a town bell. It's too high-pitched.*

Darius rode up beside her. "That's a ship's bell. We're almost there. See those long, thin sticks bobbing in the distance? Those are ships' masts. Those poles hold the sails that power ships across the waves. We're almost to Longport."

Oh, thank you, Spirit. We're almost there.

Leena tightened a death grip on her reins when her horse rose on its hind feet, screaming. She released her grip on the bridle as her mount twisted, its front hooves clawing at the sky while its wide-open mouth shrieked another wretched scream. Pushing a foot against her mount's ribs, she propelled herself from the saddle and out of the horse's path just before it slammed onto the road, burying its side with a moist flumph in the deep mud.

"Spread out!" the army lieutenant screamed. "There's six bandits hidden in the brush on each side. Don't ride straight. You'll be too easy a target. But chase them down and ensure they can never set up an ambush again."

What's the matter with this animal? Leena crawled to the stricken creature's side. The beast's head lifted in a final heart-rending grunt, then fell to the mud, silent. Its pleading eyes found hers for a few seconds. The dark brown orbs lost their sparkle when the animal's life faded. *What happened?*

Searching the animal's side, she found the last six inches of a feathered shaft buried in its chest just behind its foreleg.

On either side of the road ahead, soldiers wrestled their agitated mounts in arch-backed bursts through the deep, weed-covered roadside that allowed solid footing. Realizing their fate too late, Arvin's bandits turned to run. Blades flashed sparks of evening sunlight as soldiers' arms rose and fell among the fleeing mass. Within minutes, the bandits were lying dead in the low weeds, their lifeblood flowing out.

Arvin must be desperate to send them out into these open fields. With a last pat on her dead mount's shoulder, Leena stood and looked at the road behind them. Far in the distance, high above the road, a vast black cloud approached. Its indistinct edges seemed to flutter as it neared. *Oh no. Please, Spirit, don't let it be what I think it is.*

Darius's horse slid to a stop next to a regular army soldier. "Lieutenant, we lost too many troops at the Gundersons' farm. Can you send a runner to the knights' barracks at Midden Garrison to inform them that Lieutenant Arstead and his knights will leave with us as replacements?"

"Yes, sir, Captain."

Darius's words failed to break Leena's concentration as the lieutenant turned to relay the orders to a soldier. Darius paled as his eyes followed her round-eyed gaze at the sky. He turned back to the army lieutenant. "It looks like we have more trouble coming. Have the runner hide until it's safe to leave here. Now, take your men to the military ship at the northern pier while we load on the merchant ship ahead."

"Follow me, men!" the army lieutenant shouted. The runner spurred his mount toward concealment within Longport's buildings.

Leena scanned the surrounding fields to find that no soldier had been lost in the quick skirmish. Spurring their horses, the mounted soldiers abandoned the deceased bandits. As though fearing a horde of demons chasing them, the soldiers raced after their leader like an angry mounted mob toward the northern dock.

"Leena, grab my hand," Darius said. She locked her hand around his wrists as he slowed his horse next to her and clutched her forearm. With a quick tug, he pulled her behind him onto the horse and piloted his mount to the weed-covered road edge. "We need to get to those ships fast. I don't know what that dark cloud behind us is, but I'm certain Arvin controls it." His voice strained with effort and concern.

Her arms gripped Darius's waist in a viselike hold, and Leena looked behind them. The dark, fluttering cloud had halved the distance between them in the few minutes since they had slain the bandit archers. Beneath the cloud, a single rider raced along the road, his gray robe flapping behind him. Ahead of the rider, the road changed from mud-black to dirt-brown. Hunching over, the horseman dug merciless heels into the animal's side, urging the beast to an incredible speed.

Fear gripped her heart. *Oh, Spirit, no. That's not a cloud. Arvin's brought a massive flock of ravens with him. We don't have a chance.*

"Darius," Leena raised her voice to be heard over the clatter of shod hooves on the plank platform. "That cloud is hundreds of ravens."

Darius nodded.

"Prepare to cast off!" Leena turned to look ahead, searching for the source of the shout. The man had called from above what appeared to be a tall wooden wall bobbing up and down beyond a broad plank platform. Several wide, nailed-together boards formed a slanted wooden walkway from the platform to a gap at the wall's top. Beyond the wall, massive cloth sheets stretched in strained arcs between cross arms mounted to three large poles.

It's a ship. I can't board it. If she left Allivan now,

she'd have no hope of finding her family. Arvin might kill her parents and sister just to get revenge. She needed to stay and find some way to locate and save them.

I can't go! Despite the horse's terrifying speed, Leena slid her legs back, preparing to cast her Branch-enhanced protection spell, drop to the ground behind the galloping horse, race west into the forest, and hide until the boats were beyond the horizon. Releasing her right hand from its tight grip around Darius's waist, Leena fought to reach her wand. With each thud of the horses' hooves, her hand flapped like it had a mind of its own, making it impossible to grasp the wand.

The mount's flying rear hooves could kick her to death if she slid off the back of the horse without her spell's protection. Since she had no control over her right arm at this speed, she needed to roll to her left, drop to the ground, roll to safety, then cast the protection spell, and a healing spell if necessary. Darius would have no choice but to continue to the ship without her.

"Ride up here quick. We'll store your mounts below once we've set sail." The cry came from a man standing fifty yards ahead behind the waist-high wooden wall. Darius spurred his horse toward the ramp.

There's no time. I have to do it now. Leena began her roll.

As though expecting her attempt to escape, Darius's strong right hand grabbed her left hand, locking it to his waist. Pushing against the horse's side, Leena tried to free her hand from Daris's grip while her boots dragged across the dock and up the ramp.

"You're the last of them. Your gear's already been stowed." Shutting the door to close the gap in the wall, the man cupped his hands around his mouth and roared, "Cast off!"

Darius dismounted to the right, pulled Leena so her stomach rested across the saddle, and grabbed her wrists to hold her in place.

On board, two sailors at the front and two at the rear lifted large ropes over the rail as a small channel widened between the boat and the platform. Gathering and tugging, they curled the dripping ropes into large loops on the deck. With slow ease, the ship slid into the open sea.

"I'm Captain Elster, this ship's skipper." The large man with a heavy white beard and long hair who had urged them aboard spoke loud enough for the crowd on deck to hear above the rattle of horses being led below. "In case you've never been aboard a ship before, I am the law here while we're at sea."We'll have no problems as long as you remember that."

Leena ignored the man's speech as she glared at Darius. "Let go of me. You had no right to drag me aboard this ship."

Darius released her arms and stepped back as she slid to the deck on the horse's other side. Leena ran to the ship's rail the instant her feet touched solid planking. A wide gap of turbulent ocean separated the vessel from the receding dock.

From another platform to the north, their accompanying military ship eased from the shore to parallel their course a quarter mile away. Leena threw a leg over the rail, preparing to drop into the sea and swim to shore. A pair of muscular arms wrapped around her, pulling her back to the ship's deck.

"Stop and think of what you're doing." Darius's calm voice only increased her anger. "Look." He pointed beyond the ship's stern.

Less than fifty yards behind the vessel, Arvin dismounted at the edge of the wooden platform and stood there, staring at the ship for several seconds with his fists on his hips, watching them sail away. With a nod, he lifted his hands and sketched an intricate design in the air. The massive bird flock gathered and danced above his head.

"Wizard! Get up here!"

Leena jumped at the captain's shout. She was surprised to hear that there was a wizard onboard. *Maybe he can help me defeat Arvin for good, get us back to shore, and help me find my family.*

"Yes, Captain?" A short, ancient man in an ankle-length, dark-blue robe rose from a stairwell.

"Can you do something about that?"

The wizard stared at Arvin for several seconds, then nodded. Closing his eyes, his hands raised and flew in an intricate dance, slicing the air, creating tiny, mild flutters from his robe's broad sleeves.

Before the wizard could finish his spell, a red and orange flaming ball the size of a person's head flew from Arvin's palms toward the ship, growing as it approached. Within seconds, the sea surface hissed at the flame's base, boiling and steaming beneath it as the rushing orb dug a deepening groove through the waves. The ball's upper rim towered over the highest of the three sails. Although the ship was gaining speed and the dock was more than a hundred yards behind them, the roaring fireball would overpower them in seconds.

Leena's scalp tingled with tension. The field behind Arvin, where his bandit archers died, turned charcoal black, flowing like an unrolling dark carpet toward the distant horizon while his fireball grew.

He's using the plants' energy to fuel his spell. He doesn't care who or what he destroys to get what he wants. Leena's stomach sank when the fireball increased its speed. It towered higher than the ship now like a charging sun. *We'll all be burned to cinders. What can I do? I have no spells to counteract it.*

The wizard shot his arms straight out in front of his chest, his palms flat toward the dock, as though seeking to hold the flaming sphere back by brute force. Something stirred in the ship's wake. Like a titan rising from the deep, a thick blue and white wall rose behind their vessel, forming a seawater curtain higher than the fireball. Like a magical sea monster swallowing a smaller fish, the wall curled around the massive flaming globe, engulfing it with the violent hissing of a thousand vipers. The people crowding the deck stood mesmerized, biting their lower lips and digging their fingernails into delicate palms. Everyone knew their future depended on the battle's outcome as water and fire behemoths wrestled in a lethal duel. The encompassing liquid envelope bulged several times, thinning the seawater's smothering mass. Deadly, fiery arms thrust through gaps in the liquid shell, reaching for the vessel's cloth sails, threatening to engulf the ship in its flaming grasp. Churning blue-and-white streams lifted from the sea, growing to rivers around the orb's outer edges, rising to strengthen the grasping seawater's hold.

Arvin sank to the dock, lowering himself to his knees for a rest. The raven flock above his head scattered in disarray. For a second, hope flooded through Leena. Maybe they would abandon their master and return to where they came from. Then, the duel was all but over. A thump sounded behind her, and she turned. The wizard slumped with exhaustion, kneeling, too weak to move his arms any longer. On shore, Arvin placed a foot on the dock and, bracing both hands on his knee, rose like an avenging demon.

I can't let this be the end for all of us. Then, the realization slapped her in the face. Deep within, a small part of Leena almost chuckled at the irony of hesitating to use the Branch for fear it might bring another raven. However, it had granted her wand an enhanced healing spell. Before she could think of a reason not to, her fingers touched her hedge witch wand and cast the spell on the exhausted wizard.

Like a punch-drunk fighter, the wizard lifted and shook his head to clear his mind. Without searching for the source of the restorative spell, his hands again flowed in intricate patterns too fast for Leena to follow. Less than ten yards from the ship, the watery mass thickened around a fireball now twice the size of the vessel. The water curled into a growing, tsunami-sized wave, reclaiming the inferno in its smothering embrace. Steam rose in a thick cloud curtain from the clutching seawater as the orb dove into the ocean several yards behind the ship, its lethal cargo secured within an unbreakable grasp. A thick mist rose from the water's bubbling surface to tatter and blow away in the onshore breeze. Behind the boat, blue waves swelled toward a tranquil horizon like no battle had been fought on the sea's surface.

Limp with relief, Leena turned and smiled at Darius before she could remember her anger. They were free.

Darius's eyes widened at something behind her, the color draining from his cheeks. Leena spun around and saw Arvin standing again, raising his arms and spreading them wide. His face contorted with anger as thundering words poured from his mouth. At the commands, the black flock above his head reformed into a tight army and raced toward their vessel with the speed of a launched arrow.

Leena's mind darted in a useless search for a spell that might save them from the oncoming horde. She couldn't touch all the ravens with the Branch. But maybe it could help in another way. So far, three times when she really needed it, the

Branch had granted a new, more powerful spell, and *this* was certainly a time of need.

Her mind probed for a hedge witch spell that might be enhanced enough to defeat the oncoming raven army. She found none, and the Branch remained silent in her head. *Okay, I have no choice. I'll use what I have.* Her fingers brushed the Branch, and she called the enhanced protection spell, but nothing happened. *What? The Branch has always had limitless energy. Why not now?* The Branch kills these Ravens when it touches their breast. Could it be that the ravens absorb its energy? The power is too much when there are only one or two ravens. It over-whelms them, and they explode. Maybe when too many birds are together, the power is divided among them, and all are strengthened.

She let her mind delve into the Branch, searching for anything that might help. The Branch remained as dead as a broomstick.

Next to her, the wizard waved his arms in intri-cate patterns once again. A mighty wind grew around her, blowing her hair back and bringing tears to her eyes. The boat's speed increased. *Good, that gives me time to think. Maybe this wizard will have a spell to destroy those birds. But probably not. Surely, he would have used it by now if he had one.*

As the wizard's arms flew around, he whispered

a spell under his breath. A bird shot into the sea like a falling cannonball, disappearing beneath the ship's wake. Another bird dived, then another. The sky cleared when the last bird plunged into the sea.

Can they survive underwater? Are their beaks strong enough to penetrate the ship's timbers if they can? Is that pecking I hear? Her mind swirled into the hedge witch wand's protection spell, trying to expand it beyond its intended limits. She didn't think she could extend it far enough to protect the entire hull from the ravens, but she had to try. Her vision blurred as the spell drew energy from her mind and body like a thirsty horse lapping water from an oasis pool.

Leena concentrated on throwing all of her energy into the spell. Her mind reeled, her limbs weakened, and her energy reserves drained like mist before a scorching morning sun. Black spots swirled in her vision. *How much longer can I keep the protection spell active? Minutes at best.* Maybe I should direct the spell only where they're attacking the ship. Her heartbeat pounded in her ears like the rapid, deep rhythm of an approaching kettledrum. The overpowering noise grew so loud within her that she feared she could not locate where the ravens' hard beaks pounded against the ship's timber as they chipped away at its vital sections.

Silence settled over the ship. Leena heard only the rush of its bow wave.

Like a dark blue phantom, the wizard lowered his arms, shuffled across the deck, and disappeared down the stairwell as the accompanying military ship pulled beside them a hundred yards away. *The wizard caused those birds to fall from the sky. He knew they could not swim. It was only my imagination, causing me to hear the birds chewing away at the ship. Some hero you are, Leena. The only thing you did to help was provide a bit of extra energy to the wizard. He did all the heavy work.*

Leena released the protection spell and rested her elbows on the ship's rail. Like apples bobbing in a tub, dead ravens popped to the surface. The ocean was littered with sightless eyes staring at the sun, silent beaks open for a last peck at the hull, and lifeless claws reaching for the sky they would never know again. Feathered-covered waves washed back toward the distant shore.

Raising her eyes, Leena watched Arvin fading into the distance. Like a serf kneeling before royalty, he sank to his knees, bowed his head to the dock's planks, and fell over on his side. He might be defeated for the moment, but Leena doubted he would remain that way for long.

She had no strength left. With closed eyes, she

let the colors behind their lids swirl into blackness. Her body sagged, and she grabbed the ship's railing. Allivan and her hopes of reuniting with her family were fading dreams, lost beyond the horizon behind the boats. Only waves and the vessels' wakes followed them now.

No, I can't give up. If I go with these soldiers now, I should be back in a few months, and if I don't use the Branch, maybe Arvin won't know I've returned. It's not much, but it's the only hope I have. Darius was right. I had no hope of finding my family if I had stayed in Allivan and died.

THIRTY-ONE

"I've stored our gear below." As Darius moved to the rail beside her, her eyes watched the sea flow away behind them, her brain struggling not to think. His approaching footsteps had gone unnoticed, hidden beneath squeaking ropes and the boat's splashing passage through the water. "Since they weren't expecting any passengers, there's no extra room aboard. You and Elke will have to bunk together in one berth and Gunnar and I in another."

What can I say to him? I'm stuck on a boat I never intended to be on. I doubt he's too pleased about that, and I don't know when or how I might return to Allivan. I'm a useless appendage. Here, only because nowhere else is safe for me.

"After our trip last night and today's events, I'm

sure you're as tired as the rest of us." Darius kept his eyes focused on the sea. "I suggest we all get a good night's sleep tonight. Don't worry about missing anything. Nothing will change except for the weather and time of day. The view will be the same for the next six weeks. Let me show you to your room."

"Not just now. And I won't need your help. I'm sure I can find it on my own. Right now, I need time to think and understand everything that's happened." Leena turned her eyes back to the boat's receding wake, watching her former life slip away across the vast sea.

"Okay, your room is on the first level down the stairway. Turn right, and it's the first door on the right." Darius left without another word.

The waters were peaceful, and she tasted salt-water on her lips. Leena watched the water rushing away behind them, coming together in the distance like a flat, emerald arrowhead pointing to the horizon to be gobbled by distant waves.

Tears burned her eyes. All she wanted to do was find her family, return to Quillan, help rebuild it, and restart the life she'd always known. Now that's all gone. She'd lost her family, her village, and even her country. She didn't know where she was going. Even if she could return to Allivan tomorrow, she still had no home. She wasn't even sure if her family was still alive. She was no longer sure she trusted Darius, but there was no one else.

Placing her hands flat on the rail, Leena lowered her forehead to their soft cushion and closed her eyes. *Spirit, please help me.*

"So you're the one this fuss is all about."

Leena jumped at the deep voice's intrusion into the sea's monotonous swishing.

"What?" The word exited in a high-pitched squeal as Leena spun toward the diminutive wizard who'd conquered Arvin's ravens. Dark shadows lined the deep wrinkles of his face, and a pair of bottomless eyes stared into her soul. Clearing her throat, she struggled to speak in a more normal tone. "Who are you? Why are you sneaking up on me? What do you want?"

"Well, to answer those questions in order, I am Falchon, this ship's wizard. Although you might hear me called Falchon the Invincible. Sailors do love to give their wizards terrifying names. I guess it makes them feel safer."

Leena grabbed the railing to steady herself.

"I was not sneaking up on you. You were

studying the boat's wake with the concentration of a stalking cat, so lost in thought that you didn't hear me approach. Of course, these fleece slippers do make my steps more silent and a bit ghostly. It's good for my image.

"And what do I want? That's going to take a little more explanation. But first, I need some information from you. You see, I find it more than a little strange that you and your lot were being chased by such a powerful wizard.

"I didn't have time to scan your group when you came aboard. You might have noticed I was preoccupied. However, I've never heard of a wizard powerful enough to enchant several hundred ravens, much less control them. Usually, they'll enchant a few, maybe even a dozen, and give them specific commands to carry out a single mission each. Whoever that was, he controlled all those ravens simultaneously, which means he's a mighty powerful wizard. It also means he's after something precious to him. Perhaps something that will make him even more powerful. Fortunately, he doesn't seem to know sea magic, or we would all be raven dinner now.

"So, after we passed beyond his effective spell range and all of your people had retired, I wandered the passages below, sensing for another source of magic aboard, and found nothing until I came up on deck. You are the only other caster aboard, and your magic level is less than a hedge witch has. So, I have to ask who that wizard was, and why is he after you?"

What can I tell him? What if he knows when I'm lying? I know so little about wizards' magic. She decided she needed an ally, someone who could help her and give her answers. But she needed to find out if she could trust him first.

"My name is Leena." She paused, studying his reaction to her name, and saw none. "I'm a hedge witch with four years of training. Last Midwinter Night, I went searching in the forest. That's the night when winter herbs are most potent. In the morning, I returned to find my village destroyed. The only living thing there was a strange boy." With no mention of the Garlin Tree, Garlin Branch, or Wanted posters, Leena outlined her trek from Quillan to the ship.

When she finished, Falchon's head nodded for several seconds as his dark eyes probed hers.

"Okay, I know you've not told me everything I'd like to know, but few people ever do. I cast a truth spell on you before you started that tale, so I know everything you've told me is the truth as you know it. I'll settle for that. Now, I doubt you know anything about sea magic. But you should know that each ship needs and wants only one magic caster. A crew gets uneasy if there's more than one. Sailors are powerfully superstitious. I suppose that's because they live on an ocean that's often unpredictable. They know casters can somewhat control the sea, which makes them uneasy even though they understand why a caster is necessary. They'll only accept one caster aboard except when the wizard takes on an apprentice.

"Another problem is that you're a young and pretty lass. Don't think the sailors haven't already noticed that. It's not that they've never had a woman aboard before. Still, most of those were past their prime, accompanied by their influential husbands, or far less attractive than you. We'll be at sea for at least three weeks. That's three weeks away from the pubs and cuddle-women ashore. You're a bit young to know about these things, but sailors get somewhat...restless after a few weeks at sea.

"Now I know you cast a powerful healing spell on me just when I needed it. Without that, we'd all be fish food at the bottom of the sea right now. But that spell tells me two things. First, I owe you my life, and that's a debt I'll probably never have the chance to repay. Second, you want to keep the magic source that allowed you to cast that spell a secret, and my gratitude for you saving my life says I have to respect that.

"I've managed to stay an independent wizard, able to go where I want when I want, beholding to no one, and I've done that by repaying all of my debts. My debt to you, young lady, is enormous. I know that every person aboard this ship, myself included, owes you their life. So I can't let this voyage and these sailors threaten you.

"I propose we tell the captain you're my apprentice. I guarantee the sailors will stay far away from you then. If the captain asks why I didn't clear it with him first, I'll tell him I had no time with all that ruckus going on before we sailed. What do you think?" Falchon stepped to the rail and joined Leena, watching the ship's wake. Both stood silent, staring at the churning water burbling behind the vessel.

"I'm a girl." Leena's near-silent words flew away, almost lost beneath the turmoil of the boiling waves.

"What? I''m sorry. I didn't quite catch that." Falchon turned his head to look at her.

"I'm a girl!" she exclaimed, her words flying into his calm expression with hurricane force. "I'm a girl. You've already noticed that." Leena fought to keep her voice from growing louder. "There are no female wizards. I thought you might be decent for a few minutes, but a decent person would never stoop so low as to give me hope only to snatch it away again. We both know I can't be an apprentice wizard!"

Jaws clenched, Leena turned and stomped toward the stairway.

"Whoa, lass." Falchon's low, commanding voice rose across the deck, and Leena paused. "First, a female wizard is called a sorceress. I'll grant there are not many, and those that do exist prefer to ply their trade only in the largest cities because of the greater potential client base. Therefore, few people know they exist.

"That aside, I'm not saying I can take you on as a real apprentice. That requires about ten years of training. Granted, you might do better with the elementary stuff than most others since you've had some training. I imagine you could shave a year off. Either way, there's little I could teach you between here and our destination. I'm only suggesting you play apprentice, and I play instructor until we get to wherever it is we're going. Then you're free to choose. You can leave when we go ashore in the land we're headed to, or you can stay with me and continue playing apprentice until we return to Alli-van. Then I can tell the captain I found you unsuitable, or you're not ready for training yet, and you can go your own way."

Pondering his words, Leena shuffled back to the aft railing. His words tumbled through her mind. Falchon waited, staring at the sea. She had come so far since that Midsummer Night when she embarked on a journey into the winter cold. Arvin was still out there. She'd survived and learned what she could about the magic and power of the Garlan Branch. But there was so much more she had to learn. She needed to be at her very best if she was ever going to find her family. She didn't know why the Garlan Branch had chosen her, but maybe she could find out.

Leena watched his face as she spoke. "Okay, I can see it would be safer, but I have one question. Would you be willing to actually train me while we pretend that I'm your apprentice?"

Falchon nodded. "I will train you as much as you are willing to learn."

A breeze touched Leena's face as she stared out over the ocean.

INTO THE THROES
OF WAR

Stepping onto the deck of the military ship that escorted them, Leena shivered in the predawn darkness. Why had she, Darius, and Lieutenant Arstead been summoned from the merchant ship they arrived on to the military ship that had accompanied them from Longport? Who was this Colonel Strong?

"This way." The young lieutenant's curt tone discouraged questions as he turned and marched across the deck toward a stairway. The group's footsteps echoed in the narrow passageway leading to the ship's rear. "I advise you not to antagonize the colonel this morning. He's in a foul mood." The lieutenant stopped before the door blocking the end of the passage, raised his right hand, and gave three sharp raps on the oaken panel.

"Enter." At the deep voice's command, the lieutenant opened the door and led them into a large room.

"Lieutenant Fenland, you are dismissed." Their guide turned and eased the door shut behind him as he left.

Leena stood off to the side in Colonel Strong's office, watching the two knights standing ramrod straight in front of his desk, their eyes locked on the wall behind the senior officer. She wondered why Darius and Lieutenant Arstead stood like statues while the colonel sat behind his large oak desk, stern-faced and glaring at them as he sipped his tea. Leena studied the colonel, looking for some sign of humanity beneath the severe military haircut and time-worn, angry lines carved into his face.

"When I heard about these barbarians kidnapping our merchants," the colonel's loud voice echoed through the room, vibrating Leena's chest, "I suggested to the Great Wizard that a senior army officer command the regular army troops in the new land in case we met armed resistance when rescuing them. Since it was my suggestion, he naturally chose me to head up this mission. I arrived in Longport a week before we sailed. If you had met your sched-ule,"—he glared at Darius—"we would have been out of Longport long before that wizard arrived to try stopping us."

What? Is he blaming Darius and Lieutenant Arstead for Arvin's attack at the docks? Maybe, in some weird way, that was valid from a military perspective. Leena didn't understand nor care about the politics of it all. All she knew was that she needed to find some way to return to Allivan as soon as possible and rescue her family.

Colonel Strong tapped his finger on the desk. "So, Captain, you're the young miracle worker the Great Wizard sent to negotiate with these kidnappers for the return of our merchants? I tried to talk the Great Wizard out of sending a negotiator. After all, our merchants came here to establish friendly trade relations with them. Instead, these barbarians confiscated their goods and demanded more merchandise as ransom to return them. Still, the Great Wizard insists we try establishing mutually beneficial agreements with them.

"I have to say, you don't look like much to me." The colonel shook his head, a disgusted frown on his face. "Still, I suppose I'll have to support your efforts as the negotiator since you're under the Great Wizard's direct orders."

Darius nodded, tightening his jaw.

Colonel Strong shifted his glare to Lieutenant Arstead. "You, however, are not under the Great Wizard's direct orders," he said in a hostile tone. "I understand that you and a dozen knights boarded the other ship while you sent the army troops onto this vessel. May I see the orders allowing you to insert yourself into a regular army mission without coordinating through proper channels?"

What is he talking about? The colonel was at Longport. He had to have seen the battle at the docks. Lieutenant Arstead had no choice. What is wrong with this man?

As stiff as a board, Lieutenant Arstead continued staring at a spot on the wall behind the colonel. "Sir, hostile circumstances forced us to make instant decisions in Longport. My men and I intend to return to Allivan on the next available ship."

"I doubt that will be anytime soon, Lieutenant. However, since you have intruded where you don't belong, you and the knights on your ship are under my command for the duration of this mission."

"Sir..." Darius started.

"Silence!" The colonel's shout vibrated from the wooden walls. He raised a fist and slammed it on the desk, sending his pen and papers dancing across its surface. "I don't need you to tell me that the military charter does not permit regular army officers to command the Great Wizard's knights." The colonel stood and paced around his desk, then stopped inches from Darius, yelling into his face. "The charter also states that a senior officer may assume command of any and all troops during an emergency. Obviously, the detention of Allivanian citizens by these outlanders makes this an emergency."

Colonel Strong turned to Leena. His beady, black eyes bore into her. "And you're the witch assigned to the other ship?" His expression told her he had no place for a young, half-trained hedge witch in his organization. "You may remain in that position until we've established a presence on land. Then, you will report to Marta, the head witch for this expedition."

The colonel clicked his tongue. "You are all dismissed. I suggest you return to your ship immediately. Now that the sun's rising, we'll enter the port and teach these barbarians that it's unwise to trifle with Allivan."

Leena, Darius, and Arstead stepped from the small boat transporting them from the military ship and sped up the merchant ship's boarding ladder, propelled by the rattle of the ship's rising anchor chain clinking through its metal-lined scupper. Before Leena could race to the stairway and down to the safety of their rooms, the two ships sped toward the distant shore, with sails billowing in the onshore breeze as though in a race. Leena moved against bales of trade goods secured amidships by ropes to the deck, hoping to avoid obstructing the crew as the craft sprinted toward the dock like a sailor on shore leave. Eyes gleaming, she flowed with the deck's motion, her knees bending and straightening with the rise and fall of the waves. The chilled breeze cooling her face brought tears to her dark brown eyes. Her shadow-dark hair billowed behind her like a coal-black pennant.

It's beautiful. Leena's heart filled with wonder as she watched the land expand as they flew toward the shore. Almost three months had passed since she left her home in Quillian in search of the Garlan Branch, an ancient relic with immense power. Only two others in history had wielded the Branch—Skylar, a farmer's son, and the Great Wizard himself. But the Branch had now chosen her, a sixteen-year-old, half-trained hedge witch. She still could not believe everything that had transpired since that fateful winter's night. The shore before her faded as her mind slipped into memories of how she ended up sailing toward this foreign land. When she returned to Quillian after receiving the Garlan Branch, she found her home and the surrounding town ravaged and burned to the ground. Except for nineteen dead, all the townsfolk, including her mum, da, and sister Raina, were gone.

She had journeyed over long, cold winter days, trying to find some trace of where her family had gone. Every step of the way proved futile. In the guise of a child, the evil wizard Arvin, desperate to find the Garlan Branch, had done everything he could to get it. When his deception failed to gain him the Branch, Arvin reverted to his true self and used torture, trying to force her to reveal its location, and then attempted to murder her. Leena knew only her strength, power, and magic had brought her this far. The journey had also taught her to trust herself and to lean on others when her strength and knowledge were insufficient. She wouldn't be here without Darius, a knight in the Great Wizard's army, or Gunnar and Elke, two innocent farmers who had shown her kindness and love. She had not wanted to involve any of them, but the circumstances that brought them here had been beyond her control. Now, they were all aboard this ship, sailing toward the unknown to save Allivanian merchant hostages kidnapped when they tried to open trade with the people here.

She reached to her waist and touched the Garlan Branch, snuggled next to the hedge witch wand behind her skirt waist, using them to calm her nerves.

They were still too far from shore to see people, but the green land and gentle hills beyond the town seemed peaceful.

In the closing distance, she spotted movement. Like tiny insects swarming from a kicked anthill, people ran onto the dock and lined the shore. Several people carried torches. A dozen teams of men tugged long ropes, pulling large wooden machines and aligning them like massive wheeled statutes along the coast.

Runners raced to stack long wooden poles beside the large devices. Someone lifted a pole from the stack at each position and laid it atop the nearest machine. Torchbearers jogged past the row, lighting the rag-wrapped tip of each pole as a man turned a crank handle at the contraption's side, angling the flaming poles up and toward the approaching vessels.

Leena stiffened when she realized what was happening.

"Clear the deck!" the captain shouted. "Prepare

for an attack!"

The crew rushed all around her, preparing the ship for battle. Sailors sped by her, shifting bales and wooden crates out of the way. Leena stepped back, hoping to avoid the surrounding chaos. Each shift to a new position pushed her closer to the ship's rail. Her back connected with the latched gangway's firm boards.

I can't stay by the gangway. What if the bombardment doesn't work, and they send a boarding party from shore? This is where they'll try to board? I have to get to my room. But there are too many sailors racing around. I'll just be in their way.

Muted shouts rose from shore over the swish of the speeding ship's bow wave. Leena spun forward to see several dozen fire-tipped poles launched in graceful arcs, rushing toward the boats like a swarm of flaming wasps.

"Hard astarboard!" The ship's captain's voice rose above the bedlam on deck. With the ease of an experienced dancer, the merchant ship turned away from the shore. Watching a last volley of flaming arrows plunge into the ocean behind the vessel, Leena breathed a relieved sigh.

They must know the maximum range of their weapons. Those had to be warning shots.

Motion on the ship's port side caught Leena's

eye. Following the merchant ship's lead, the military ship also turned south, moving to take a port position ahead of the merchant ship. No one aboard spoke as the vessels sailed away from the city.

LEENA GOODWIN returns in *The Unchosen Life Saga: Into the Throes of War*! Coming soon in eBook and paperback. Join the epic journey today!

ACKNOWLEDGMENTS

Foremost, I wish to thank Jonathan Yanez, not just because he is a longtime friend and highly talented author but because his encouragement, guidance, and dedication to the writing craft have provided shining examples of skill and commitment to uncountable authors. I also offer heartfelt thanks to his brilliant wife, Jynafer Yanez, for her support and guidance, without which this book would not have been possible.

Above all, I thank my wife, Mary Ann, the most wonderful person I know. She not only endured long hours of separation while I hammered away at the keyboard in seclusion but also tolerated my many tirades against unfeeling editors while gently leading me back to writing it as I should have.

STAY CONNECTED

Hello, fellow adventurer! I'm Franz McLaren, a lifelong fantasy enthusiast who started with *Alice in Wonderland* and has since explored 48 states and countries like England and Japan, gathering inspiration for my own tales. Now, I invite you to step into the worlds I've created, where reality takes a playful detour.

Want to join the journey?

Sign up for the Guild of Sword & Sorcery newsletter at franz-mclaren.com for updates and exclusive offers.

Connect on Facebook or Instagram for more fun and mischief.

And if *The Unchosen Life Saga* has sparked your imagination, share the magic with a friend and let's grow this Guild together!

BOOKS IN THE UNCHOSEN LIFE SAGA

A Simple Task

(A Short Story)

Hedge Witch Rising

Into the Throes of War

www.ingramcontent.com/pod-product-compliance
Lightning Source LLC
Chambersburg PA
CBHW020308160726
47992CB00004B/1443